I asked, 'So what's all this about?' but Duncan ignored me and went on rummaging. After a minute or so, he found what he was looking for. I just had time to clock the *Bellini* logo before he turned to a page somewhere in the middle, smoothing it flat on the bench in front of me.

I looked, and my blood pressure leapt a few notches. The words *Night People!* were printed in dripping crimson across the top of the page. It was some sort of fashion spread, glistening with saturated colour. The model, of course, was wearing black. It was a dress cut low at the neck, made out of that clinging fabric you could only wear if you were prepared to spend half your waking life in the gym. But the dress itself wasn't so extraordinary; Lulu had a dozen or so like it in various shades of pink. What was extraordinary was the rest of the picture.

The model's face was dead white, and it appeared frozen with shock, which wasn't so surprising since somebody, not entirely in frame, was ramming a sharp stick through her chest. The dark fabric of the dress was gleaming even darker where the stick went in. A trickle of blood ran from one corner of her immaculately painted mouth. Her brilliant teeth were bared in a snarl, and there was no doubt that two of them were fangs.

Anne Billson was born in 1954 in Southport, Lancs. She is a distinguished journalist and film critic and works as a contributing Editor of *GQ* magazine and as a film critic for *New Statesman and Society*. Her published works are *Screen Lovers, Dream Demon* (a film novelization), and *My Name is Michael Caine*. Anne Billson now lives in Cambridge.

SUCKERS

ANNE BILLSON

PAN BOOKS
LONDON, SYDNEY AND AUCKLAND

First published 1993 by Pan Books Limited

a division of Pan Macmillan Publishers Limited
Cavaye Place London SW10 9PG
and Basingstoke

Associated companies throughout the world

ISBN 0 330 32806 9

5 7 9 8 6 4

A CIP catalogue record for this book is available from
the British Library

Typeset by Intype, London
Printed by Cox & Wyman Ltd, Reading, Berkshire

PART ONE

ONE

It wasn't murder, in my opinion. Some people might have
had trouble understanding that. I might have had trouble
myself if I hadn't been there when it happened. Afterwards,
Duncan sank into a depression and stayed depressed for the
next five years. By the time he managed to snap out of it, he
had almost succeeded in convincing himself the whole thing
had been a dark trick of his imagination. Almost, but not
quite. Each time he noticed my left hand, he couldn't help
remembering what had happened to the top joint of the little
finger. I caught him looking sometimes, but we never talked
about what he was thinking. We didn't have to. I just knew.

After thirteen years we were different people, leading
different lives. Duncan had turned into a non-smoking tee-
total vegetarian. And he had gone right off horror movies;
he would turn the television off as soon as it threatened to
broadcast anything with old dark houses, or women in black,
or ooh-whee-ooh music, and no one thought this odd, least
of all Lulu. She was squeamish too, and naturally assumed
he was switching off on her account.

3

But the main difference was that we were both making money now, and lots of it. Duncan made more than me, but then he worked a lot harder than I did. I'd gone for the soft option, starting out as a Stylist, then altering my job description to Creative Consultant, which sounded more impressive and pretentious – more in tune with the times.

There was no shortage of work, because there was a flash new magazine title on the newsstands every couple of weeks – all style and no content, packed with features dealing with 'image' and 'life style'. It was down to people like me to keep publishers informed about their target market of upwardly mobile young adults with disposable incomes. I took the 'Creative' part of my job description literally. Most of the information I provided was completely fictitious.

Duncan and I weren't the only ones on a roll. Pubs and clubs were jam-packed full of people with too much money to spend, all standing elbow to elbow and jogging each other's drinks. You had to queue to get to the bar, and you had to queue to get to the Ladies Room as well. If you strained your ears to hear beyond the sound of flushing cisterns you could sometimes pick up the discreet chip-chop of credit cards against porcelain, followed by gentle snuffling as fine white lines were hoovered up into hovering nostrils.

These people took their pleasures seriously. In pubs, clubs, or restaurants, they talked about money and work, work and money, all the time. And they dressed like guests at a funeral. It made me uneasy sometimes, so it must have made Duncan uneasy too. Everywhere you looked, there would be women dressed in black – white faces, black hair, mouths painted scarlet. It was The Look. You saw it on the street. You saw it on the covers of magazines. You saw it presenting arts programmes on TV.

4

And some of us saw it in our nightmares. I made sure I didn't look like that. It was thirteen years since I had gone out dressed in nothing but black. And I made sure there was more to my life than money and work, work and money. I had a wide range of interesting hobbies. Gardening, for instance. I didn't do much digging – you could only dig so far on a balcony – but there was plenty of honeysuckle, most of it covered in aphids. Aphid-hunting was another of my hobbies. The black ones were easiest to spot, but the green ones were juicier, more fun to pop. At the end of a serious aphid-squishing session my fingers would be stained the colour of lime juice.

I collected plastic construction kits as well, though not the aeroplane ones. I had a pterodactyl with a battle-scarred wing, a life-size skull which glowed in the dark, and a Visible Woman with a detachable foetus. I watched videos, and I did crosswords, and sometimes, just to keep my hand in, I dressed up and went out and socialized, like everyone else.

But my favourite hobby was persecuting Patricia Rice. I knew her name because she had written it on a small piece of card and slid it into the little slot next to her doorbell. She had no idea who *I* was, of course, but I knew *her*. She lived in a ground-floor flat in a Victorian terrace just south of Waterloo Station. She was a lucky girl; she had gas-fired central heating, new wiring, and a freshly injected damp-proof course. I knew all this because I had seen it for myself. The estate agents had shown me round. They had even given me a set of keys and later, when my offer had been accepted, I had gone back on my own to wander from room to room, deciding where to put the furniture. I had paid my surveyors. I had run up a tab with my lawyers. I was all set to exchange contracts when Patricia Rice came along out of nowhere and gazumped me.

5

It wasn't as though I'd had trouble finding somewhere else. I took out a mortgage on a first-floor flat across town. The main drawback was the lack of soundproofing; it was a cowboy conversion, and the people upstairs drove me nuts with their noise. Besides, one of them was German. Up until then, I had properly encountered only one German in my life, but he had been more than enough to leave me with a distinct anti-German bias.

Even so, I liked my flat, because it was only a brisk ten-minute walk away from Duncan's. So in a way, Patricia Rice had done me a favour. But that didn't mean I was going to let her get away with it. For three years after the gazumping, I was too busy to care, but then I found myself with time on my hands. I thought about Patricia and how she had made a fool of me, and every so often I would nip down to SE1 to see how she was getting on. The lifts at Lambeth North tube station always seemed to be out of order, and it warmed my heart just to think of her toiling up and down that grimy staircase every day. I thought long and hard about how I could make things even worse. As soon as the Channel Tunnel opened, I'd decided, I would send her address to a selection of Belgian youth groups, with the message *Cheap rates, towels provided, backpacks welcome.*

I also liked to dial her telephone number and once she'd answered leave my handset lying on the table; that way, her phone was all tied up so that no one could call her, nor could she ring out until I hung up again. I couldn't be bothered with any of that heavy breathing nonsense, though I would occasionally pipe Def Leppard down the line. I didn't particularly care for Def Leppard; I'd bought the tape especially for Patricia.

But the most rewarding part of this particular hobby was the correspondence. It was one way, but I didn't mind. I had hours of fun cutting up magazines, and Cow-gumming letters on to blank sheets of Basildon Bond. Having to wear rubber gloves made it even more of a challenge. Once or twice, I got up early so I could loiter outside Patty's flat and watch her mail being delivered bang on eight, just before she left for her boring nine till five job in an employment agency – I knew where she worked because I'd followed her there. Opposite her front door was a small construction site; the workmen never showed up before ten, and the cement mixers provided excellent cover. That way I could enjoy the spectacle as Patricia emerged, tense and nervous after opening the latest in the YOU ARE A SLUT AND YOU WILL DIE HORRIBLY series, or the slightly more colourful variations on BURN IN HELL YOU VILE NAZI BITCH.

The subject of Patricia Rice came up one afternoon while I was hanging around in Duncan and Lulu's kitchen. Lulu had been making it obvious she didn't want me there. She was fussing over her chickpeas, never passing up an opportunity to remind me that she and Duncan were expecting people for dinner, and that I wasn't on the guest list. Everyone else I knew bought their hummus ready-made from the supermarket, but Lulu liked to make things difficult for herself.

She kept asking, 'What do you think, Dora? Do you reckon this'll be enough?' until I felt like ramming the ruddy chickpeas down her throat. 'You know Jack's a real Bunter,' she said in that little-girl way of speaking which got on my nerves. 'If he doesn't get enough, he'll just start scoffing everyone else's.'

'Crumbs,' I said, rocking back on my chair. 'You'd jolly well better make lashings of it, then.' Even Jack, I thought, might lose his appetite once confronted by this khaki-coloured mush, but I stopped myself from saying so out loud. Lulu might have been a pain in the neck, but Duncan, for some reason best known to himself, was fond of her. And I didn't want to upset Duncan.

As usual when Lulu was being obnoxious he was keeping a low profile. He was sitting at the far end of the kitchen table, retouching a print he'd promised Jack as a belated birthday present. It was a photo of Alicia draped in a black veil, standing among the tombstones in Kensal Rise cemetery. Duncan might have gone off horror movies, but he had never quite managed to kick the cemetery habit. It was a striking photograph – made even more striking by his signature, which automatically added a bob or two to its market value.

Duncan had once stepped out with Alicia, and he had the photos to prove it. He made a habit of keeping in touch with his ex-girlfriends, even when they insisted on marrying jerk-offs like Jack. Duncan and Jack seemed to get on quite well – they were always discussing manly topics such as fast cars and football. You had to know Duncan as well as I did to realize that fast cars and football didn't interest him at all. He was just trying to keep up appearances.

Alicia was usefully photogenic, so long as you overlooked her weak chin, and Duncan still used her as a model in some of the arty, non-commercial work he liked to turn out occasionally. He had photographed her in the nude when she'd been pregnant, and then he'd done some more nude studies of her with the new baby; the baby had been nude,

8

as well. Alicia had framed one of the pictures and hung it over her dining table. Jack and Alicia were a thoroughly modern couple, and to look at them you would never have guessed that he had bribed her to give up her career so she could concentrate on breeding.

Lulu started chopping up parsley with a wicked-looking knife – rather closer to me than was necessary. 'Watch out, Dora,' she said. 'Better move back, or you'll lose another finger.' Out of the corner of my eye, I saw Duncan glance up sharply. Lulu was being spiteful, but he refrained from giving her the ticking off she deserved. Once again, it was left to me to show her up.

'It's only the last joint,' I said. 'All the best villains have the top joint of their little finger missing.'

Lulu paused in her chopping and said 'Huh?' I adored making her look stupid in front of Duncan. Every so often, he would have to be reminded that he had more in common with me than with her.

'*The Thirty-nine Steps*,' he said without bothering to look up again. 'Or is it *The Yakuza*?'

Lulu repeated 'Huh?' and, pretending not to care, went back to her parsley. When she'd reduced it to a sloppy green mulch, she forced me to move even further away from the table so she could reach the blender. I'd been rocking my chair so much that one of the legs had worked itself loose. Now when I scraped it back across the floor, there was a faint but ominous splintering sound. The chair didn't give way, not quite, but I sat quietly for a while, not wanting to push my luck.

To my face, and especially in front of Duncan, Lulu was all intimacy, but I knew she disliked me almost as much as I despised her. On her side, at least, it was nothing personal;

she was the sort of woman who regards all other women as rivals. She hated leaving me alone with Duncan, even for a short while, imagining I was ready to jump on him the minute her back was turned. If she'd been at all perceptive, she would have realized it wasn't his body that interested me. He was too thin and pale and neurotic-looking to qualify as beefcake. But she sensed there was something between us, and she was envious of that. Duncan and I had been through something she could never be a part of.

Like Duncan, Lulu didn't talk much about her past. Unlike Duncan, this was not because she had something to hide, nor was it because she wanted to forget – it was because she realized her past just wasn't terribly interesting. Her real name was Lorraine. Once, as a joke – because I knew she wouldn't have the faintest idea what I was talking about – I asked her if she'd called herself Lulu after the heroine of the Frank Wedekind plays. She looked blank and said no, as a little girl she'd been rather partial to a pop song called 'I'm a Tiger', and had named herself after the singer.

It had been easy for her to get modelling work, but she had never had the luck or drive to make it into the top ranks – only as far as one or two of the middlebrow women's magazines, the sort you find on sale next to supermarket checkouts. I always reckoned she could have had a successful career posing topless for some of the cheesier tabloids, but she was too much of a snob. She had masses of streaky blonde hair and enormous breasts, and liked to pretend she was even more dimwitted than she really was. She was convinced that all men fancied her, and equally convinced that all women hated her because they were jealous of her face and figure. She was right about women not liking her, but wrong about the reasons. Women didn't like her because she was a complete bonehead.

She'd latched on to Duncan because he was famous. Not a household name, exactly, but he was getting there; he'd already appeared on one or two TV chat shows, moaning about how tedious it was to be constantly jetting off to the Seychelles to take pictures of fifteen-year-old cuties in string bikinis. At twenty-five Lulu was too old for this sort of lark, but she was still offered work when occasion demanded the sort of dollybird who could fill out a bodice. I suspected it wouldn't be long now before she decided to pack in the career altogether in order to concentrate on family life. She was already pouncing on the flimsiest of pretexts to steer the conversation round to babies. Come to think of it, this was probably why Jack and Alicia had been invited over. Lulu would be able to display her maternal tendencies by cooing over Abigail.

When I had first caught up with Duncan again, eight years or so after all the unpleasantness, I found him living in the same building, but the place had been transformed. Previously, it had been a gloomy warren of rooms painted in bright peeling colours left over from the sixties: red and black, or purple, with gold stars stencilled on to the bathroom ceiling. The communal hallway, with its crumbling cornices and soggy carpet, had always been packed with bicycles and stacks of junk mail. Then an uncle had died and Duncan had inherited the leasehold, and he had started to do the place up. It was partly the physical effort of that which had hauled him up out of the slough of self-pity.

One by one the tenants had moved out, mostly because they were fed up with the constant hammering and drilling. Duncan sold the other flats at a vast profit and used the money to refit his own. Some of the interior walls had been removed to make one enormous living room with floor-to-ceiling windows and stripped-pine floorboards. When I first saw the changes, the place was barely recognizable. Which was probably the whole idea; he was trying to obliterate all trace of what had happened there.

Lulu didn't bring much with her when she moved in – just a couple of Swiss Cheese plants and a trunkful of clothes and make-up. She insisted that Duncan sell two-thirds of his book collection so the remainder fitted neatly into a couple of alcoves instead of cluttering up the entire room. Each month she bought *Vogue* and the rest of the glossies and arranged them in neat stacks on the coffee table. She also bought a lot of imported Italian fashion magazines, though her knowledge of the language was limited to words such as *l'uomo, donna,* and *lei.*

Now she was bustling round the kitchen, dressed in her customary leisure wear of pink Lycra leggings, oversized pink T-shirt, and pink towelling headband. There wasn't much in Lulu's wardrobe that wasn't pink or red. She never wore black. As far as I was concerned, this was her one redeeming feature. She thought it made her look sallow.

She finished messing with the blender and started peeling the paper from a big slab of ricotta. I told her about Patricia Rice because I knew it would upset her. To my delight, she made little tutting noises of disapproval. 'Dora, that's *awful,*' she said. 'I'm not sure that you realize how awful that is. It's *really* mean. You wouldn't like it if I did that sort of thing to you.'

'But you wouldn't *do* that sort of thing,' I said. 'You're much too nice. Besides, you and I know each other, and the whole point is that Patricia and I have never met. This way, even if she called the police in – even if they could be bothered to launch an investigation into a couple of harmless anonymous notes – they'd never know where to start looking.'

'Not unless someone tipped them off,' Lulu muttered, just loud enough for me to hear.

Duncan looked up from his retouching. 'Dora, you're wicked,' he said. 'We'd better ask her to dinner, Lu, or we'll start getting poison-pen letters.'

Lulu shot him a look of exasperation. 'Duncan! I'm not sure there's enough food as it is.'

'That's OK,' I said brightly. 'I don't eat much.'

Lulu gritted her teeth and pretended not to sulk.

'That's settled, then,' said Duncan, like a referee.

'Yes,' she said. 'That seems to be *that*.' She ploughed her fork through the cheese so vehemently that a large clod of it flew out of the bowl and landed on the table, just missing the edge of his photograph.

'Jesus, Lu!' he snapped. 'For Christ's sake watch what you're doing. That was nearly half a day's work down the tubes.' His expression was thunderous, and for a minute I thought he was going to scrunch up the photo and chuck it at her. On the whole, he managed to keep his temper, like a lot of other things, under wraps, but sometimes it got away from him. These days, though, he was better at controlling it, and now I could see him taking a deep breath and staring hard into the middle distance until the storm clouds dispersed. He wiped the cheese up with his finger and ate it, then looked pointedly in my direction, as if to punish Lulu by deliberately excluding her from the conversation. I tried not to smile as I saw her lower lip quivering.

'Dora,' he said, 'I really need your advice.'

'About what?'

For a moment, he was lost for words, as though my response had thrown him off balance. 'Work,' he said at last. 'Photos and stuff.'

I hadn't expected this. I'd done a short stint in the photographic department at college, but Duncan was aware I didn't know anything like as much about photography as he did.

Lulu muscled in. 'Maybe *I* could help.'

'I doubt it, love,' Duncan said. He only called her 'love' when he was being patronizing. 'It's technical.'

'What do you want to know?' I asked, hoping for another chance to get Lulu to demonstrate her stupidity.

'Show you later,' he said.

Lulu turned to face the stove, still looking as though she was about to burst into tears. As soon as she'd turned her back he gave me a look, a glance so naked in its desperation that it knocked me for six. It was just for a moment, and then it was gone. Then he bent his head back down over the print and continued to dab away at the shadows with his fine-pointed brush, filling in all the flaws with tiny black dots. Years of point-blank brushwork had taken their toll on his eyesight. Sometimes, for watching television and so on, he was having to wear spectacles.

For a while there was silence. Lulu continued to pout, and Duncan continued to dab. I sat without moving, trying to resist the temptation to start rocking my chair again. I had a feeling deep inside which at first I had trouble identifying, because it had been years since I'd last felt it – thirteen years, to be exact. It took me some time to recognize it as excitement.

TWO

Lulu had swapped her pink leisure wear for pink formal wear. She swayed from side to side in time to the music, if you could call it music.

'What *is* this noise?' I asked.

'It's New Vague music, Dora. Recommended by my yoga teacher. It's supposed to relax you.'

'Sounds like whales,' said Alicia.

'I think it's got whales in it somewhere,' Lulu said.

I picked up the cassette case and scanned the notes. 'Nope, no whales here. Ethereal flutes, yes. Haunting pan-pipes, yes, not to mention the gentle ebb and flow of celestial oceans. Oh, and we mustn't forget the cosmic tinkle of inter-galactic glockenspiels.'

Lulu snatched the cassette case from me and read out loud, 'This music creates the perfect ambience for those pre-cious contemplative moments.'

I yawned, which probably convinced Lulu the New Vague was working. I'd already had my fill of precious con-templative moments. Over on the other side of the room

Duncan was listening intently to Jack. I wished he would get to the point and tell me what was on his mind.

Alicia was flicking through magazines. You couldn't blame her; the repartee, so far, had not been sparkling. Over pre-dinner drinks, Jack and Duncan had talked about Ferraris and Grand Prix racing, while Alicia had listed the pros and cons of Pampers versus Peau Douce. Then, while Lulu was slopping out the hummus, Jack launched into a monologue about office politics on the weekly magazine where he was Features Editor. He worked with a load of degenerates who seemed to do nothing but snort cocaine and misspell the names of world-famous celebrities: Stephen Speilberg, Eddy Murphy, Arnold Shwarzenegger. Everyone listened politely as he fulminated about his co-workers' habit of using up all the office biros – throwing away the ink-tubes and leaving the outer cases crusty with a mixture of white powder and snot. I noticed he scrupulously avoided mentioning Roxy, his *zaftig* personal assistant. I'd seen them in Gnashers together, but they'd been too busy snogging to see me back.

At this point I started to cast despairing glances in Duncan's direction, but Jack was getting into his stride. He surrendered the floor only when he came up against someone even more self-centred than himself. The first we heard was a faint spluttering from the bedroom, like water gurgling through an ancient plumbing system. Then came an ear-splitting wail which persisted all the way through the pasta course. Eventually, Alicia noticed I had dropped my fork and jammed fingers in both ears, so she brought the baby to the table and rocked it into semi-silence.

Once everyone's attention had been drawn to Abigail, the rest of the evening disappeared swiftly down the plughole. After the tagliatelle Lulu related in meretricious detail the plot of a film which none of us had seen nor even wanted to see; she herself had watched no more than a TV trailer in which the three leading actors made comical attempts to change a baby's nappy. Lulu interpreted this as a challenge for her to demonstrate that she could do what highly paid Hollywood actors pretended they could not. We were duly treated to a round of nappy-changing between the pasta and the pudding. We were also treated to a round of full-frontal breast-feeding from Alicia. I almost expected Lulu to have a go at that as well, just to prove she had what it took.

And now it was decaffeinated coffee table time. Alicia was cradling the baby with one arm and using her free hand to leaf through the magazines. Abigail's tiny fingers made a grab for the nearest page and scrunched it into a rudimentary origami design. 'Abigail, *no*. Mummy's *reading*.' There was a sound of glossy paper rending as Alicia prised the chubby little fist away.

Lulu brandished another magazine. 'The second issue of *Bellini*,' she chirrupped. 'I'm going in to see them. Amanda says they pay really well.'

Alicia glanced at the cover. I caught a glimpse of it too, and wished I hadn't; it was a larger-than-life close-up of a heavily made-up model winking at the camera. It gave me the heebie-jeebies whenever I saw anyone winking; it never failed to remind of things I preferred to forget. I looked away and counted slowly to ten – my well-tested method for wiping unwanted images from my mind. When I looked back, the magazine lay open on Alicia's lap and the picture was no longer visible. She was studying the masthead on the contents page. '*Bellini*,' she cooed, rocking the baby gently. '*Bellini* . . . Never heard of it.'

'It's a champagne cocktail,' Lulu said helpfully.

Alicia looked as though she were biting back a sharp comment. 'Up to a point, Lu,' she said, in that tone she sometimes used, the one which periodically reminded me why I quite liked her. She flicked through the pages, eventually coming across something which made her stop and flick back. 'But these girls are all topless,' she said.

'So?' I said. 'It's no worse than the *Sun*. Or *Vogue*.'

'No no,' she said. 'When I say topless, I mean they *don't have any heads*.'

I was about to lean over and see what she was talking about when Lulu snatched the magazine away from her and riffled through it. 'It's all very surreal,' she said grandly. 'Surreal' was one of her favourite words. 'Look at this,' she said, flattening the pages at what appeared to be a fashion feature about lingerie. From where I was sitting it didn't look very surreal at all. She and Alicia bent their heads down over it and started to make bitchy remarks about the models.

I was dying for a cigarette, but I was stuck in a room with four non-smokers. My thoughts turned to alcohol instead. I had drained my glass of wine, and no one was breaking their neck to offer me a refill, but there was a bottle of cheap brandy sitting untouched on the table. Duncan had bought it some months before, duty free from Barcelona airport, but he never went near alcohol these days, and Lulu drank spirits only when she was trying to impress somebody. Alicia didn't want her milk contaminated with noxious substances, and Jack was sticking to moderate quantities of white wine so that later on he would be able to point the car in the direction of their flat, which was all of two hundred yards away.

No one was paying me any attention, so I poured myself a large measure and gulped it, slooshing the liquid around my mouth so it wouldn't inflict third-degree burns on my palate. Jack and Duncan were talking about Ferraris again. I began to wish I hadn't stayed.

The New Vague warbling stopped. Lulu was sifting distractedly through her pile of magazines and didn't notice. She was looking for something. 'Duncan?' she asked. 'Where's the first issue?' She raised her voice. '*Duncan?*'

Duncan broke off his conversation.

'*Bellini,*' Lulu insisted. 'Where did you put the first one?'

'It's somewhere around.'

'I want to show Alicia.'

Duncan paused, and then he said, 'You can show her another time.' There was a note in his voice which hadn't been there before. Oh-*oh*, I thought. Watch out, Lulu.

'*Duncan,*' she said.

Usually he did whatever she asked – anything for a quiet life. But now he was glowering. I hadn't seen him so edgy and bad-tempered in ages, but I really didn't mind, not if it was directed at Lulu. She was pouting again, but with her chin thrust out, determined to stand her ground in front of Jack and Alicia, who were both looking slightly embarrassed.

'Please, Dunc,' she said in her whiniest voice. 'Duncan *Doughnut.*' This was her pet name for him. He had never actually *said* that he hated it, but you could sometimes see the muscle in his jaw twitching.

For one glorious second I thought he was going to gouge her eyes out, but instead he sighed, and got to his feet. 'I think it's somewhere in the darkroom,' he said.

Lulu laughed triumphantly and clapped her hands together. 'Alicia, wait till you see this,' she said. 'It's really *gross.*'

As he went past my chair, Duncan spun on his heel and looked me straight in the eye. The effect was like a mild electric shock to the base of my spine. I got the message immediately and leapt to my feet. 'Now?'

He nodded, all of a sudden looking ten years older. 'Might as well get it over with,' he muttered, more to himself than to anyone else. Then he raised his voice. 'We've just got to go over this stuff. It won't take long. A couple of minutes.'

'Can't it wait?' asked Lulu.

'No,' he said. 'No, it can't.'

Jack and Alicia exchanged glances. They thought I was a pest, hanging around Duncan all the time. Lulu was acting like an abandoned puppy. I permitted myself to flash a quick grin in her direction as I followed Duncan into the office. Once the door was shut behind us, I toyed with the idea of making loud and interesting party noises, but he didn't seem to be in the mood for japes.

The office was cramped, with no windows; there was barely enough room for a desk and filing cabinet. One of the walls was taken up by a sliding door; Duncan pulled this open and we went through into the darkroom, which was only slightly bigger than the office and stank of stale chemicals. He tugged a cord and the light came on, and somewhere an extractor fan whirred into life. He dragged a stool away from the bench and insisted I sit down. While he was rummaging through the contents of a filing tray, I twisted round to peer into the sink behind me; it was full of black-and-white twelve-by-tens which eddied slowly as the water level repeatedly rose and fell. The topmost picture was of a nude girl wearing a hat shaped like a dead seagull.

I asked, 'So what's all this about?' but Duncan ignored

me and went on rummaging. After a minute or so, he found what he was looking for. I just had time to clock the *Bellini* logo before he turned to a page somewhere in the middle, smoothing it flat on the bench in front of me.

I looked, and my blood pressure leapt a few notches. The words *Night People!* were printed in dripping crimson across the top of the page. It was some sort of fashion spread, glistening with saturated colour. The model, of course, was wearing black. It was a dress cut low at the neck, made out of that clinging fabric you could only wear if you were prepared to spend half your waking life in the gym. But the dress itself wasn't so extraordinary; Lulu had a dozen or so like it in various shades of pink. What was extraordinary was the rest of the picture.

The model's face was dead white, and it appeared frozen with shock, which wasn't so surprising since somebody, not entirely in frame, was ramming a sharp stick through her chest. The dark fabric of the dress was gleaming even darker where the stick went in. A trickle of blood ran from one corner of her immaculately painted mouth. Her brilliant teeth were bared in a snarl, and there was no doubt that two of them were fangs.

I read the accompanying column of text out loud. *'Smart vamps only come out at night in the slinkiest fabrics, but stakes are high when the claret begins to flow and the chips are down.'* Beneath this was a list of labels and prices.

I could hardly believe my eyes. But I calmed down and studied the photograph objectively. 'Decadent chic,' I sneered. 'So *passé*.'

'Go on,' Duncan urged. I flipped the page. The next picture was even more tasteless: the same model in a different dress, black with sequin trimming around the neckline. The same anonymous co-star was applying a hacksaw to the dotted line which had been drawn round her neck. There was even more blood than on the previous page. I read, *'Toothsome cuties dress in black, and keep their heads when all around them are losing theirs.'*

I tried to summon up another sneer, but my heart wasn't in it. I looked through the rest of the feature. It was the same story in each: a white-faced, raven-haired, scarlet-lipped woman, clad in an assortment of little black dresses, being subjected to violent and potentially lethal indignities. I wondered how much it had cost to have the fake bloodstains removed from the clothes after the photo session, though not all the pictures had blood in them. In one, the model's mouth was being stuffed full of lettuce and radicchio. *'Le dernier cri de French Dressing,'* said the text, *'but remember to go easy on the garlic.'* Another shot depicted the unfortunate girl being dunked in a bath: her eyes were bulging and her long hair swirled like seaweed around her head beneath the force of the water cascading from the taps. *'Still waters run deep,'* intoned the text. *'Careless dress codes can lead to an early bath.'*

The last photograph in the series was relatively restrained, but somehow that made it all the more unpleasant. The model was bound to a chair, directly in the path of a beam of sunlight which was slicing through a gap between the curtains. She was snarling again, straining at the ropes which held her fast. Where the shaft of light fell on her bare arm, the make-up artists had applied an unpleasant-looking weal, and the blackened flesh appeared to be smouldering. *'Sunburn can be fatal,'* said the text. *'Smart vamps prize their pale skin and use barrier cream to shield their features from the ultraviolet.'*

A dreadful idea occurred to me. This was Duncan's work, his idea of a public confession. He had finally gone and flipped. 'Don't tell me these are *yours*,' I said, not wanting to hear the answer.

'Good Lord, no.' He shook his head rather more violently than was necessary, jabbing his forefinger at the small print at the bottom of the page. 'Dino, it was Dino.'

'Sick-*o*,' I said. I'd seen Dino's byline before, but had never met him. I didn't have to, I'd seen enough of his work to know he was a pretentious, obnoxious git – he liked to photograph naked women in compromising positions, adorned with lots of tasteful bondage and tight leather corsets. The prints were usually hand-tinted.

Duncan was now looking down at me with a faint smile, but I could see he was smiling only from a misplaced sense of bravado. The sight of the blood, fake though it was, had turned him pale and sweaty-looking. It was hot and stuffy in the tiny room, but not *that* hot and stuffy.

'Duncan?' I whispered. 'Duncan? Are you all right?'

He wasn't listening. He was staring past my head, at the wall.

He said, 'I think she's back.'

THREE

The occasion demanded a cigarette, so I pulled one out and lit up. There was no ashtray, so I used the floor. Duncan didn't object. I wasn't sure he'd even noticed. He was too busy staring at that last picture, looking as though he'd seen a ghost.

I inhaled, exhaled, and coughed. 'Not her,' I said at last. 'Doesn't look anything like her.'

'Of course it's not her.' He sounded peevish. 'What do you expect? But *look* at them.'

I looked again. 'Just some people in a studio. Just a way of showing the clothes. Some stupid fashion editor had what she thought was a bright idea.'

'You know there's more to it than that,' he said, adding – quite unnecessarily – 'You were there.'

I protested, 'You did most of it.'

'You helped.'

'Only because you *asked* me to.'

'Christ, I wish . . .' His voice trailed away.

'These are just photographs,' I said. 'Stupid ones. These

people think they're being deliciously witty, but they've got it wrong. I mean, *we* could cook up something much heavier if we put our minds to it. This is much too restrained. I can't see any limbs being hacked off. What about the chiffon scarf? The body bags? The burial at the crossroads?'

At each word, Duncan flinched as though white-hot needles were being inserted into his flesh. He had to prop himself up against the edge of the bench. I offered my seat, but he shook his head and instead helped himself to a cigarette. It was a long time since I'd seen him smoking. That, as much as anything, brought home the seriousness of the situation.

When he spoke at last, it was slowly and carefully. 'I don't believe this is a coincidence. These photographs are here for a purpose. She's back, and she wants me to know it.'

I told him he was reading too much into the pictures. There was no need to panic. There had never been any need to panic. We had always covered our tracks. But he wasn't listening to a word I said. 'It was the worst day of my life,' he muttered, staring bleakly at the fashion spread. 'I don't know what went wrong.'

Neither did I.

'I blew it,' he went on. 'I don't know what got into me.'

It occurred to me he might *welcome* the chance to feel guilty all over again. It was high time to nip *that* in the bud. 'Don't be silly. You did what you had to do. So did I.' I closed the magazine with finality and stared at the cover. A big white baby-soft face winked back at me. 'Jesus Christ! Do they do that *every* month?'

Duncan nodded sympathetically, though I'm not sure he

grasped the precise nature of my phobia; I'm not sure I even grasped it myself. 'Gives you the willies, doesn't it?' he said, smiling sadly. I forced myself to take another look. Wink or no wink, the cover-shot was not particularly unusual, neither was the *Bellini* logo. On the face of it, the magazine was interchangeable with any of the other new publications cluttering our newsstands: *Eva, Riva, Diva, Bella, Nella,* and *Stella,* and so on.

I turned to the contents page and checked the masthead. The publisher was Multiglom, a name I recognized as one of the first big companies to plant its headquarters in the Docklands area. None of the other names were familiar. The editor was either Japanese, part-Japanese, or pretending to be one or the other. It figured; Japan was still deeply trendy in media circles. I flicked through the pages. Faint perfume wafted up from scratch 'n' sniff advertising inserts which Lulu had already peeled open and rubbed against her wrists. There was a report on the Milan fashion shows, and an interview with a famous film director who had been com-missioned to shoot a cosmetics commercial with a budget exceeding those of all his feature films combined. There were pictures in which débutantes in white satin ballgowns stuck their tongues out at the camera or hoisted their skirts up to expose their legs, and an amusing photo-feature in which the fashion editors had lured some of the Have Nots off the street and into the studio where they'd been decked out in designer clothes. After the shoot, I assumed, they'd had their smelly old rags restored to them and been thrown back into the gutter.

The *Night People!* fashion feature seemed an aberration, as though it had been thought up by a different editorial team. I was surprised the publishers hadn't demanded it be toned down; those centre pages were not the sort of thing normally considered suitable for the shelves of a family newsagents.

'OK,' I allowed grudgingly. 'It might not be a coincidence.'

Duncan said nothing. He was fiddling with his thumbnail, doing something unbelievably vicious to the cuticle.

I said, 'If you're *really* worried, I could check it out.'

He looked up at last. 'How?'

I dropped the end of my cigarette on to the floor and ground it out with my heel. 'I could go and see them. They look as though they could do with some creative consultancy. Lulu says they pay well.'

'*Lulu* says? How in hell would she know?'

'She said she was going to see them.'

'Like *hell* she is. She'd better keep out of this.'

I didn't think this was entirely fair, and said so. Lulu might have had half her brain missing, but she was still entitled to make her own decisions.

'Lulu knows nothing,' Duncan said, perhaps more truthfully than he intended, 'and I want it to stay that way.'

'Look,' I said, 'I'm sure there's nothing to worry about, but I'll go in and talk to whoever thought up those photos. Or maybe I can talk to the editor.'

'The editor,' he echoed. All of a sudden there was a faraway look in his eyes. 'That name. Did you see?'

'See what?' I turned back to the masthead. 'Rose Murasaki? Never heard of her.'

'Murasaki Shikibu was a Japanese writer of the Fujiwara era. Eleventh century. She wrote *The Tale of Genji*.' I'd almost forgotten Duncan had once been an avid Japanophile. He'd had a big thing about martial-arts movies, had seen *Sanjuro* ten times or more, trying to work out how Toshiro Mifune had managed to draw his sword and plunge it into Tatsuya Nakadai's heart, all in a single movement so the blood spurted out like a geyser. I wondered whether he'd been able to watch it again at any point over the last thirteen years, what with his latterday aversion to gore. Maybe he still found it bearable; the film was in black and white, after all, and he'd told me the gushing blood was nothing but chocolate sauce.

'So this is a distant relative,' I suggested. 'Or more likely someone's idea of a hip literary reference.'

'That name,' said Duncan. '*Murasaki.*'

'So?'

'It's the Japanese word for purple.'

This was so rich I started to laugh, but I forced myself to stop before I got carried away. Even in my own ears, the laughter sounded too loud in that cramped space.

Duncan was beginning to ramble. 'Pink and purple. Did you know the Japanese don't have blue movies, they have *pink* ones? And did you know the French title for *Pretty in Pink* was *Rose Bonbon*? And did you know *Rose Bonbon* was the name of a striptease at the Crazy Horse?'

'No,' I said.

'Isabella Rossellini told me that.'

'Really?'

'And she also said that—' He stopped in mid-sentence and picked up whichever thread it was he had lost. 'It's the ultra*violet*,' he said, jabbing the magazine with his finger. 'Sunburn and ultra*violet*. Purple. Violet. Murasaki. That's why she picked the name.'

'Do you really think so?' I asked doubtfully.

'I *know* so.'

'Duncan, you don't *know* anything.'

He looked wounded. 'I knew *her*. You didn't know her at all. To you, she was less than human.' I bit my tongue to stop myself blurting out that it wasn't just my verdict – she was less than human whichever way you looked at it.

'Be careful, Dora,' he said, so solemnly that I almost started laughing again. It was the first time anyone had ever told me to be careful of . . . what? A magazine? The colour purple? Someone who had been dead for thirteen years?

'You're probably right,' he went on in a rush. 'It's probably just coincidence. But of all the things I've done in my life, that was the most evil, the most awful, the most unforgivable, and someone, somewhere, is wanting to make me suffer for it, and – do you know – I think we *deserve* to suffer, because I don't feel good about what we did at all . . .'

'I *know* I'm right,' I said in what I hoped was a reassuring tone. 'I *know* there's nothing to worry about. You're getting worked up over nothing. Look, I'll go and see these people and find out what's going on, but I promise you: it will be nothing. *Nothing.*'

I didn't believe what I was saying for an instant, I was just saying what I thought would shut him up, but he took a deep breath and was back to his normal charming self. 'What on earth would I do without you, Dora?' He smiled and dipped forward and pecked me on the forehead. 'You don't mind? I never wanted to drag you into any of this. I wasn't thinking straight. I'm still not thinking straight . . .'

I tried to make my face glow with sincerity. 'You'd better get back to your guests. Lulu's imagination will be running riot.' I felt like kissing him properly, none of that pecking,

29

but he would have been shocked. Not because he was afraid of being unfaithful to Lulu, more because it wasn't the sort of thing he expected from me.

'Oh, yes,' he said. 'Lulu.' He picked up the magazine and rolled it into a thick tube and held it up to his eye, like a telescope. 'She wanted Alicia to have a look at this, didn't she.' He hovered uncertainly, as if waiting to be told what to do next.

'If I were you,' I said, 'I wouldn't show Alicia. Too tasteless. It might upset her.' I eased the magazine from his grasp. 'Tell Lulu you've lost it. Tell her you'll buy another one tomorrow.'

'Oh yes. Of course.' As he was moving towards the door, I added, 'And don't forget to tell everyone we just had great sex together.'

He smiled warily, unsure whether this was supposed to be a joke. 'You shouldn't be nasty to Lulu. She really likes you.'

'Oh, I bet she does.'

'She does,' he insisted. 'Only the other day she was saying how much she admires how you always get what you want.'

'She does all right for herself.'

'She's been having a hard time of it lately, only you'd never know it. She keeps things bottled up.'

I was fed up with all this talk about Lulu. She didn't interest me in the slightest. 'Why don't you go back into the other room,' I said. 'I'm going to stay here and have another cigarette.' I couldn't have one outside; Alicia would have killed me for contaminating the baby's airspace.

'Right,' he said, backing through the door into the office. He paused again. 'Dora . . .'

'It's OK, Duncan. Really it is. It's not her. She hasn't come back. There is no way on earth that she *could* come back. Not after everything we did.'

'You're right,' he said. He seemed relieved, as though my word was law. 'And you won't mention any of this to Lu?'

'Don't be daft. She'd get us locked up.'

He forced a smile. 'See you,' he said. He went out, and I heard Lulu saying something as the office door opened. Then it closed again, and the sounds of the outside world were cut off, and I was left alone with my thoughts. I finished that second cigarette, and promptly lit another one. I reckoned I had every right to chain-smoke. My cigarette hand was shaking. The more I tried to hold it steady, the more it shook. I stared at it detachedly. It belonged to someone else.

It was all so obvious. I hadn't been convinced, not to begin with, but that was because I hadn't *wanted* to be convinced. Duncan was paranoid, but then he had every reason to be, because there was no doubt about it, none at all. The fashion spread was a joke, a ridiculous gesture, but it was also as good as a calling-card. She was back. She thought she could waltz right back into his life, after all these years.

I didn't know what she wanted. I just knew I was going to stop her from getting it.

It was one of those nights. The Krankzeits had visitors. They were on good form, twisting the night away until well past three. I needed to blot out the day's events to make a fresh start in the morning, but I couldn't even get to sleep. I tried to think instead, but I couldn't concentrate on my thoughts.

The noise from upstairs got me stuck in a mental groove which flickered pink, purple, violet, pink, purple, violet, until the colours took on a life of their own and started dancing the can-can in my head. I knew from experience it was no good banging on the ceiling with the end of a broom; the Krankzeits were making so much noise it would have taken a bomb to attract their attention. Many times I'd toyed with the idea of sending them one.

After an hour spent trying to stuff the corners of the duvet into my ears, I gave up and sat down at my desk, donned my rubber gloves, and cut up some magazines to compose a letter to Patricia Rice. It wasn't a particularly inspired letter; I was too bleary-eyed to summon up much creativity at that time in the morning. But I called her a CoMmIE LEsBiAN CoW, even though I knew perfectly well she was neither commie nor lesbian, and I informed her that her every move was being watched by mR BoNes and his BoDy ROt CReW, members of a Californian killer-hippy cult which was plotting to take over the whole world, starting with Lambeth.

Gripping the fibre-tip pen in my left fist, I laboriously printed Patty's name and address on one of the plain brown envelopes I'd bought from Woolworths. The Krankzeits' visitors yelled goodbye and clomped laughing and weeping into the night, but Gunter and Christine continued to drop concrete blocks on their floor at regular intervals, so I took the opportunity to compose an angry letter to the council about the recent proliferation of rubbish on the street. From force of habit, I withheld my identity but listed the names and addresses of my next-door neighbours who had once held an all-night party and told me to fuck off when I'd complained about the noise, followed by the name and address of the drug dealer who owned the four Alsatians which sometimes howled all night because they were kept in a tiny backyard which was never cleaned, followed by a postscript in which I hinted that the noisy community centre down the road was allowing drugs to be sold on the premises. As an afterthought, I signed myself Gunter Krankzeit.

By this time, the noise had subsided into the to-and-fro-ing I recognized as normal bedtime routine, so I thankfully sealed the envelopes and crawled back into my bed. The last thing I remembered thinking about was Alicia, and the way she'd sniffed the air as I'd come out of the darkroom and asked if anyone had been smoking. That had got me so mad I'd almost told her about Jack and Roxy.

I fell asleep watching the light-fitting sway in time to the last dwindling thuds from upstairs.

FOUR

I dreamt about a boardroom where a dozen or so people were sitting round a table. They looked like regular executive types, but I knew they were not.

'She can't handle it,' said one of the men. He looked familiar. In my capacity as dream director, I zoomed in for a close-up and saw it was Burt Reynolds. 'She could easily lose control.'

'Give her a chance,' said someone else. It was Robert Redford – I had evidently assembled an all-star line-up.

'But she'll lose her head,' Burt said. 'And it'll be a disaster, like before.'

'I think you're wrong,' said a woman with startled eyes. Good grief, I thought, what was Liza Minnelli doing here? 'She's learned her lesson.'

'I wouldn't be too sure.' Burt coughed, as though embarrassed by what he had to say next. 'I don't know whether any of you are aware of this, but she still thinks she's in love.'

There was some snickering at this. 'Love?' sneered Liza,

and I saw now her eyes were not just startled, but glittering cruelly in a way I'd never seen before. 'She doesn't know the meaning of the word. She's interested in nothing but power, and the wielding of it.'

I wanted to chip in and tell them no, they'd got it wrong, I really did love Duncan, I'd loved him for years. Perhaps not in the accepted sense, but my feelings for him were stronger than they appeared. But the role of dream director was limited to lining up the shots. I wasn't really there, I could do no more than watch and listen as they went on discussing my case.

'Nevertheless,' said Burt, 'she maintains he is still important to her, especially after Paris. We should keep her under surveillance. She might still do something rash that would jeopardize the entire project.'

'In that case,' said Robert, 'may I suggest we contact the Hatman? Andreas Grauman has reasons of his own for wanting to keep an eye on her, which in my view makes him all the more trustworthy.'

There was a ripple of approval. 'An excellent idea,' said Liza.

Mention of Grauman made me feel uneasy. I hoped he wasn't going to turn up in my dream. But then the debate took a weird turn, and they all started talking about Israelis and Palestinians. There was a time and a place for politics, I thought, and it wasn't in my dreams. I listened for a while, tried in vain to vary the camera angle or cut to another scene, but succeeded only in waking myself up.

Next day my instincts were telling me things. I needed a holiday. I *always* needed a holiday, but, unfortunately for me, I was the conscientious sort. There were half a dozen deadlines looming up – one of them for Jack's magazine – and I prided myself on being reliable. Unreliability would lead to no work, would lead to no money, and we couldn't have that, not while the Have Nots were roaming the streets as a reminder of what it would be like.

But most of all, I didn't want to leave Duncan. Especially not now, when he was paying me more attention than he'd paid me in years. So I did what I'd promised; I headed for Multiglom Tower. It was a long haul. To get there, I had to go to Tower Hill and transfer to the Docklands Light Railway. It was years since I'd been anywhere east of Aldgate, and the city had changed. The railway was fun, like a slow-moving roller-coaster trundling through a half-finished theme park. Sticking up from the otherwise uniform acres of gutted warehouse were the developers' party pieces: toy town halls made from primary-coloured building blocks, Lego pyramids covered in shocking pink scaffolding, and Nissen huts decorated with Egyptian murals. Viewed from the comfort of the train it was amusing, but as soon as I emerged from Molasses Wharf Station I found myself trapped in a pedestrian's nightmare. Progress was thwarted at every turn by fenced-off building sites or gloomy basins of stagnant water. Concrete mixers blocked the pavements. The ground was coated with a layer of pale mud, and every so often a truck would thunder past and splash the backs of my legs. The only other people I saw were distant figures in yellow helmets. My A–Z of street maps was obsolete; streets that were supposed to be there no longer existed, and new ones had sprung up in different configurations. I buried the book in my bag and tried to dust off the instincts that were still sulking from having been dismissed earlier on.

Fortunately, I could see where I wanted to go. It would have been impossible to miss it. Had it been a sunny day, the shadow would have fallen across my path. Multiglom Tower loomed up out of the drizzle like a gigantic monolith, its summit swathed in wheeling seagulls and wisps of grey cloud. The building was controversial, less for its design than its height; it had buggered up half of east London's TV reception. I had seen photos, but now I had to admit they didn't do it justice. It reminded me of a sound system: a stack of tape-decks, amplifier, and CD player in black glass, opaque except for odd little pinpoints of red and white glinting deep within the walls. But who could tell what kind of music it would be playing? I steered towards it, or tried to.

After about half an hour of dodging traffic and sneaking through gateways marked with signs of men being struck in the chest by lightning bolts, I found myself within spitting distance of my destination. I circled it warily, craning my neck to stare upwards, feeling like a lost tourist trying to get her bearings in the middle of Manhattan. There were two entrances. There was a service door big enough to swallow a fleet of trucks, but while I was there I saw only one vehicle emerge – a navy blue Bedford van with a tinted windscreen and the words DOUBLE IMAGE stencilled (twice) on to the side.

At the main entrance the word MULTIGLOM was chiselled into marble over three sets of revolving doors. Each door was flanked by uniformed security guards who looked as though they might have cut their teeth on Treblinka. I tried to peer past them, but all I could see in the black glass was my own distorted reflection. The guards watched me with hard, unblinking eyes. They made me nervous. It was getting on for lunchtime, so I decided to postpone my investigations and seek out some Dutch courage.

Over the street was something which had once been a warehouse, but which was now a brasserie-cum-art-gallery called the Bar Nouveau. From what I had seen of the area, it was the only watering-hole for miles. I assumed it would be doing a roaring trade in Multiglom workers, but it turned out I was the sole customer. There was a sign saying *Barsnacks*. I bought a half of lager and a Gruyère bagel, and asked the barman how he managed to stay open. 'You'd be surprised,' he said, polishing a glass with his tea-towel. 'Evenings, we're packed out.'

'Don't they eat lunch? Where are they now?'

'How should I know?' Now he was looking vexed, as though I were distracting him from his polishing manoeuvres. I left him to it and wandered away with my drink and bagel to examine the small collection of oils hanging on the far wall. They were primitive in concept and execution, but there was one painting I liked: a picture of a tower-block, not in the Multiglom mould, but the chunky type to be seen on any sixties-built housing estate. Half-way up the building a big white ghost was leaning over a balcony, howling and flapping its sheeted arms in the air. I didn't know why, but the picture made me laugh.

I settled down at a table near the window and watched people going in and out of Multiglom. I sat there for half an hour, sipping my lager and smoking cigarettes, and all in all, only two people went in, and only one came out. The one who came out was one of the two who had gone in, and he came out again pretty smartly, as though he'd been turned away at reception. I wasn't sure I could get much further, but it was time to give it my best shot. A last cigarette for luck, and I was strolling, ever so casually, across the street.

One of the guards looked me up and down as I approached, but concluded I wasn't an interesting enough specimen to be dragged off to the nearest death camp and watched impassively as I wrestled with the heavy revolving doors. I plunged through them into a different world. The daylight was blotted out and replaced by flat white lighting which bounced off the white marble and made me pull up, dazzled. It was like being in an empty cathedral. The floor was as vast and as slippery as an ice-rink, and the walls stretched upward for fifty feet or more, branching out as they rose into a high-vaulted ceiling. There were no chairs, no potted plants, no ashtrays on stems, and no magazines to flick through. Visitors, like diners in McDonald's, were not encouraged to linger.

It took me about fifteen seconds to walk from the doors to the reception desk, but it felt like five minutes. So white and shiny was the floor, I found myself sneaking backward glances to check I wasn't leaving a trail of dirty footprints. The reception desk itself was built on a sort of dais, designed so the receptionists could look down their noses at me as I approached. Both of them were dressed in black. I felt like kicking myself; I should have gone back to black, just this once, to blend in. But it was too late: here I was in Prince of Wales check, and it was obviously a serious infringement of the dress code.

I found myself gazing up at the nearer of the women. There was something unnatural about her skin. It was too smooth, as though the foundation beneath the powder had been a thin layer of liquid latex. Or perhaps it was the lighting, which made everything look flat and white and dead. Her facial expression would have made her a fortune at poker. She arched an eyebrow, no more than a fraction of a millimetre. 'Yes?'

'Uh,' I said. 'Which floor is *Bellini*?' As the words came out of my mouth I realized the acoustics made my voice sound high-pitched and squeaky, like Mickey Mouse. The receptionist's reply, on the other hand, bore all the hallmarks of one who had majored in voice projection.

'Do you have an appointment?' she boomed.

'I didn't know I needed one.'

'You have to have an appointment.'

'I want to see Rose Murasaki. I knew her back in '75.'

Poker-Face barely cracked. She turned and punched out some numbers on a telephone. 'There is a person here,' she said into the receiver, 'who says she used to know the Editor.' She spoke as though she didn't believe a word of it.

There was a faint buzzing. Poker-Face turned back to me. 'What do you do?'

I explained. 'Creative consultant, freelance,' she echoed into the phone as though the words were descriptive of some unpleasant disease of the digestive tract. Then she hung up and said, 'Thirty-second floor. Lifts over there.'

I smiled weakly, and went off to summon a lift. While I was waiting for it, I scanned the small print on the floor guide. Micromart, Superdish, Pharmatex, Hi-Vista, Deforest, Double Image . . . and there, up against numbers thirty-two and thirty-three – *Bellini*.

The lift arrived and I stepped inside. The walls were

stainless-steel inlaid with strips of solid black Perspex. It was a bit like a hi-tech microwave. I pushed the button for the thirty-second floor, half expecting my head to explode, but instead the doors closed. I didn't normally feel nervous in lifts, but this one made me feel as though a troupe of flamenco dancers were stomping all over my grave. The upward movement was as quick and smooth as the speed of light, but it was accompanied by an unpleasant clanking sound which set me thinking about all the movies I'd seen in which elevators plummeted down shafts so fast their occupants were plastered against the ceiling or sliced in half by steel cables snapped free from their moorings.

Not before time, the doors slid open. I stumbled out on to thick green carpet, into another reception area, though this was cosier than the one downstairs. Here there were no right-angles, only curves, but the same flat white light as below. And the receptionist looked as though she had graduated from the same charm school, except she was blonde, like Eva Peron. She was perched over some kind of Starship Enterprise console fitted with monitors and a couple of keyboards. From somewhere beyond a doorway to her left came a faint flutter of electronic sound. The place wasn't exactly bustling.

She looked up as I approached. 'You want to make an appointment.'

'I'd like to see the Editor.'

'That's right. You want to make an appointment.'

'Is she in?'

'She can't see you today. You need an appointment.'

'Oh, all right.' There didn't seem any other way of getting to meet Rose Murasaki. 'I'll make an appointment.'

Eva Peron was checking one of her screens. 'When?'

'Tomorrow?' I said hopefully.

She laughed derisively. '*Impossible*. I can't fit you in until next week, at least.'

So why ask, I thought. Out loud I said, 'That'll have to do.'

She tip-tapped at the keyboard and inspected something which came up on her monitor. I leant forward and tried to inspect it too, but she flashed me such a look of fury that I shrank back, grinning fatuously and pretending my action had been part of a neck-flexing exercise.

'Next week. The 14th,' she said finally.

'Nothing before that?'

'The 14th. Take it or leave it.'

'OK, OK. The 14th. What time?'

'Nine.'

I winced. Nine was pushing it. I wasn't used to doing business until well after ten, with my brain kick-started by at least two jugs of strong black coffee. 'Can't you make it a bit later?'

She sighed as though I was putting her to enormous trouble. 'Ten o'clock? Midnight?'

'*Midnight?*' It took a while for this to sink in. 'You mean nine o'clock *in the evening*?'

She blinked. Once. Twice. 'Our Editor has a very full schedule. She often takes meetings at night.'

'In that case, nine o'clock will be just fine.'

She sighed again. 'Name?'

I missed a beat, but not so as she noticed. Something inside me suggested it would be prudent to keep a low profile. On the other hand, I might just have been fibbing out of habit. 'Patricia Rice,' I said.

'Address?'

I gave her Patricia's address and telephone number, and she punched them into the computer. As I watched her fingers on the keys, I had what seemed like a smart idea. 'Any chance of some back issues?'

She stared at me as though I'd asked her to remove her clothes. 'There have only ever been two issues of the magazine.'

'Well, perhaps you could spare a couple.'

Her mouth twitched. I thought she was going to tell me to get lost, but she didn't. 'Please wait,' she said, and disappeared through the door to her left. I could hear her talking, but I couldn't hear what was being said.

I have never been computer literate. I could operate simple word-processing software, but the finer points of bytes, pips, and programs left me at the starting-point. Still, Eva Peron didn't appear to be in the Albert Einstein class, and she was coping. I hovered long enough to check she wasn't coming straight back, and then I leant across the reception desk and examined the monitor – just in time to see Patricia Rice's name and address flicker on the screen, and vanish.

I thought I'd stopped being the sort of person who takes risks. I'd taken a few back in the early days, when I'd been younger, with an imagination which had not yet expanded to encompass the full range of unpleasant things that can happen to a person. But once again I was experiencing the weird sensation of the world shifting beneath my feet. Rocky times called for reckless behaviour. I slapped the EXIT key and the screen ticked over until we were back in the basic LAUNCHPAD system. Quickly, I scrolled through the databank to see if I recognized any of the names. ARTEMIS. ARTISTIC

AGENCIES. ARTISTS, INC. ARTO. ASTRA. ASTROPOLOUS. They unfurled on the screen at a rate of knots. I zapped through the Bs and Cs. One or two companies I'd heard of, but nothing of interest. I had the vague intention of getting as far as M for MURASAKI. But then I saw DINO.

I could still hear the murmur of voices beyond the door, so I punched into what I thought was inspection mode. A load of indecipherable rubbish came up. I pressed EXIT and ENTER and RETURN and I ended up with an address: Studio E, 174 London Bridge Road. I tried punching my way back into the main file, but I must have pressed the wrong key. The screen went blank except for a single word in the top left-hand corner: ROTNACHT. I pressed what I thought was the correct key (but hadn't I pressed that one before?) and the word disappeared, but then it was back again: ROT-NACHT. Now it was flashing on and off. ROTNACHT. ROT-NACHT. ROTNACHT. I panicked, pressed EXIT and ENTER and CANCEL and STOP and the word disappeared again and I was just wondering whether I'd erased all the other data in the process when I realized the murmur of voices in the next room had died away.

I straightened up with a sinking feeling. Eva Peron was leaning against the doorframe, watching me with her arms folded. She smiled, but I wished she hadn't. 'Seen anything you like?' she asked, sauntering over, holding out my two back issues. I took them, even though I didn't particularly want them any more.

'Not really,' I said. 'I was just trying your computer, but I don't think I'll buy one like this. It's much too complicated.'

She sat down and scrolled back through the files, trying to work out how much I'd seen. 'This is a specialist machine,' she said frostily.

'I thought as much,' I said, shuffling towards the lifts.

'Thank you . . .' she said, looking directly at me. '*Miss Rice*,' she said, as though she'd always known it wasn't my real name, and smiled again.

'Bye,' I said, pressing the down button. The microwave door slid open. I remember thinking how odd it was, in a building that size, with that capacity, that the lift I had come up in was exactly where I'd left it – ready and waiting to take me down again.

FIVE

Duncan and I had arranged to meet in one of the few Soho streets which had not yet been redeveloped as a parade of upmarket eateries, which could still boast one or two *Girls in Bed* signs, and a sex shop full of inflatable dolls and crotchless panties. The café was next door. It was a lousy café; it didn't even do cappuccino, but it had the advantage of being undiscovered by bright young media folk and it had never been written about in the *Good Food Guide*, so there were always plenty of empty tables.

In thirteen years nothing had changed. The radio was tuned to a station which played nothing but Slade and Showaddywaddy. In the corner, the same faded poster for a peach-flavoured aperitif called Sex Appeal. On the walls, the same bleached prints of the Bay of Naples. The contents of the sweet-trolley looked suspiciously familiar as well: the same strawberry gateau with its dusty Quick-Jel filling, the same primordial slime the waiters claimed was Tiramisu, and profiteroles which had calcified into geological specimens.

'The place hasn't changed at all,' I remarked, stirring

46

sugar into my cup. I didn't usually take sugar, but the coffee hadn't changed either; it was so disgusting it needed all the help it could get.

'Hasn't it?' Duncan said absent-mindedly. 'I wouldn't know. I've never been here before.'

My jaw dropped. 'Yes, you *have*.'

He was puzzled by my insistence. 'No, I don't think so.' I felt like shaking him. *Wake up! What kind of spell did she put on you?* Not for the first time, I wondered what was going on in his head. Was all the time he spent with me so forgettable? Which pieces of the past did he bring out and mull over in his private moments? Did *any* of them include me, or were they all memories of Violet? Maybe all the booze and pills had given him brain damage. My own memory wasn't so hot, but I'd always been able to recall certain occasions in the minutest detail. I could even remember what people had been wearing. That Saturday, thirteen years ago, for instance: he'd been in a green corduroy jacket; I'd been wearing a black crape dress which I had bought from an Oxfam shop. That had been back in the days when I'd still been wearing black.

I buried the memories and described my trip to the Multi-glom Tower. This was what Duncan had been waiting for. He'd heard some of it on the phone already, but now he leant forward, listening intently as I ran through it again. I gave him a fairly straight account, but played down my feeling of having been caught trespassing in a high-security morgue.

'But you didn't get to see *her*,' he said at last.

'Who? Murasaki? You're kidding. It's like getting an audience with the Pope. I've got to stand in line with everyone else. But I made an appointment for Monday.'

47

'It's *her*. I know it is. It *has* to be her.'

'If it is, she's come up in the world. Her standard of living has improved.' I was on the verge of saying too much, and swallowed the rest, but Duncan didn't appear to have noticed anything. 'Those offices are pretty plush,' I added quickly.

'She always did have resources.'

'I should say. I was looking through those back issues. You should see the bylines – all the really big guns.'

'That's what I was afraid of,' Duncan said. He reached across the table and took one of my cigarettes.

'I thought you'd given up.' That was the trouble with non-smokers. They invariably helped themselves to other people's cigarettes, never bought their own.

'I have,' he said, lighting up. 'I just feel like one.' He took a couple of puffs, grimaced and stubbed it out so heavily there was not even the possibility of my being able to straighten it out and slide it back into the packet. 'There,' he said. 'I just gave up again.'

I thought I deserved a pat on the back, at least, for having trekked all the way to Docklands on his behalf. 'There's Dino's address,' I reminded him.

'Dino,' said Duncan. 'Yeah, maybe we should talk to Dino.'

'Have you met him?'

'I've run into him once or twice. He's a wanker.'

'You can see that from his work.'

'A runt. His real name is Phineas Dean.'

'I thought he was Italian–American.'

'He wishes.' Duncan examined the sugar bowl and stewed silently about something. By the time he spoke again,

48

he'd made up his mind he wanted to go straight round to London Bridge Road and give Dino the third degree. When I said I had work to do, he tried to get me to postpone it and tag along as moral support. He didn't have to try very hard. He called for the bill and began to sort through the change in his pocket.

'Hang on a minute,' I said. 'At least let me finish my coffee. There's no rush.'

'Yes there is. There is now. Lulu had a summons.'

'Oh Lordy, not again.' I thought he was referring to Lulu's habit of stuffing parking tickets into her glove compartment and forgetting about them. She had been sent a clutch of summonses for non-payment, but she forgot about them as well. Stern men had been sent round to deal with her, but she always won them over with entreaties and promises and much fluttering of her eyelashes, and they always patted her on the head and went away satisfied. She never did pay up.

But Duncan wasn't talking about that sort of summons. It turned out that someone from *Bellini* had contacted her agent that morning. There was a lot of flu around; the model they'd booked had gone down with it and they needed a replacement at less than a day's notice. They'd come across Lulu's card and she was exactly what they were after: blonde hair, blue eyes, 34C–22–34, 5′ 10″, 110lb. Face like a Botticelli bimbo and bosoms like a tit-man's dream. Jack had once described her like that. To her face. And she had taken it as a compliment.

'She won't listen to me,' Duncan said. 'She's got it into her head this is her big break.'

'Isn't she a bit old?' I asked, and I wasn't trying to be

catty. By modelling standards, Lulu was well past her sell-by date.

'That's what I said, and she just got mad. I said I didn't want her to go, and she got even stroppier, said I was trying to tie her to the cooker. I said I was game if she was, but she didn't think that was very funny.' Duncan tipped a small amount of sugar on to the table-top and, apparently without thinking, arranged it into a small, neat line. 'Only the other day, she was wanting to start a bloody family. Now she's wanting a bloody career again. How can I tell her that it might be *dangerous*?'

'Duncan, it's a *magazine*, for Christ's sake. How could it be dangerous? I've been there: the security was tighter than a duck's ass, and – you know how these things work – she'll be the centre of attention. There'll be make-up people, and hairdressers, and stylists and fashion directors and photographers and assistants, and PRs and lots and lots of hangers-on. Anyway, Lulu can look after herself. She's a big girl.' And in all the right places, I wanted to add but didn't. It was odd taking her side against Duncan, but I thought he was being excessively cautious. He had never been that worried about me.

'You don't know her,' he said. 'She's far too trusting.'

I wanted to say, Oh no she's not, she's a calculating bitch. Instead, I asked, 'You sure you're not jealous they've asked Lulu and not you?' Judging by Duncan's reaction, I'd hit the nail on the head. He huffed and puffed and declared he only had Lulu's best interests at heart.

'Oh, let her do it if she wants,' I said, draining my coffee cup and getting a mouthful of bitter sludge. 'The worst thing that can happen is Dino will take her clothes off and hand-tint her. Then you'll be able to act like a real man and punch his face in.'

We went down to London Bridge Road in Duncan's car, which was small and black and flash-looking. Dino's studio turned out to be only a few blocks away from Patricia Rice's flat, in a row of old office buildings which had been knocked through into one big hangar and tarted up with green paint. We stepped through the door into an open reception area. I'd had enough of receptionists to last me a lifetime, but at least this one looked human. She was lolling behind a chunky metal desk, twirling a fibre-tip pen between her fingers and looking incredibly un-busy. The direct route to the desk was blocked by a large, empty cardboard box which was standing in the middle of the floor; we walked around it.

I went straight to the point. 'Where's Dino?'

She shrugged. 'How should I know?'

'Because you're the receptionist.'

'I'm the *manager*,' she said sniffily. 'I *manage* this place.'

I'd made a *faux-pas* and she hated my guts already. Duncan was forced to take over. 'He's an old friend,' he said. 'We went to the same school.'

This was news to me. I wondered if he was improvising. Meanwhile, the receptionist who said she was a manager was looking at him with goo-goo eyes. 'I know you, don't I. You're Duncan Fender.'

Duncan nodded, pretending to be embarrassed but in fact enormously flattered. She got to her feet and held out her hand. 'I really like your work.' As he clasped it she suddenly leant over and kissed him full on the mouth. He winced and pulled back in some alarm, though not *too* far, because she was the kind of girl men like Duncan always find attractive: a wild mane of hair, a dress which fitted like cling-film, and enormous squishy please-hit-me lips.

'Absolutely thrilled to meet you,' she said. 'I've always been a fan of yours, ever since I first started in this business. I'm Francine, by the way.' She delivered an appreciative résumé of Duncan's career, called him a genius more often than was good for him, and popped one or two technical questions about F-stops and fill-in flash. She described some photographs she had recently had published in a music paper. It was obvious she had taken on this administrative job in the hope of meeting people and making contacts. She was the kind of girl who would go far; I sincerely hoped it would be somewhere like the Outer Hebrides.

But she and Duncan were getting on like a house on fire; he was radiating charm like a chat-show host. She offered to make tea, rounded up three or four dirty mugs, and disappeared. Duncan turned to me and winked, even though he should have known better.

I scowled. 'Were you really at school with Dino?'

'Mmm, he was one or two years below me.'

'Why didn't you *say*?'

He shrugged. 'It didn't seem important. I don't think we ever spoke. Oh, except one time when a couple of us beat the crap out of him.'

'You did *what*?'

'He was a disgusting little toad, even then.'

'You *beat him up*?' I couldn't believe what I'd heard.

He shrugged again. It was no big deal. 'He insulted my mother.'

He fell silent as Francine came back and picked up where she'd left off with the flirtatious chit-chat. I was still stunned. I'd always imagined Duncan as a sensitive and artistic little boy, a loner who preferred library books to the rugby field. Never in my wildest dreams had I seen him as a violent and obnoxious bully.

When the tea had brewed, Francine poured some for Duncan and offered him biscuits as well. As an afterthought, she poured a cup for me but forgot to hand it over, so I had to go round to her side of the desk to get it. She stood up to allow me past her chair, and a blast of garlic caught me full in the face. No wonder Duncan had recoiled from her kiss.

From my new vantage point, I was able to read the scribbled notes on her memo-pad. She had doodled a baroque framework of leaves and flowers around a small clearing in which the name *Dino* had been scored and scored again in fat black letters. I could also see a partly opened drawer containing a number of large brown envelopes. The name *Dino* was visible there as well. I sipped at my tea and decided to stay put. For an instant, my eyes met Duncan's; it was almost as good as sex. He bit into a custard cream. 'And how is Dino? What's he up to?'

Francine lost some of her self-composure. She looked genuinely upset. 'He's gone,' she said in a small voice. Duncan asked what she meant.

'I mean he took off. Doesn't work here any more.'

'This is a recent thing, right?' I said, in case Duncan was thinking I'd made a mistake with the address.

Francine took a deep breath. 'I came in one morning last week and found him trying to burn the place down.'

'You're kidding.'

'It's true. He put all his negs in a pile and set fire to them. It could have been a major disaster if I hadn't come in. Look, you can see the burn marks.' She went over to the cardboard box and pushed it to one side to uncover an expanse of scorched carpet.

'Crikey,' said Duncan. 'The whole place could have gone up.' He glanced at me and I nodded. He examined the scorch marks closely, all the time keeping up an inane patter and contriving to stand so Francine was forced to turn her back on me – just for a second, but it was enough.

'He was in a frightful state,' she was saying. 'Hadn't shaved or changed his clothes for days. God, he was *smelly*.'

I thought that was rich coming from someone with her garlicky breath. Mission accomplished, envelope tucked safely beneath my jacket, I moved away from the desk with my best butter-wouldn't-melt expression.

'Did you call the police?' Duncan was asking.

'Didn't seem worth it,' said Francine. 'He was only trying to burn his own property.'

'What happened then?'

'I put the fire out.'

'No, I mean what happened to Dino?'

'He called me a stupid cow and stomped off.'

'Do you know where?'

She shook her head.

'Well, where does he usually hang out? Where would I be most likely to bump into him?'

She frowned. 'Gnashers, I suppose. And there's some place in Covent Garden, I can't remember the name. Oh, and he took me to the Foxhole a couple of times.'

'The Foxhole?' queried Duncan.

'I know it,' I said. 'Over the river.' I'd had quite enough of Francine, so I grabbed Duncan by the elbow and steered him towards the door. 'Just the place for a quick drink,' I said. I looked back over my shoulder and was delighted to see that Francine was glowering. She'd got the message. Duncan belonged to me.

SIX

We were driving north over Blackfriars Bridge when Duncan remembered the envelope and asked what was inside. I peeked in and saw negatives.

'No contact sheets?'

I checked. 'Just negs.'

Duncan whistled the first few bars of the theme from *The Third Man*. 'So he didn't burn them all.'

'Francine was lying.'

'Of course she was. She's in with Violet. So's Dino. They're all in it together.'

'She can't be in with Violet,' I said. 'Didn't you smell her breath? The girl reeked of garlic.'

Duncan mulled over this. 'I'm still not letting Lu go off on her own tomorrow.'

I told him he was overreacting. One photographer may have been behaving strangely, but we had no proof that working for *Bellini* was going to turn Lulu into a pyromaniac as well. I tried to put things into perspective. 'This is a *magazine* we're talking about. A fashion *magazine*, all about clothes and make-up. Not some sinister East European agency which jabs poisoned ferrules into people because they refuse to wear the autumn colours.'

Duncan said, 'Do be serious.' I hated it when people told me to be serious, especially when I *was* being serious.

'I feel responsible for her,' Duncan went on. 'I know she gets on your nerves – and she gets on mine too sometimes – but she's a genuinely *nice* person, Dora. There is not an ounce of maliciousness in her, and these days that's remarkable. She's not as dumb as she looks, either, even if she hasn't got round to reading Proust. Neither have I, come to think of it. We can't all be intellectuals like you.'

He said 'intellectuals' the way one might say 'fascists' or 'serial killers'. I protested I wasn't an intellectual, I just happened to have read a few French authors, but he was getting into his stride now. 'I owe her so much. She saved my life, and I mean that literally. I don't think you've any idea what shape I was in.'

I was fuming. This was his selective memory at work again. He hadn't noticed all the things *I'd* done for him. And I'd done a *lot* – a hell of a lot more than Lulu. 'It seems to me,' I said, choosing my words carefully, 'that you're less worried about Lulu's welfare than about the possibility of her running into one of your old flames, and maybe learning rather more about your sordid past than you would care to have her know.'

That hit him where it hurt. By the time he'd found somewhere to park in one of the narrow streets around the Savoy we were both sulking. I flounced out of the car, intending to catch the tube home. I was annoyed when Duncan tagged along behind me. I walked faster, but couldn't shake him off.

We got almost as far as the railway arches, where the Have Nots huddled in their newspapers and cardboard boxes. I stopped and wheeled round to face Duncan and asked where he thought he was going.

'I thought we were going in there,' he said, pointing to the top of a staircase visible through a nearby doorway. I recognized it as the entrance to the Foxhole. 'You look as though you need a drink,' he said, adding, 'I could do with one too.' I reminded him he'd given up drinking a long time ago. He said maybe it was time he started again, and gave me a peculiar little smile which crinkled the corners of his eyes. When I saw that smile, I almost forgave him everything.

The Foxhole was a murky cellar with walls moist enough to support several species of fungi. It was already getting crowded, and we had to do some nifty manoeuvring to grab the last vacant table. As I'd expected, it took only one glass to knock Duncan back against the ropes. Perhaps I should have put a stop to it, but I was still so annoyed at the 'intellectual' gibe that I encouraged him to have another. And another. Besides, it was good to have him to myself for once, without Lulu or Alicia around to be disapproving.

After three glasses he started singing selections from *South Pacific*. In all the time I'd known him, Rodgers and Hammerstein had never struck me as his kind of entertainment, but you live and learn. The people on the next table joined in on *Bali-Hai*. Duncan got chatty with them, and we learned that the man with the bow-tie and red-framed spectacles was Dexter, who was in advertising, and that his girlfriend with the Rita Hayworth hair – she *wished* – was Josette, a publishing PR, and that their companion with the stammer and the name I didn't catch was an accountant.

SUCKERS

They were impressed when they found out Duncan was a famous photographer. No one took much notice of me, which was the way I liked it. I was content to sit back and wait for Duncan to lose interest in them. It was only a matter of time and it happened even sooner than I was expecting. He started singing again, only to break off midway through *Some Enchanted Evening* and lurch to his feet, announcing he had to go and make a phone call. He began to weave his way through the tables, banging into one or two of them and slopping people's drinks. Then he turned round and wove back again, fumbling through his pockets, and asked if I had any change.

I found some ten pences in my bag, instructed Dexter and Josette and their friend to save our table, and trotted after Duncan to the payphone. It wasn't a very exciting telephone call. I should have realized he'd been going to check on Lulu. I could hear him arguing with her in a basic yes/no mode. After a few minutes of this, I was itching to get back to my drink, even if it meant having to make polite conversation with Dexter and Josette.

'You just can't,' Duncan kept saying. 'Because I don't *want* you to.' By the time he'd inserted the last of my ten pences, his shoulders were sagging and his voice was trailing off into a hoarse whisper. He'd argued himself to a standstill. Then he heard something which made him hand the receiver out to me. 'Lu wants a word,' he said.

'Hello?'

Lulu sounded anxious. 'Dora? Is that you? Where are you? What's the matter with him?'

'He's all right,' I said, trying not to slur my words. 'He just heard some bad news about an old schoolfriend.'

ANNE BILLSON

Lulu wanted to know who it was, but I deliberately kept
it vague. 'But drinking's bad for his liver,' she wailed. 'For
God's sake don't let him drive.'

'Of course I won't.'

Then, unexpectedly, she said, 'Thank Christ you're there.
Thank Christ it's you and not Jack or Charlie. Those guys
just egg each other on.' I was surprised, even a little touched
in my tipsyish state.

'He's pissed off because I'm working tomorrow,' she
said. 'I don't know what's got into him, he never tried to
stop me working before.'

In a conversational tone, I asked, 'You mean you're going
to take that Multiglom job?'

'I'd be mad to turn it down.'

'That's the spirit. Don't let him push you around.'

'He *can* be incredibly bossy sometimes,' she said, slipping
into a confidential tone. 'I don't think he realizes.'

'We girls have got to stick together,' I said.

'I wonder if . . .' she began, but changed her mind. 'Give
him my love, won't you? Tell him I love him.'

'Oh yes,' I assured her. She said something else, but I
didn't catch it because I was already returning the receiver
to its cradle.

Duncan was slumped against the wall, staring at his
shoes. I said to him, 'You need another drink.'

He looked up sharply, as though only just remembering
where he was. 'What did she say?'

'She said you needed another drink.' It was time to move
on. I frogmarched him up the stairs and over the Strand to
another bar, mildly amused by the notion of Dexter and
Josette being left to defend our empty table against all

comers. This new place was even more crowded than the Foxhole, but by now we were beyond caring. We squeezed aggressively on to a red-plush banquette and commandeered half of someone else's table.

After a couple of beers Duncan started babbling, and I encouraged him. He told me how much he valued our friendship. He observed the colour of my eyes, and informed me what I already knew – that there was a speck of hazel in one of the irises. He became sentimental and said what an extraordinary person I was, what a wonderful singer, and asked how on earth I had managed to learn so many languages. He waxed lyrical about my tiny, tiny feet, and, at this point, I experienced an uncomfortable sensation of *déjà-vu* and realized he had long since stopped talking about me. I started to feel very depressed and switched from white wine to Scotch and soda.

Duncan, meanwhile, had switched from second to third person. 'She's been away for a long time. A *long* long time. And now she's back and it's all going to happen again.'

I shushed him. It wasn't prudent to bring up such things in public. 'It's finished. *Over.*'

'No, no, no,' he said, shaking his head. 'No, no, *no*. *Not* over. Because you know what? She's not like *us*. She's *different*. Very, *very* different.' He shook his head some more, in case I hadn't seen him shaking it the first time.

I said, 'We're each of us different in our own little ways.' The conversation had taken a dispiriting twist. The alcohol had loosened his inhibitions, but not in the way I'd anticipated. It was the same old story: all that effort, and all of it swept aside so easily.

'It's beginning again,' he was saying. 'And you know

what? You know what? I *want* it to begin again. Oh yes I do.'

'Oh no you don't,' I said. 'That's the last thing you want. It wouldn't be a good idea, not *at all*.' He persisted, so I tried talking sense. 'Let us suppose that – contrary to all laws of medical science and Middle European mythology – let us suppose you *are* right and it really *is* beginning again. Do you *really* think she'd want to shake you by the hand? Remember what you did? Remember how you left her without a hand to shake? She'd be fairly pissed off at you, don't you think?'

'Don't care.'

'Oh for Heaven's sake, use your head.' I could have wept. I was in that sort of state, but Duncan's drunkenness was way ahead of mine; it had passed through the maudlin stage and had now entered the rowdy.

'Want to know the quickest way to a woman's heart?' he asked loudly. 'Through the thorax with a Kitchen Devil!' Heads swivelled in our direction. He started to laugh uproariously. I shushed him again, and he lowered his voice so only about half the people in the pub could hear. 'It was the next best thing to fucking my mother, you know?'

'No, I don't know. Nobody wants to hear about your Oedipus Complex.'

'Not Oedipus,' he complained. 'You've got it upside-down.'

'I don't care *who* was on top. Just keep your voice down.'

'I've done nothing to be ashamed of. That's what you kept telling me, wasn't it? That I've done nothing to be ashamed of.'

'Not much,' I muttered.

'Don't you think I did the right thing?'

'Yes,' I said, in what I hoped was an authoritative voice. 'Imagine if you'd let her get away with it. Imagine what would have happened then. Think of it as being like a contagious disease. If you hadn't put a stop to it, it would have spread like wildfire. Of course you did the right thing.'

Duncan started to laugh again. 'Like AIDS, you mean?' His voice had acquired an eerie penetrative quality and sliced through the smoke and noise. At mention of the word *AIDS*, there was a pause in the hubbub, and a few more heads swivelled in our direction. 'No, Dora, you've got it wrong again. It was a great and glorious gift, and she wanted me to have it.'

This was way out of order. I tried to calm him down. 'Don't talk rot. You can't even stand the *sight* of blood.'

'That's what I mean,' he said. 'That's what she did.'

I told him not to be so silly. He was fine. His course of treatment had been interrupted. I hadn't noticed him turning down shooting assignments in sunny Tenerife. He was still eating garlic, wasn't he?'

'Takes time,' he said.

'What? Thirteen years?'

'No, no, no,' he said, rather crossly. 'You don't understand at all, Dora. It's not like a one-night stand. It's a mona ... moga ...' He paused and took a hop, step, and jump at the word. 'A *mono-ga-mous* situation, that's what it is.'

We continued in this vein for a while, repeating ourselves and going round in circles and generally not making a great deal of sense, until even the eavesdroppers grew bored and went back to their own conversations. Closing-time came and went, and no one seemed in a hurry to turf us out. Eventually Duncan excused himself and staggered off to find a toilet. Twenty minutes later I was wondering whether he'd left without me when a complete stranger announced that my companion had passed out in the Ladies. Duncan had evidently reached the third and last stage of the stages of drunkenness: unconsciousness. I went off to find him.

He was wedged beneath the washbasin, groaning. I splashed cold water on his face and roused him sufficiently to steer him out of the pub. He wobbled down the road, patting the pockets of his jacket. 'Keys...' he muttered. 'Car keys...'

I'd forgotten the car. 'Oh *no*,' I said. 'No *way* are you driving.' I pulled him towards the tube entrance, but it was later than I'd thought – the stairs were barred by a criss-cross metal grille. An entire evening had slipped away and we hadn't eaten so much as a pretzel. No wonder we were both legless.

On the Strand I attempted to hail a cab, but they were all heading east with their lights off. Duncan clutched my arm in a determined fashion. 'S'all right, I'm *perfectly* sober.' This was patently untrue, but I allowed him to lead me back to the car. I couldn't think what else to do.

It was a wild drive. Haves and Have Nots were out in force. Crowds milled on pavements outside clubs, queueing to pass the dress code inspection and spilling into the road. Along Shaftesbury Avenue I was rather pleased to see two shaven-haired thugs heaving a paving stone through the window of a shoe shop. We pulled up at some lights and I shouted, 'Yo!' They waved back, then, grinning like escaped mental patients, started walking across the road towards us.

'Jesus!' I said, but just then the traffic started rolling again. I craned my neck, looking back. The thugs were wading through the cars like a couple of teenage Godzillas, heading back up the road to Cambridge Circus.

The streets were swarming with drunken drivers pretending to be sober, all pointing their hood ornaments in what they hoped was the right direction and praying like mad they wouldn't get stopped. Duncan would have failed a breathalyser at fifty paces, and there was a nerve-racking encounter with a night bus in the vicinity of Marble Arch, but we managed to get as far as Queensway without knocking down any little old ladies. Then, south of Westbourne Grove, just as I was starting to relax, he gave a little sigh and drove into a wall.

We were taking a corner at the time. As I saw his hands lift ever so slightly off the wheel, it flashed through my head that he had judged it an excellent way of committing suicide. Fortunately, our speed was too low to inflict anything other than minor damage to the front bumper and one of the headlamps. We ground to a halt with the engine still running. The wall came off without a scratch.

My head was instantly clear. I tipped Duncan on to the pavement and took his place behind the wheel. I'd given up learning to drive a long time ago, but now I remembered enough to trundle around the corner in first gear and park the car so it didn't stick out at too crazy an angle. One of the wheels ended up on the kerb, but it wasn't bad for an inebriated amateur. I yanked the handbrake up and switched off the engine.

When I got back to Duncan, he was sitting on the wall, kicking it with the backs of his heels. 'That's quite enough driving,' I told him, burying the car keys in his pocket. Behind me, there was the sound of someone clearing his throat. I turned. Just across the road, standing beneath a lamppost, was a man in black.

'It's all right,' I called. 'He's not hurt.'

But the man didn't react. There was something about his stillness which made me uncomfortable. A window opened somewhere over his head and he tilted his face so the light fell on it, and I saw he was having a heavy nosebleed. It made me wonder if he too had been involved in a minor accident, but I didn't want to hang around to find out. I hauled Duncan to his feet and marched him along the street, risking a single backward glance before we reached the corner. The man hadn't budged; he was staring after us with a fixed look on his face as blood gushed steadily from his nostrils. I was relieved when we rounded the corner and he couldn't see us any more.

'You'd better come back with me,' I told Duncan. My flat was only a few blocks away, a five-minute stagger as opposed to the fifteen-minute trek required to reach his place. Quite honestly, he didn't seem up to it. He could walk, but he had no willpower; I was having to propel him.

Lulu had left several anxious messages on my answering machine. 'Dora? Are you there? Is Duncan there?' and 'Dora, please call.' It was too late to ring back; I figured she would have gone to bed early on the eve of her big day.

By the time I'd gulped down a couple of glasses of water, Duncan had passed out fully clothed on top of the bedclothes. I undressed and slid beneath the quilt next to him. Once or twice I dozed off, but mostly I lay propped on one elbow, examining his face at close quarters. I hadn't had him so close for ages. I stared into his face and puzzled over it. He wasn't so good-looking. His hair needed cutting; it flopped all over the place. I'd known men who were more talented, funnier, cleverer. So what *was* it about this one? As far as I could see, he had failed to enhance the quality of my life in any way whatsoever. All he had done was bring me grief. So why did I stick with him? The only way I could make sense of it was by thinking of him as a type of addiction. He was a drug.

At some point during the night, he regained consciousness long enough to remove his clothes and clamber on top of me, though I'd not sure he realized who I was. After a bit of unresolved fumbling, he rolled over and went back to sleep. He may well have been a drug, but he certainly wasn't a hard one. If it hadn't been the grand physical reunion I'd had in mind all those years, what the hell – it was better than nothing.

Feeling quite pleased about it, I fell asleep.

SEVEN

The next day started off badly and got steadily worse. First of all, Duncan went home without even stopping for breakfast. It was one of those mornings when breakfast wasn't exactly on my agenda either. We'd been wrenched awake at about half-past ten by the sound of the Krankzeits hurling furniture at each other. My first attempts at getting vertical convinced me that while I had been sleeping someone had levered my brain out of my head, pulped it repeatedly against a rock, and stuffed it back into my skull the wrong way round. It was a fair bet Duncan would be feeling even ropier, but that was no excuse for bad manners. While I was groaning at my reflection in the bathroom mirror he snuck out of the flat without even stopping to thank me for having him.

In between heavy doses of Alka-Seltzer and fruit juice, I had to deal with a series of bothersome phone calls. The first was from the editor of a women's magazine called *Flirt*, wanting to know if I'd finished compiling their readership profile. I said I hadn't and she made tutting noises and told me she needed it for a meeting in the morning. There was no way out. I sighed and promised it would be on her desk first thing. The second call was from Jack, wanting to know what had happened to the research I owed him. I told him it was ready, which was sort of true, though I still had to type it out. I agreed to drop it round that evening. The third call was from Ruth Weinstein, inviting me to a party she would be holding the following Saturday. I said I didn't think I'd be able to make it, but I'd try, and she remarked that, when it came to parties, I was always noncommittal, but everyone always knew I'd turn up anyway. That pissed me off; I didn't like being thought of as predictable. 'OK,' I said crossly, 'I'll come.' I had no intention of doing any such thing – all I wanted was for the conversation to end – but Ruth chattered on about work, and Charlie, and the gallery, and asked after Duncan like she always did, because we'd all been to the same art school and she'd never stopped being curious about him and me, though I had never told her a thing.

All I told her now was that I had a humungous hangover in the hope she would take the hint and shut up. Instead she said, 'Oh, what were *you* up to last night, then?' I ignored the question, which was impertinent, and said I'd call. She reminded me that I always said that, but never did – *she* always ended up having to call *me*. This was true enough. Ruth refused to let our long-lasting acquaintanceship follow its natural course and shrivel up.

The fourth call was from Duncan. I was pleased to hear him until I realized he wasn't calling to apologize for his bad manners after all. He wanted a sympathetic ear, and he didn't care who it belonged to. 'I missed her,' he said. 'I didn't get back in time, and she'd already left. She didn't even leave a note.'

'What did you expect?' I asked, and tried to jog his memory. 'You spent the night with another woman.'

He moaned. 'Don't I know it. Dora, I feel *dreadful*. Where did we go? Where's the car?'

Thanks, I thought. Thanks a *lot*. 'Our happy hour turned into a lost weekend. You drove the car into a wall.'

There was a shocked pause before he said, 'Jeez, I was wondering about the bruises. We didn't kill anyone, did we? How's the car?'

'The *car*'s just fine,' I said, 'just a few small dents.' I told him where I'd parked it. Nice of him to ask after *me*. I could hear him smothering a sigh. He knew I was being terse, but couldn't work out why, unless maybe I was having my period. Whenever members of the opposite sex failed to respond to Duncan's boyish charm, he always concluded it was their time of the month. But it wasn't mine, not yet.

'I didn't get breathalysed or anything?'

'No.'

'Thanks, Dora.' There was an awkward pause. 'I guess I'd better go and rescue the car. Before it gets clamped.'

'Why don't you do that,' I said, and hung up.

Duncan's call left me in a rotten mood. For about the billionth time I made up my mind never to talk to him again. Let him worry about Lulu all he liked. See if I cared.

I spent the rest of the day trying to work. I typed out some lists and *vox pop* quotations for Jack, and concocted some readership survey results for *Flirt*. I looked upon these things as conceptual art. They may have been made up, but they seemed no less accurate than any other form of market research. I prided myself on my knowledge of human nature, and my attitude was that I *was* the market. I told everyone my readership profiles were composite portraits, compiled from data gleaned from hundreds upon hundreds of telephone interviews – interviews which were constantly having to be updated in order to reflect the minutest fluctuations in the state of the economy. No one ever queried an invoice; they just coughed up.

At about eight o'clock, as I was making last-minute corrections to Jack's research, Duncan called again. In my frail condition I found myself talking to him before remembering, too late, I'd decided not to.

'She's still not back.'

'So? The night is young.'

'She hasn't even called.'

'She won't have had time. You know what it's like.'

'I'm really worried.'

'Duncan, I've got to rush, I'm going out. I'll call you in the morning.' Feeling deliciously hard-hearted, I hung up on him and set off for the tree-lined crescent where Jack and Alicia lived.

'How's Roxy these days?' I asked.

Jack glared at me. 'Fine.'

Alicia was knitting an unidentifiable garment on large wooden needles, somehow managing not to stab Abigail, who was gurgling and wriggling on her lap. The needles ceased clicking as she looked up. 'I didn't know you knew Roxy.'

'We went to the same school,' I lied. 'She was a real bully. She used to beat the crap out of me.'

Alicia returned to her knitting. 'Ooh, what a cow,' she said, rather absent-mindedly. I didn't pursue the matter. My initial question had been a test, to find out if she knew her husband was being unfaithful. From her reaction I concluded not, but I held my tongue. I enjoyed making Jack feel uncomfortable, but I wasn't about to ruin his marriage.

'Let's have a look at these papers,' he said pointedly. 'Want a drink?' I asked for a gin and tonic, and he stayed where he was, sifting through the typed sheets. After a few seconds, Alicia dutifully gathered up her knitting, hefted the baby on to one arm and struggled to her feet.

'I'll have one too,' Jack said without looking up.

I couldn't bear it. 'Stay where you are,' I said to Alicia. 'I'll do it, save you getting up.' She beamed and sat down again in a tangle of baby and wool.

Jack and Alicia kept their liquor in an art deco cocktail cabinet. I wondered how much cocaine had been chopped up on the mirrored shelf over the years. Not a lot recently; apart from the occasional joint, Alicia was now completely illegal-substance-free, and was trying to make Jack follow suit, though I suspected he and Roxy sometimes depleted the office Biro collection after hours.

I thought about how much Alicia annoyed me, all the more so because she was settling for less than she deserved. Once upon a time she had earned herself a first-class degree, had written articles for a couple of heavyweight literary reviews, had seemed poised for some sort of brilliant career.

According to Duncan, she had always been surrounded by so many admirers he'd considered himself favoured when she finally agreed to go out with him.

Then she married Jack, and everything changed. He had taken her on a Grand Tour – France, Italy, Greece, Spain – before bringing her home to install her as a baby-maker. Things hadn't gone quite as planned – Jack, of course, blamed Alicia for the delay – but now they were back on course. He was saying they wanted a two-year gap between babies.

They weren't short of money, but had never got round to hiring a nanny, so Alicia was left holding the baby while Jack went out on the town; it was an arrangement which suited him down to the ground. Alicia's reward was a gold American Express and frequent weekends in a remote part of Dorset, where they'd just bought a cottage. I was angling for an invite, though wary of ending up stuck in the middle of nowhere having to listen to Jack's monologues.

I handed Alicia her gin and tonic. She adjusted Abigail's position so the baby's head wasn't lolling, and turned her concerned maternal gaze on to me. 'Is everything all right between Lulu and Duncan?'

'As far as I know. Why do you ask?'

She paused, and had the grace to look embarrassed. 'Lu said she thought there was another woman.'

The blood rushed to my head, but then I realized she couldn't have been talking about me. News didn't travel *that* fast. 'She hasn't mentioned anything to me.'

'I can't believe Duncan would be so stupid,' said Jack, so smugly that I wanted to hit him. 'Lulu's a corker.'

There was another uncomfortable silence. 'There's some

problem with tax, I think,' I said, damaged brain working overtime. 'He's been having a lot of meetings with his accountant. Maybe that's it.'

'Maybe,' said Alicia, but she didn't look convinced. I thought I saw her raise an eyebrow in my direction, but I may have been mistaken.

Five minutes after getting home, I had yet another call from Duncan. It was the same old stuff – no Lu, no fun, no future. By the time I'd summoned sufficient resolution to terminate the one-sided conversation, my mood, which had been jiffed up by the gin, had plummeted back into the pits. There was only one thing to do in the circumstances. It was a foolproof method of cheering myself up. I dialled Patricia Rice's number.

At the twenty-fifth ring – just as I was about to give up and go to bed – she answered. I heard a little gasp, as though she were anticipating some fresh new hell, then realized it had not been a gasp but a yawn. I had probably got her out of bed. She was just the sort of person who would be turning in before eleven o'clock.

'Hi there,' I said in what I hoped was a Californian accent. 'Am I talking to Patty? Patty Rice?' I'd decided to give her some more of the weird hippy subcult.

Immediately she was on her guard. 'Who is that?'

'You don't know us,' I said, 'but we sure as hell know you. We were kind of wondering if you'd gotten our latest letter.'

I should have known something was wrong as soon as I heard Patricia laugh. She usually swore, or hung up, or both things at once, but she never laughed, not ever. 'Yes,' she said. 'I got it this morning. And you know what?' She laughed again. 'This time you really screwed up.'

The sensible thing at this point would have been to hang up. But my brain was still feeling like something battered against a rock by a Greek fisherman, so I didn't. I kept on babbling, my accent veering from California to Brooklyn and back again, taking in the Deep South *en route*. I had never been terribly good at accents. I gave her some poetry: 'Once upon a midnight dreary, while I pondered weak and weary, de dum de dum de dum de dum de dum forgotten lore . . .' I stopped. Something she had said finally sank in. 'What do you mean, *I screwed up*?'

Patricia's voice quavered with righteous triumph. 'I don't know why you've been doing this, and I don't care, but at last I can put a stop to it. *You've finally given yourself away*.'

I racked my brains, but I didn't know what she was talking about. 'Hey, what did I do? Use headed notepaper?'

'Not quite.' I could see her smiling in that mean, thin-lipped way she had. 'But almost. You sent me something you didn't mean to send.'

I was impatient, but uneasy. 'And what's that?'

'Oh yes, it must be nice, living in *Notting Hill*,' she said. 'Shame about all the *rubbish* on the streets, though. And the *noisy neighbours*. And the *Alsatians*. I know you're not really *Gunter Krankzeit*, are you, it's just another of your poison pen-names, but this time I've got your address and I'm giving it to the police. You're sick. You should be locked up, and I'm going to make sure you—'

I slammed the receiver down on her. Or she slammed it down on me, I'm not sure which. What had I done to deserve this shit? My stomach lurched as I realized what had happened. I wondered how Kensington and Chelsea's Environmental Health Department was coping with the threatening letter from the weird hippy subcult.

I sat completely still, trying to control my breathing by slowly counting to ten. It was all the Krankzeits' fault. If they hadn't kept me awake, I would never have written that letter, and I certainly would never have been dozy enough to put it in the wrong envelope. I blamed Duncan, as well. I couldn't think why, exactly, but I did.

My first instinct was to march straight round to Patricia's and threaten her with GBH until she returned the evidence. Then I decided this wasn't such a sensible course of action. She might have known, approximately, where I lived, but she still didn't know who I was, and there was no point in showing my face. Besides, she was bigger than me. But I couldn't let it rest. There were fingerprints, handwriting, and, for all I knew, traces of saliva on the gummed flap of the envelope.

I smoked three cigarettes, thinking hard all the while, then plumped for emergency action. Somewhere in the top drawer of my desk, amongst all the spare boxes of staples, hotel stationery, novelty erasers, and rubber stamps, there were various old keys I had never had the heart to discard. I rooted around and found what I was looking for – the Yale to Patricia Rice's flat. I hadn't kept it on purpose; I just hadn't got round to returning it. And the estate agents, embarrassed by the gazumping, had never asked for it back.

EIGHT

It was raining hard. I wrapped myself in a large mackintosh and set out for the offices of *Flirt*. It was far too early for the Notting Hill flotsam to be up and crawling, but there were plenty of reminders of the previous night's rumba session: rubbish all over the streets, dog shit and broken bottles and ripped-up garments with revolting stains all over them, a paddy field of old newspapers and sodden cigarette packets. The usual stuff, only it seemed to be getting worse each day. In my head, I composed yet another why-oh-why letter to the local council. I thought grimly that while I was at it I could send a copy to Patricia Rice as well.

Two out of the three down escalators at Notting Hill station were out of order, the platform was covered with litter, and the train was running late due to a signal failure at Edgware Road. It arrived a couple of centuries later, and another couple of centuries after that, after I'd read my newspaper (including the financial, sports, and small-ad pages) and completed all but two of the cryptic crossword clues, we rolled into Embankment station. I headed up Villiers Street, past the entrance to the Foxhole, and plunged into Covent Garden. Since it was not yet ten thirty, the *Flirt* office was deserted except for a lone receptionist. I deposited my fun package on the appropriate desk and took the opportunity to dial Patricia Rice's number, just in case she'd stayed home sick. No answer, just as I'd expected. She was a creature of dreary routine.

The coast was clear, but the sky wasn't. The rain was pelting down as I crossed Hungerford Bridge. The drainage was so bad it was like walking on the beach when the tide wasn't fully out; water darkened the leather of my shoes until they made squelching noises at every step. Before I'd got half-way across I was so wet it didn't matter any more. I paused and leant against the railing, facing east to where the sky was darkest. Squinting against the rain, I could just make out some brightly lit buildings in the City. I couldn't see as far as Molasses Wharf, but in my mind's eye was a picture of Multiglom Tower, even darker than the sky, a long way beyond Lloyd's, but big and very sinister, surrounded by black flapping things which might have been seagulls but were probably not.

I shook myself out of this reverie and moved on, past the Festival Hall, feeling wetter and colder all the time. There weren't many people around, only a few figures scurrying towards the nearest shelter, huddled beneath umbrellas or shielding their heads with newspapers. The streets around Waterloo were busier, though not by much. I stopped off at the station to warm my bones with a cup of coffee before striking out through the downpour for Lambeth North.

Patricia's flat was a conversion job, but one of the things I had liked was its position on the end of a terrace, which meant it had its own separate entrance on the side street around the corner. Lucky Patricia; no awkward neighbourly encounters in the hallway, no having to sift through other people's fishy-looking mail, no Krankzeits to thunder up and down.

I pressed her doorbell. Of course there was no reply. I hadn't expected one. I looked around; the building site across the road, like the *Flirt* office, was deserted. I went on to check out Patricia's back yard, which backed on to a tiny corner of scrubby public land. There was a bench right under her back wall. I clambered up to peer through the tangle of barbed wire. Before the gazumping, I'd planned to fill the yard with shrubs and creepers; Patricia had filled it with dirty milk bottles and an old kitchen cabinet. It was clear she had failed to exploit the property's full potential on the outside; now, letter or no letter, I wanted to see what she'd done to the inside. I climbed down and strolled back to the front door. There was no one around, but even if there had been they wouldn't have noticed me. I was an old hand at looking casual. I inserted my key, turned it, and stepped inside.

What little light there was came through the small panel of amber glass in the front door. I didn't much care for the way Patty had decorated the hall. The wallpaper was turquoise, and reminded me of the décor in a Tandoori restaurant. There was a framed reproduction of Rousseau's *Sleeping Gypsy* on the wall.

I stood for a while, ears straining, but apart from my own breathing the only sound was that of water dripping slowly off the bottom of my raincoat. I took it off and left it draped over the Rousseau. The first door led to the kitchen, where there were little jars of dried herbs and some recipe

79

books on a shelf above the fridge. Hanging from some red plastic hooks were an apron with *Supercook* emblazoned across the front, an oven-glove shaped like a penguin, and a tea-towel decorated with characters from Mabel Lucie Atwell. It was all preternaturally tidy, except for a single unwashed mug – not at all like my kitchen, which was rarely without a sinkful of dirty crockery.

The bathroom smelt of fake pine, and the predominant shade was lilac. There were no interesting prescription drugs in the wall-cabinet; just aspirin, and Listerine, and tampons manufactured in Havant. I retraced my steps along the hall-way. The bedroom had been decked out in lemon yellow, in that bland style witless folk called 'feminine' – floral-patterned quilt, brass bedstead, and fluffy toys. The bed hadn't been made; apart from the mug, it was the only evidence I had seen of sloppiness. On the dressing-table were a couple of pinkish-beige lipsticks, a bottle of Dior perfume, and some blemish concealer. I sneered and went into the last room. This was the room which faced on to the street, and it was darker than the rest of the flat because the blinds were closed. I could just about make out the outlines of furniture, and that was all, so I went over to the window and yanked on the cord to let in some light.

I should have realized something was up as soon as I felt the scrunching beneath my feet, like the sensation you get from walking on a crisp layer of snow. As I let the light in, I turned away from the window and saw a lot of things. Not all of them registered immediately. But I saw enough to make me snap the blinds shut, quickly, before the smell of burning could get any worse.

The first thing I saw was the mirror over the mantelpiece,

or what was left of it. There was hardly any glass left in the frame – most of it lay in pieces on the carpet; I'd stepped on some and shivered it even further. It was impossible to tell precisely what had happened, because the floor was covered in debris; as well as glass, there were pieces of broken china, scraps of fabric, and feathers. I remember thinking how odd it was this room should be so untidy when the rest of the flat had been so neat. Patty had slipped up there.

Then I saw exactly where she had slipped up. One of her slippers had fallen off, and I saw her bare foot before I saw the rest of her. She was lying alongside the sofa, one cheek pressed into the carpet, hair spread out like a fan. There was blood on her dressing-gown, but not much.

And that was it. That was all I saw of her as she was then, because the exposed part of her face was already turning a shiny plum colour, even as I looked. The light came in through the window from the north. What with the clouds and rain it was fairly feeble, but it was still enough to make her skin blister and pop. Patricia Rice was fortunate it was not a sunny day.

Her limbs twitched. There was movement beneath the dressing-gown, but I knew it was involuntary. There were sounds, but they were involuntary too, like the bubbling and hissing when milk boils over and splashes on to the hot-plate. And there was a smell like lamb chops cooking beneath the grill; it was a smell which under normal circumstances I would have liked, which made it worse. It took me a split second to see all this and then I fumbled for the cord and pulled the blinds shut.

I was thinking practical thoughts, and lots of them. My brain was a different creature from the battered cephalopod of the day before; now it was whirring through the options like a well-oiled fruit machine. Carefully, I trod back across the room and switched on the lamp by the telephone. I was quite calm. I was calm because I knew what was going on. I'd seen this sort of thing before: open wounds on the neck, glassy-eyed stare.

Definitely Violet.

Violet had been here.

And Violet would be back, this night or the next, to complete what she had begun. It was this certainty, more than anything else, that stopped me from leaving the blinds open, though I couldn't for the life of me imagine why anyone should bother to preserve someone as boring as Patricia. I craved nicotine, but I didn't dare light up. I wanted to leave things as near as possible to how I'd found them. As it was, I knew that Violet, as soon as she came back, would smell that someone else had been present. I wondered whether she would be able to identify the source of the scent; I wondered whether her olfactory recall went back that far.

But I had other unfinished business. I crossed the room again and rifled the bureau. Patricia's papers were not as organized as the rest of her life. I found a mass of unpaid bills: gas and electricity and television rental. There was an uncompleted insurance form, and a half-finished letter to someone called Moira, and a small red address-book notable only for the number of blank pages. I thought of my own personal organizer crammed with names and addresses and telephone numbers, and for a few seconds I almost felt sorry for Patricia. Then I decided it served her right. Nice girls don't gazump.

But there was no sign of my letter. I scanned the rest of

the room, reluctant to touch any more than was necessary. I especially didn't want to touch what was left of Patricia. There was a sudden hiss of tyres on wet tarmac as a car went past the window. I checked my watch, thinking I'd been there ten minutes, but more than half an hour had passed since I'd inserted the key. It was time to beat a retreat and devise a plan of action. As I pulled my raincoat back on, I heard the muffled thud of a pneumatic drill starting up across the street. The building-site boys had finally turned up for work. They didn't see me letting myself out. No one did. No one had seen me go in. And no one saw me leave.

PART TWO

PART TWO

ONE

I was an only child, brought up in a semi-detached, three-bedroomed house on the outskirts of Havant. This is a place which rings bells with people who like to read the small print on packaging; Havant is best known for its tampon factory.

I never gave my parents any trouble, at least not to begin with. I never stayed out late with unsuitable friends, because I didn't have any friends, unsuitable or otherwise. I didn't really fit in at school, but I managed not to make too many enemies, and I worked hard. I was seventeen, studying for A-levels in French and Art, when my mother suddenly got it into her head to search my bedroom. She found all sorts of interesting things: a sheep's skull I'd found in a ditch, a collection of adult magazines shoplifted for research purposes, a diary which was more fantasy than fact, and some of the drawings I'd done to illustrate my favourite French set book, *Les Fleurs du Mal*.

I came home from school that afternoon to find a bonfire blazing in the garden, my mother stoking the flames hysterically as my most valued possessions turned to ash. It was the diary that had set her off. She burst into tears, called me an unnatural child, and told me I was no longer welcome in her home. She wept even more when she saw I was only too eager to leave. There were streaks of grime on her face, and her hair, usually so neatly permed, frizzed around her head like a tangle of live wire. She appeared to be having some sort of nervous breakdown. I was hugely embarrassed, and disowned her on the spot.

I spent the night in a neighbour's garage, curled up in a nest of oily rags and yellow newspapers. I was in a state of shock – this was the most exciting thing that had ever happened to me. In the morning, my father rather sheepishly gave me some money and I caught the next train to London. For the next five nights I slept on the sofa in a flat belonging to a friend of his secretary, who had also supplied me with some of her old clothes. In the daytime, I roamed the streets, living off coffee and sandwiches, and loitered in the British Museum, sketching and making notes. On the fifth day I strayed into University College and jotted down some phone numbers-from the students' notice board. Two days later I moved into a small room in Camden Town.

The following weekend, my father drove up to deliver all my unburnt earthly goods: clothes, record-player, records, and boxes of books and papers. My mother had sent bedlinen, a towel, and a tear-stained letter in which she begged me to come home. I told my father this was out of the question, and he agreed to send me a small allowance each month, at least until I found my feet. It wasn't much, but it took care of the rent.

I found a part-time job in a West End shoe store. Every

evening at closing time the manager would search his employees' bags to make sure we weren't walking off with items of stock, though the shoes were so awful (patent plastic, buckles, platform soles) no one in their right mind would have wanted to steal them. Besides, the store practised its own type of aversion therapy. We assistants had to wear turquoise nylon smocks; the carpet was nylon too, and the display units were metal, and every time we touched a shoe, it would give us a small, sharp electric shock.

On days when I wasn't trying to squeeze misshapen feet into plastic shoes, I was busy doing all the things my mother had never let me do at home – like staying up half the night, or staying in bed till noon. I assembled intricate collages out of pictures cut from magazines. Other than a weekly trip to the cinema, I didn't go out much. I played records at maximum volume, until the student in the next room tapped timidly on my door and asked if I could turn it down because she was trying to sleep. Sometimes I laid traps for the mice which would come out to play every night, squeaking excitedly as they abseiled down the back of the wardrobe on my loudspeaker wires.

It wasn't long before the shoe shop and I parted company. One day I got into a scrap with another assistant – an Argentinian girl who called me a 'beach' when I innocently directed the manager's attention to the bulge in her sweater. It turned out to be a packet of tights she was smuggling out on her lunch break. She swore at me in Spanish and ripped out a handful of my hair, so I punched her in the stomach. Customers looked on in amazement as we rolled around the floor, biting and scratching and crackling with static. It wasn't my fault, but the manager sacked us both on the spot.

I was so outraged I rang up Lunar House in Croydon with a visa enquiry, and ten days later my Argentinian friend was shipped back to Buenos Aires.

My next job was in a Soho patisserie. Here, the staff were positively encouraged to help themselves to any merchandise left unsold at the end of the working day. Other assistants would gratefully tuck a Chelsea bun or two into their shopping-bags when they went home. I took this policy a step further by consuming what I wanted, when I wanted it: doughnuts, Danish pastries, éclairs, almond slices, strawberry tartlets. No one objected. I didn't get fat, exactly, but I got sort of plump.

But I had no intention of spending the rest of my life flogging croissants and custard tarts. I needed to broaden my horizons. I wanted an education in the University of Life. Before long, I'd built up quite a collection of scribblings and collages, so I shuffled them into some sort of order and managed to bluff my way on to a three-year diploma course in Fine Art.

I started making friends, but slowly. For a while, I floated along in my own little world, dropping into class whenever the fancy took me, but mostly skiving off and wandering through the back streets, eating sticky buns and peeking through windows, watching the people inside, wondering how much money they had, and what sort of lives they were leading. But as soon as I set my sights on Duncan Fender, my life snapped into focus. I started putting in long hours over my easel, attended as many tutorials as I could. At first I didn't run into him very often, but it didn't take me long to realize this was because he spent most of his time down in the darkroom. I began to spend time down there, too.

SUCKERS

I knew I wanted him as soon as I laid eyes on the photographs which came peeling off the dryer. He'd been taking pictures of cemeteries: Highgate, Kensal Rise, Norwood, Brompton, Nunhead, Abney Park. All sarcophagi and skeletal trees, ruined chapels and crumbling stone angels. He spent a lot of time and effort printing up those negatives, burning in the sky so it glowered, dodging in all the shadowy details. Sometimes there would be figures flitting through trees in the background, but mostly it was nature in a state of shock, petrified and overgrown. One could tell he was deeply sensitive just by looking at his work.

I had to borrow a camera. I was one of the few students who didn't have a Pentax or a Nikon of their own. Sometimes it felt as though the college was being turned into an alternative finishing school for people on private incomes. By a cruel twist of fate, some of the wealthier students received full grants from local authorities befuddled by their parents' estrangements and remarriages and complicated custody arrangements. The extra cash came in useful for throwing parties, or buying clothes, or nipping over to Paris at weekends, while I was plugging up the holes in my own allowance by working Saturdays at the cake shop.

In my year, we had Susannah Stukeleigh of the Stukeleigh sales rooms, and Jane Appleby, whose father owned a string of racehorses, and Nancy Manners, whose coat of arms was familiar from a certain well-known brand of tea, and Ruth Weinstein, whose father was rumoured to be some sort of arms dealer. I insulted these rich girls to their faces, but they were always nice to me, because they found me colourful — except for my clothes, which were black. I wore black all the time back then, though in those days it required some effort to find black items – not like ten years later, when all the shops would be stocked to the hilt with fifty-seven varieties of little black frock. Back in the seventies, all-black attire was considered suitable only for widows and New Zealand rugby-players.

Susannah and Jane and Nancy and Ruth adored Duncan, because he had charm and he knew how to use it. They were flattered when he wanted to take pictures of them looking ethereal in graveyards. And they were fascinated by his back-ground, because he came from genuine bohemian stock. His real name wasn't Duncan; it was something fancy like Done-can, or Duncannon, but he'd changed it because he was fed up with it being misspelled. Duncan's great-uncle had hung around with Kurt Schwitters, the Dadaist, and Duncan's father had also been a famous painter – though not so famous that any of us had heard of him. Even better, there was a rumour that his parents had once been involved in a *ménage à trois* which had scandalized *tout Paris*. Duncan didn't talk about his family at all, but his reticence made the little that leaked out all the more tantalizing. Politely but firmly he discouraged all attempts at intimacy, and concentrated instead on his art. He worked hard, he always worked so hard, battering away at his personal muse, turning out beauti-fully photographed cemeteries by the score.

My own muse wasn't quite so complicated. It came in fits and starts – mostly waiting in the wings until I felt the need for attention. Then it would take centre stage and dance the fandango. One time, for instance, I added pieces of broken razor-blade to my latest collage. It was hailed as an artistic triumph, especially when one of the tutors slashed his finger and had to be rushed to hospital. Another time, I constructed a landscape out of calves' liver. Before the day was out it was swarming with flies and there were complaints about the smell, but still it was acclaimed as another *tour de force*. No one ever thought to ask how I was going to make a living out of artistic arrangements of offal and razor-blades. The tutors believed in Fine Art as a pure concept unsullied by commercial opportunism. They didn't care what happened to us in the world outside.

But the art served its purpose. No one could ignore it, not even Duncan. He took the bait – though hooking him was one thing, reeling him in was another. It became the central obsession of my life. He was the last thought I had before going to sleep, he was present in my dreams, and he was there in my head as soon as I woke up. And in the studio one evening, as I was packing up to go home, he came up to me and asked me out. Afterwards, I danced home in triumph. This was what I'd been waiting for. This was all the proof I needed – I was not an ordinary person, I possessed the *power*, and Duncan belonged to me.

And life, for a while, was like a dream. He was the teacher I'd been looking for; he showed me around town, gave me books to read, took me to Chinese restaurants and Japanese films – he liked samurai movies, and did a great impersonation of Toshiro Mifune in *Yojimbo*. He showed me round his favourite cemeteries, and I watched him take photographs, though for some reason he never took any of me. He always said he was going to, but he never got round to it. He promised that one day he would show me Père Lachaise, in Paris. It was the best cemetery in the world, he said. Oscar Wilde and Jim Morrison were buried there.

The funny part was – I'd fantasized about him so much

that, in the flesh, he was disappointing, not nearly as exciting as I'd first imagined. Sex was no more than satisfactory, conversation brittle and superficial. We traded trivialities, and talked about popular culture, and that was it. I wanted passion and intensity, but he kept that part of himself locked away. Given time, I would have decided he wasn't worth the effort. Given time, I would have extracted what I needed, and moved on.

But time was what I didn't get.

One evening, I was alone in the etching department, up on the top floor. I had signed up for a crash course in etching because Duncan was going to be there all week, transferring some of his photographic designs on to plates, and I liked to keep an eye on him. That afternoon he had left early to return some borrowed equipment, but I'd stayed on. I'd rolled a layer of etching-ground on to a fresh plate and blackened it with one of those medieval-looking torches they still used in the department, the sort I imagined would be carried by villagers when they stormed the Transylvanian castle. I was working on the latest in a series of severed heads. I'd already done Salome, and Isabella with her pot of basil, and now I was more than half-way through Medusa.

I could hear the faint noise of traffic outside, but the room seemed cut off from the rest of the world. The air was heavy with hot wax and lavender, and the smell was making me sleepy. I'd just finished scratching the last of the snakes into the lampblack and had slipped the plate into the acid. I was engrossed in the tiny bubbles when I heard someone humming. The tune was familiar, but I couldn't place it.

I looked up just in time to see her come in, and go directly to the desk where Duncan had been working. She stopped humming and studied his half-finished plate. Her head was bowed, and I couldn't see much of her face because her hair fell forward in a dark curtain, and she was bundled up to her chin in big fur. She was dressed all in black, like me, but her clothes didn't look as though they came from the Oxfam shop. She was smaller than me, and skinnier too, beneath all the wrapping. She had the tiniest hands and feet I'd ever seen; they were encased in black leather gloves, and in black leather boots with pointed toes and peculiar curved heels – I had never seen boots quite like those before. She was dressed as if for winter in Siberia, though the evening was unusually mild. The weathermen were attributing the unseasonably high temperatures to a drifting band of volcanic dust which was giving us a series of spectacular blood-red sunsets.

She bent over Duncan's desk, and – without removing her gloves – scribbled something on a scrap of paper. Then she stood up straight again, and the way she held herself you would have thought she was taller than she really was. As she turned to leave, her gaze met mine for the briefest instant. There was no surprise, because she'd known I was there all along – those eyes knew everything there was to know.

But she wasn't interested in me, not in the slightest. She broke eye contact almost immediately, and just before she disappeared she started to hum again. It wasn't until the humming had faded that I finally put my finger on the tune: one of Verdi's greatest hits, the drinking song from *La Traviata*.

I felt cold all of a sudden, as if she had left a breath of winter behind, but there was no particular sense of dread. Just fuzziness, as though I were coming round after anaesthetic. I went over to read her note. The handwriting was spindly, a trail of ink left by wandering spiders. 'Duncan – the DeMille, tomorrow night, nine o'clock. Violet.'

Violet, I thought. *What an unusual name.*

TWO

D uncan said, 'I think I've in love,' and the blood rushed to my head. For a few seconds I was flying higher than I had ever flown before – higher than I would ever fly again as long as I lived. I thought he was talking about him and me. This was the Age of Innocence, before the Fall.

I could be forgiven for getting it wrong, because for the last half hour we'd been discussing my favourite topic of conversation – me. Or rather, Duncan had been talking, and I'd been lapping it up. He'd been telling me what an extraordinary person I was, how rare, how talented, and how privileged he was to know me. I should have guessed something was up.

He might have been trying to soften the blow, but only succeeded in making it that much more crushing, when it finally came. He should have been brutal to start with. Here we were in this sandwich bar, and in between eruptions of steam from the Gaggia, I could hear Steve Harley singing 'Come up and see me, Make me smile', and I could hear Duncan saying how terribly fond he was of me, and he didn't want me to get hurt, and that was why we should stop seeing each other.

I couldn't believe my ears. I thought I was going to have a hysterical screaming fit, right there in the sandwich bar. Then something snapped, very quietly, like an old elastic band which had been stretched too long and too tightly in my head, and I felt my entire life shift into a different gear. I could see Duncan's lips moving. I could hear the traffic, and the patter of feet on the pavement, the murmur of voices and the distant wailing of a siren, and all these things were leaving vapour trails of noise. In that instant, my mind separated from the rest of me and struck out on its own. From then on, I was like a movie to which the wrong subtitles had been added; the written words bore no relation to what the voices were actually saying on the soundtrack. I was screaming inside, but it was with detached fascination that I could hear myself saying in a mild and reasonable voice, 'Yes, but we can still be friends.'

This was about a week after the note. When Friday evening came, I'd tried casually to entice him away from his rendez-vous. With what had seemed like genuine regret he told me he had a prior commitment, an arrangement to meet with an old family friend, and in the morning he had to leave for Yorkshire – something about visiting his sick uncle, the one who owned the flat he was renting. Next Saturday, he promised, it would be different. Next Saturday we would go somewhere nice.

All right, I thought, let him go out with this woman if he wanted. An old family friend – maybe even old enough to be his mother. I thought of the bridge-playing turkeys my parents had always hung around with and decided she could pose no possible threat to me. I felt secure in the knowledge that I was someone special. Women like me didn't come along twice in one man's lifetime.

I was already aware of Duncan's habit of keeping in touch with ex-girlfriends. There were several of them around – strange women who drifted in and out of his life, who made guest appearances in his photographs every now and again. He said, only half joking, he had always found it difficult to let go of the past – he worried that a clean break would make him lose his grip on the present as well. So it didn't seem odd he should want to keep in touch with an old family friend. Especially since there didn't seem to be a lot of family left.

The Casa DeMille was an upmarket spaghetti house. It was only later (much later) that I found out nine o'clock on Friday night was when it all began. It wasn't the first time they'd met, not exactly, but it was the first time she'd had a chance to talk to him properly, adult to adult as it were. If only I'd tried harder, I could have put a stop to it before it had even begun. If only I had destroyed the note – no one need ever have known. There were many 'if onlys'. In the days and nights to come I would be replaying them ceaselessly in my head.

And now I could hear myself saying, 'Yes, but we can still be friends.'

He looked embarrassed. 'Dora, it's finished. I feel really bad about it.'

I reached across the table and squeezed his hand. He started to pull away, then thought better of it. 'When I say friends, I mean *friends*,' I babbled, 'no strings attached.' The words tumbled out. I was surprised at how easy it was. 'There's no point in us going on if you're in love with someone else. But I don't see why we shouldn't see each other again.'

He looked doubtful. I was no longer of any interest to him, and now all he wanted to do was extricate himself as tactfully as he could. But still I ploughed on. 'I mean, I never thought we were going to get *married* or anything. But I don't see why we can't meet for lunch, and things. Unless of course you can't stand the sight of me . . .'

'Good God, Dora, no.' Oh no, Heaven forbid I should think something like that. 'But I wouldn't want to take advantage of you.'

But you already *have* taken advantage of me, I thought. He was sounding like a character from a Victorian novel. 'You couldn't take advantage of me if you tried,' I said in a flippant, slightly breathy way, my every word weighted with lightness. 'Of course, it goes without saying I'm immensely jealous of this person, whoever she is, and I wish you'd told me about her before.' And I paused, and added, 'What's she like?'

I'd caught him on the hop. He frowned, and for the first time I noticed that little crease between his eyebrows, the one that would get deeper over the years. For a moment or two, he looked as though he'd forgotten what we were talking about. 'You mean Violet?'

'Is that her name?' I asked ingenuously. 'How unusual.'

'I don't think it's her real name, but it's what she calls herself.' He looked at me pleadingly. 'I never intended to fall in love.'

I couldn't think of anything to say to that. Haltingly, in

order to fill the ghastly silence, he told me what he knew, which wasn't much, though I gathered they'd already spent an entire weekend in each other's company. So much for the sick uncle. By the time we'd finished our third cup of coffee, and he'd pecked me goodbye on the cheek, and we'd parted to go our separate ways, I'd formed a clearer picture of what I was up against.

She called herself Violet Westron because her real name was too difficult to pronounce – she was part-Czech, or part-Romanian, or part-Russian, he wasn't sure which. She was fluent in several different languages, including English. She had once been a singer, but she'd got fed up with it and retired. She'd told him she'd been around – she'd spent time in Prague, and Paris, and Berlin, and she knew Venice like the back of her hand. She'd had affairs with one or two famous artists and musicians, and even with a head of state, but she was cagey about their names. She let slip she'd once had her portrait painted by Fernand Khnopff, a painter whose name sounded vaguely familiar, though he wasn't what you'd call a household name. She'd appeared in a couple of films by a well-known German director, though when Duncan had demanded to know which one she'd shaken her head and laughed. It was almost certain all the prints had been destroyed, she'd said, and she thanked the Lord for that.

I said she sounded like a busy little bee.

She wasn't enormously wealthy, Duncan reckoned, but she had resources. He couldn't tell whether it was a wealthy patron, or an employer, or an ex-lover, but there was defi-nitely someone in the background who was bankrolling her expensive taste in clothes. She had come to London in order to set up some sort of business deal, but when Duncan had pressed her further she'd laughed again and changed the subject. He'd asked how long she would be staying, and she'd said, 'For as long as it takes.'

And that was all he knew about her, though she already seemed to know everything there was to know about him. It was uncanny, he said, they'd only just met and already she knew him better than he knew himself. But then she *was* an old family friend.

I wondered aloud whether she would be going away once her business had been completed. Duncan wasn't sure, but I didn't have to ask what he would do then. I knew, because I knew all about obsession. He would follow her, even if she went to the ends of the earth.

She would be a tough nut to crack, but I didn't think she'd be impossible. In my more optimistic moments, I saw Violet Westron as a challenge.

I was besotted all over again, and it was worse than before. I couldn't concentrate on anything else. I went home and drank a bottle of cheap wine. For the first time in my life I bought a packet of cigarettes and painstakingly smoked every last one of them, even though they made me cough and splutter. I awoke in the middle of the night with a parched throat and a throbbing headache, and all I could think about was the memory of those eyes. There had been danger in them, yet I had chosen to ignore it.

That night I sat up in bed, browsing fitfully through some of the art books I had taken out on more or less permanent loan from the college library. Somewhere at the back of my brain was something I knew I had to try and remember, but I couldn't think clearly enough to keep it in focus. I turned the pages of *Symbolist Painters*, making faces at the sphinxes and shady women. I'd always liked those pictures before, but now they reminded me of *her*.

My subconscious must have been working overtime, because suddenly what I'd been trying to remember was right in front of me. The picture of an abandoned city, water gently lapping against its closed doors. The artist's name was *Khnopff*. I scanned the text until I found what I hadn't known I was looking for. '*The great painter of the Sphinx-Woman was the Belgian artist Khnopff (1858–1921).*'

Perhaps I'd remembered it incorrectly, or perhaps Duncan had got the name confused. I leafed through some of the other pages. Perhaps it had been Kubin (1877–1959) or Kupka (1871–1957). But no – he had definitely said Khnopff. 1858–1921. I had to read it several times before the significance of the dates sank in.

Khnopff had died in 1921. If she had been telling the truth, if he really had painted her portrait – even if she'd been a child at the time – it would mean she was a lot older than she looked.

I reckoned she was at least sixty.

In the weeks that followed, I would occasionally spot Duncan wandering around with a somnolent expression on his face. Sometimes he noticed me and said hello. More often he seemed lost in his own little world, hardly speaking to anyone. Once or twice I heard him humming – that drinking song from *La Traviata* again, and something or other from

La Bohème, and one or two other things I didn't recognize. Duncan had never much cared for opera, but now he was obviously getting an education in it.

At the end of the day, I would hang around long after everyone else had gone home, hoping against hope that he would come by and invite me out for a drink, just for old times' sake – but he never did. As far as he was concerned, I'd ceased to exist. Entire days would go by when I didn't see him at all. People noticed his absence, and made comments. Ruth, one of the few people aware we'd been seeing each other, asked me if he was all right. Then she saw something in my expression and asked me if *I* was all right. 'I'm *fine*,' I snapped, and she knew better than to ask again.

I went for long walks, trying to fill the empty hours. I revisited places where Duncan and I had been together. I couldn't understand why being there without him should make me feel so unhappy. On the face of it, nothing had changed – I was still walking, on the same two legs, across the same stretch of the park, stopping at the same pond to watch the same ducks. I was still sitting in the same pubs, drinking the same drinks and munching the same brand of crisps. But it wasn't the same. I tried to pretend it was, but it wasn't. There was something missing, and it wasn't just Duncan.

I was still going to the same cinemas, too, though for obvious reasons I couldn't watch the same movies, not all the time. I pored over film textbooks, searching in vain for mention of lost German masterpieces. I sat through all the German films I could find, just in case, but never once did I see those eyes up on the screen. The films, being German, did nothing to lighten my mood.

The good news was that I lost my appetite. Cakes and croissants no longer gave me pleasure. The weight fell off until, for the first time in my life, I discovered I had cheekbones – they'd been buried there all along. I stared at them in the mirror. The face that stared back was pale and interesting. It was some consolation, but not much. What was the point of cheekbones? What was the point of anything, when I couldn't have what I really wanted?

I couldn't sleep. I would lie there, fretting and perspiring in a shallow fever of helplessness. I wrote long, rambling letters to Duncan, and tore them up. I wrote long, rambling letters to myself, and to this Violet person, and I tore them up too. My room was strewn with stream-of-consciousness confetti.

One night, the fever got so bad I felt like banging my head against the wall. The only way I could stop myself was by getting up and getting dressed. I went for a walk, with no idea where I was heading. My feet took me all the way up the High Street to the Grand Union Canal. I clambered over the locked gate and walked alongside the water, thinking how easy it would be to step into the dark reflection. I heard the night-time noises of the zoo, and walked and walked. Sometimes the path tried to lead me away from the water, but each time I found my way back. I walked for hours, until I found myself at the north end of Ladbroke Grove. I had never meant to go there, but my feet had developed a mind of their own. Now they took me south, overland. They took me straight to Duncan.

I stood beneath the trees on the opposite side of the road and stared up at the light in his second-floor window. It was the only light in the block, the only light in the street. I wondered what he was doing, up at such an unsociable hour. I debated whether to call in and demand a cup of tea. It was four in the morning, but that wasn't what stopped me from ringing the doorbell. He wouldn't care what time it was – he didn't care about things like that any more. I didn't ring because I knew what his reaction would be; polite, as always, but thinking, all the time, about someone else. It would have been unbearable.

One or two cars went past. I walked round the block three or four times, doing a brisk pin-step, then stopping again in the shadow of the trees. I didn't know what I was waiting for, but after half an hour or so, the front door opened. He stepped out, and of course she was with him, wrapped in her furs. I couldn't see so well from where I was standing, but her movements were not those of a sixty-year-old woman. She was petite and childlike, not wizened and old. I'd made a mistake, or Duncan had, or perhaps she'd told him a downright lie.

He stooped and she kissed him. At least, I think that's what she did. Her hair fell across both their faces so that I couldn't see properly. I think he started to say something, but I couldn't be sure. She left him there, staring at her back as she walked away, pulling her hat down over her face and folding herself tightly into the fur. He drank in one last look, as though she was all the sustenance he had, and turned round and went back inside the house and shut the door.

I wondered why she was leaving so early, why she was walking, why hadn't she phoned for a cab. I had nothing better to do, so I followed her. It was the first time I'd ever followed anyone, and in those days I wasn't too good at it. I did all the things I'd seen them do in movies – stopping to tie my shoelace, ducking into doorways, turning to gaze into shop windows. It was ridiculous; we were virtually the only two people on the streets, and still she gave no indication of having seen me.

She walked surprisingly fast, all the way down Ladbroke Grove and along the Harrow Road. She looked neither to left nor right as she went, and I stuck with her all the way. And that's how I found out what she really was.

THREE

I thought at first the gates had been left unlocked, because she slipped between them. When I got there I found they'd been padlocked after all, but the chain was slack and left enough of a gap for a skinny person to squeeze through. Thanks to my recent weight loss, I made it.

So she liked cemeteries too. She and Duncan made a fine pair. Inside, the faint moonlight illuminated ranks of tombstones glowing softly in the undergrowth. Violet was a dark and distant blur on the path ahead. After a few seconds I lost sight of her, but now I could hear her singing softly to herself. '*Libiamo, libiamo* . . .' I couldn't understand the Italian, but I knew it was that bloody drinking song again.

What the hell was she up to? I had to find out. Whatever it was, I would be able to use it against her. I trod cautiously, avoiding the gravel and sticking to the grassy verges, trying to make as little noise as possible. Vandals had passed this way before me. Monuments had been daubed with graffiti, angels had lost their noses, graves gaped in preparation for the day of judgement. I wondered how I'd allowed myself to be lured into this stupid place, at this stupid time of night. But it never occurred to me that I might be putting my life in danger.

A pale grey mass loomed ahead: a mausoleum. I climbed the steps to the portico and was greeted by the stench of urine, and of something else, something familiar I couldn't quite identify. I was wondering which of the three paths Violet had taken when there was a clatter of metal which echoed and clashed – I stopped dead, ears straining, hardly daring to breathe, but the echo died and the rest was silence. I homed in on the source of the sound, and found myself creeping along a passageway lined with pillars; to the right they opened on to a moonlit courtyard; to my left they stood guard over the dim outlines of family tombs.

I had my ideas, most of them far-fetched. I thought she might be involved in espionage, or terrorism, or a spare-parts surgery racket. Or a black-magic cult whose members danced naked and sold their stories to the *News of the World*. I was an incurable romantic with a vivid imagination, but it stopped short of embracing the paranormal as a part of everyday life. I had always liked horror movies, but had never imagined the creatures they depicted were real. I didn't believe in vampires. But the process by which disbelief turned to acceptance was fairly swift, and it started around the next corner.

There was a soft rustling sound, like dry leaves trembling in the gentlest of breezes. I turned the corner, and what I saw was this: the moonlight casting pale strips across the floor, and a writhing shape slumped against one of the pillars. I knew the shape wasn't human because it had too many limbs. An arm flopped sideways on to the ground, and I heard the rustling again as the hand involuntarily tightened its grip around a crinkly plastic bag. Then a leg kicked out, also involuntarily, and once again a thick crêpe sole came into contact with the tin and sent it spinning away on its side. As soon as I spotted the red and white label, I knew what the other familiar smell had been. Cow Gum had always been a vital factor in my collage assembly.

I took another look at the shape, and realized it was not a single entity, but two separate figures conjoined in an unnatural manner. The first figure was hunched over the second, which was skinny and male and slumped on the ground. The first figure was Violet, and she was making small bobbing movements – rather suggestive movements, I thought, only it wasn't a blow job because whatever she was doing was concentrated around the head and neck. I could see by the way the other figure sagged that she hadn't been giving him the kiss of life – the closely cropped head lolled in a state of open-mouthed narcosis. One of his legs was locked in a violent spasm, the other crooked back at an unnatural angle. Then she stood up straight and wiped her chin with the back of her hand. She gazed down at him impassively, as though getting her breath back, before gripping his shoulders and dipping her head once again.

Then it all got confused, but for a few seconds I'd had a grandstand view, and I'd seen what had been left of the side of his neck. The blood which was still pumping gently out of the wound – which was turning his white shirt dark and his dark anorak even darker – had been black and not red in the half-light, so I don't think it was that which was now making me feel queasy. I might have been hyperventilating, and I hadn't been eating properly for the past few days, but more probably it was sheer physical shock. Just because I believed what I was seeing didn't mean I was taking it in my stride. I felt a sound forming in the back of my throat. I knew I had to stop this noise from happening, so I jammed my fist into my mouth and retreated as far as I could into the deepest shadow. I would have turned and made a run for the gates, but I didn't altogether trust my legs.

Then she looked up again and I almost choked. She was looking right at me – but she didn't appear to see me at all. Later on, I would learn it wasn't the shadows which saved me. They can see in the dark, these *people*, like cats, and Violet had been around for so long she could scent dinner at fifty paces. If she'd been operating at full throttle, she would have been on to me in an instant, ripping my throat out with her teeth, or slicing my jugular with her fingernails, or cracking my head open on the flagstones, laughing as she did so. I found out later she was capable of all these things, and that there were several circumstances which combined to save my neck. First, she hadn't fed for several nights, and now this over-hasty blow-out was blunting the sharp edge of her senses. Nor was she behaving in orthodox undead fashion: she was ignoring all the recommended procedures, pursuing impromptu strategies of her own, taking risks, leaving herself wide open. Just because she was in love for only the third time in three hundred years, she thought it gave her the green light to behave like a complete idiot and forget what she was being paid to do. But then Violet didn't care about that. She didn't care about anything, except maybe Duncan.

And she had deliberately picked nourishment she knew would be contaminated with additives – Cow Gum and, at a guess, Lamb's Navy Rum, Carling Black Label, speed – whatever the pathetic squirt had managed to pour down his gullet prior to having it ripped out. Later, I realized she had provided him with most of these substances herself. It was how she had lured him there in the first place.

So when she stood up straight and wiped her mouth and looked around, she didn't see me, and neither did she pick up my scent. I didn't know it then, but she was completely out of her skull. For the next few minutes she stood over the crumpled body, staring down at him as if to establish the state of play. He was either dead or dying, and she didn't give a damn. She brushed her hair back from her face, and, for the first time, I saw colour in her cheeks. She looked astonishingly beautiful in a predatory sort of way, but I thought she also looked weary. It was the weariness of someone who needed to catch up on a few hundred years' worth of sleep. It was then I knew she wasn't just old, she wasn't just weird – she wasn't even human.

This time I didn't think I could suppress the noise. It really had nothing to do with me, but it was coming up anyway, and now I knew for sure it was about to turn into something louder than a whimper or a gurgle – it was going to be a howl. I decided I could no longer fight it, and it would have been all over then and there, if my mouth hadn't suddenly been clamped shut so abruptly I felt the sharp edges of my front teeth slice into my gums. The howl died, smothered at birth by a hand smelling of whisky and tobacco and soap. I plucked at it feebly, but a tentacle wrapped itself around my waist and I was being pulled up and away, and I was kicking my feet in the air. My first thought was that she'd got me, but I could see Violet was still somewhere up ahead, and the tentacle wasn't a tentacle at all – it was an arm. I felt, rather than heard, a wet whiskery mouth pressed up against my ear and a hoarse whisper, '*Don't move. Don't make a sound. Do anything and you are dead.*'

Up ahead, in a foggy vignette, I saw Violet delve into her coat pocket with a leisurely, almost dreamlike movement. When her hand emerged, there was a small cylindrical object in her fingers. I didn't realize what it was, not until she swivelled the gilt casing and began to apply the lipstick to her mouth. Her hand was sure and steady; she had no need of a make-up mirror. Which was just as well, because even if there had been a mirror she would not have been able to see herself reflected in it.

Andreas Grauman was tall, but he was made even taller by the snakeskin boots with stacked heels and platform soles. They were the most ridiculous boots I had ever seen. Grauman told me later they were not particularly to his taste, but Violet had taken a fancy to them and bought them for him, and he had worn them ever since, out of respect.

The last thing I remembered was Violet putting on her lipstick, and the next thing I knew I was lying on the back seat of a car and a long-haired hippy with wire-rimmed spectacles was leaning over me with his hand up my skirt. My reaction was instantaneous and unthinking. I slapped the offending hand as hard as I could, and said, 'Stop that *immediately*!'

He laughed. But took his hand away.

I suddenly remembered what I'd seen and sat up in a panic. 'Where is she? Where am *I*?' I twisted around, trying to look out of the windows, but they were all misted up.

'You are in my car,' he said, 'which is parked near the cemetery.' There was a slight accent. He wasn't English.

I thrashed around, trying to find a way out, but we were in the back seat of a Ford Cortina and the doors were at the front. 'Let me *out*,' I said. There wasn't a whole load of room to manoeuvre. One of my elbows caught him on the edge of his jaw, and he reacted as though he'd been cuffed by the heavyweight champion of the world, shying abruptly away, rubbing his chin and gingerly feeling around inside his mouth. 'Shit,' he said. 'Please be careful.'

'Sorry,' I said without thinking. Then I did think. This man was going to rape me, or worse. 'I've got to go,' I said, tipping up the driver's seat and lunging for the door handle.

He grabbed my wrist and hauled me back. 'Go where? After *her*? Oh no, you stay here with *me*.'

'I left a note; my parents know where I am; they'll call the police . . .'

'Bull*shit*,' he said, peering into my face. His attention made me feel uncomfortable and I quickly looked away. 'You are on something, yes? I can see from your eyes. What have you been taking?'

'Nothing,' I said, pulling my wrist free and rubbing it sulkily. 'I think you'd better let me out.'

He chuckled. 'Maybe later. Tell me, have you been introduced to Violet, or is it just the guy you are interested in?'

'Neither.'

'Don't lie to me. You were following her tonight, yes? How much do you know? Who is the guy?'

'And who the fuck are you?' I asked, outraged. 'Why don't you tell me what's going on?'

He said he would, all in good time, if only I behaved myself and sat quietly in the passenger's seat. On the way to Kensington Church Street we stopped several times at red lights. I had several chances to open the door and make a run for it, but something held me back. I had already decided that if I was going to be horribly murdered, it would have happened already, back in the cemetery where it had been nice and quiet. In fact, I had the feeling the man with the foreign accent had probably *saved* me from being horribly murdered. Not for the first time that night, curiosity got the better of me. I snatched a couple of sideways glances at him as he drove. He was dressed in brushed-denim flares and a brocade jacket, but something told me he was not of the peace and love persuasion. He had longish straw-coloured hair with sideburns, a beaky nose, and wire-rimmed spectacles. The hair looked bleached. I decided I didn't like him one little bit.

We parked in a side street. He frogmarched me to an anonymous brown door and pushed it open. Inside, a steep flight of stairs led downwards. I hovered warily. 'Well, go on,' he said. 'I have no sinister intentions. Here is the only place I know that is open at this hour. London is bad like that.' I started down, and he followed.

We were greeted at the bottom by a man in a shabby dinner jacket who asked to see a membership card. The man with the foreign accent said he'd forgotten it, but dropped several different names and that seemed to do the trick because we were waved in. It was a drinking club, unremarkable apart from its opening hours, decked out in peeling brown and maroon like any shabby old bar in urgent need of refurbishment. There were three or four middle-aged couples sitting around, talking quietly in advanced but practised states of inebriation. I slid into a corner booth and my companion, if you could call him that, fetched a bottle of red wine and two glasses. I sniffed the wine.

'It is not so bad,' he said in an offended tone. 'It is not German.'

'But you are?'

'My name is Andreas Sigismund Grauman.'

'Dora Rosamund Vale,' I said. We shook hands.

Andreas Grauman was not a vampire. He told me later that Violet called him her 'Hatman'. He never wore hats, he said. It was an ancient Moldavian term meaning Commander-in-Chief. He said this with a straight face, and I couldn't for the life of me tell whether or not he was having me on.

He was one of the creepiest people I'd ever met, but I was naïve enough to think I could pump him for information. We circled each other warily for a while, smoking cigarettes (*his* cigarettes – I'd long since run out) and sipping wine, each trying not to give too much away while trying to find out how much the other knew. I got the impression that none of this conversational shuffle was strictly necessary – he was teasing me and enjoying it. I asked how long he'd known Violet. He told me they had a sort of working partnership which went 'way back'. Meanwhile, he was trying to find out more about the 'guy'. 'Do you know that guy? Is he your boyfriend?' I assumed he was referring to Duncan, and said no, we too had a sort of 'working partnership'.

Grauman grinned sarcastically. 'We are not getting very far. Why don't you tell me? You can trust me, you know. I am on your side.'

'Oh yes,' I said.

He gazed at me earnestly. 'You want to have your boy-friend back. I *want* you to have your boyfriend back. So – we both want the same thing.'

I squinted at him through the smoke from my latest ciga-rette. 'Don't tell me that *woman* – that *thing* – is your . . . *mistress?*'

He laughed. 'No, no, no. That would be like *die Blut-schande.* Like fucking my own mother. But Livia is very precious to me, like my favourite aunt, and I do not want her to continue to meet with your friend. It is *bad* for her, you understand. Bad for health, bad for business. There are certain things she must do while she is here in London, and she is not doing them. Because of him. He is fucking every-thing up.'

'Livia? That's her real name?'

'She has many names.'

'How old is she really?'

He leaned forward conspiratorially. 'I tell you what. I tell you her age, and you tell me all about your boyfriend.'

'Not a very good bargain. You tell me her age *and* where she comes from *and* where she gets her money from.'

'OK.'

'And you go first,' I said.

He didn't know exactly how old she was. She either habitu-ally lied about her age, or had genuinely lost count. But he put it at somewhere between two and three hundred years.

'Fernand Khnopff,' I said, more to myself than to him.

He stared at me in amazement. 'You have seen that painting?'

116

'I've heard about it.'

He looked grim. 'Well, there you are. It is like I told you. She is becoming careless.'

'Go on.'

She came originally from Moldavia, he said, which was now a part of the USSR. She had led a normal, respectable life as a daughter of Bogdan until, in a port on the Danube, she encountered a certain Italian aristocrat.

'Then what? Who was the aristocrat?'

'I have told you my story. Now you tell me yours.'

'You haven't finished. Where does she get her money?'

He sighed. 'There is a very old man who lives in Colorado, in the United States of America. He is extremely rich. There is another old man who lives in a castle in Mexico. He too is a millionaire. There is an old woman, I think, who owns a small island off the coast of Japan. There are others, I am not sure where – maybe in the Aegean, or Nepal. But I know they are all very old, and all very rich. They give her money.'

'Why?'

'Because they are vampires too.'

'Good Lord. How many vampires are there?'

'Not many. Like many species, they face extinction.'

'Why don't they spread it around, then? Bite more necks?'

Grauman sighed, his eyes glazing over. 'It is not so simple, not like in the movies. One bite may be enough to infect you, but it will not bestow on you the full range of powers. That process is long and arduous, and extremely dangerous, as the recipient will hover on the threshold of death for six or seven days, while fluids are still being exchanged. And, so long as this recipient exists, the original vampire is unable to bestow his or her gift on another. At least, not in its entirety.'

'How inconvenient.'

'Yes, it is. Most inconvenient.'

'So what is Violet being paid to do?'

His eyes snapped back into focus. 'I have kept my part of the bargain,' he said pleasantly. 'Now you will keep yours. Tell me your story, or I will break both your arms.'

I looked at him to see whether he was joking, but I didn't think he was. 'What was it you wanted to know again?'

'Tell me about your boyfriend. What is his name?'

I sipped some wine. 'Duncan.'

He snarled. For a second I thought he really was going to lean across and break my arm. 'Duncan *what*?'

After the first shock of waking up to find him there, I had found him simply creepy. Now he was beginning to frighten me again.

'Duncan Fender,' I said.

A look of such ferocious anger crossed his face that I quickly estimated the fastest route to the door, just in case I had to make a run for it. But then he sighed and sat back and lit another cigarette.

'Duncan Fender,' he said. 'I thought as much.'

FOUR

I saw a lot of Andreas Grauman in the next few weeks. Or rather, he made sure I saw a lot of him. He was keeping tabs on me, but I was careful not to give too much away. I refused to tell him where I lived, for example – I didn't want him springing any nasty surprises. But it was true I was spending more time in W11 than in NW1. I had a friend called Matt who was attempting to run a tiny independent record company from a couple of rooms at the dingy end of Blenheim Crescent. I talked him into giving me a set of keys so I could use the place as a makeshift base at night. It was somewhere to make coffee, chop up sulphate, and smoke cigarettes – all fast becoming my favourite hobbies. And it was only a short walk away from Duncan's.

Violet killed people. I knew that now. She wasn't turning them into other vampires; she was tearing their throats out and drinking their blood. Down and outs, drug addicts, people who wouldn't be missed – but they were still *people*, and I wasn't happy about it. The cemetery was obviously a favourite dining area. I followed her as far as the gates, once or twice, but I had seen it once, and had no desire to see it again, and I couldn't bring myself to follow her in. I never found out what happened to the corpses, but there was never any mention in the press of a serial killer at large. I had the impression, from something he let slip, that one of Grauman's duties was to clear up after her. This struck me as a demeaning task, and I wondered why he put up with it.

Sometimes, I wondered if I were transferring my obsession from Duncan to Violet. I couldn't get enough of her. I felt cheated during the daylight hours, when she disappeared into the basement of her big empty house in Holland Park. It was as good as a fortress, and it needed to be. The windows were barred, and the door was solid as a rock. Without keys, or a bulldozer, there would be no way of getting in. Grauman warned me not to try; the place was rigged, he said.

While she slept, I browsed in libraries, mulling over books and taking notes. I made lists, concocted theories. I theorized, for instance, that the traditional effectiveness of garlic as a deterrent was due to its playing havoc with the finely tuned sense of smell, triggering off some kind of debilitating migraine. I was curious about how people were turned into vampires in the first place. It would be a long drawn-out process requiring more than one blood-draining session – probably a whole series of them. I began to look even more closely at Duncan when I saw him, but while he was obviously having trouble keeping normal hours he didn't seem particularly distressed by the garlic I waved under his nose.

I still dropped in on the occasional college seminar, justifying my absences by dropping hints about the grand designs in which I was engaged at home. In fact, I was turning my dealings with Violet into a sort of artistic project. Matt let me fix up a bulletin board on his wall and, since it was quite decorative, never asked what it was all about. I constructed a collage of maps, coloured cotton, and drawing-pins to record Violet's movements. The blue drawing-pins recorded her wanderings, the green stood for her meetings with Duncan. Fatalities were red.

My main reason for going in to college, though, was to keep myself supplied with drugs. Ruth Weinstein had lots of hippy friends and had consequently become our resident dealer. Mostly she supplied various forms of hash, but the rich kids liked to splash out on cocaine for special occasions, and she turned a tidy profit on the side. I had never had the money to fritter away on recreational drugs, but I needed to stay awake at night. Ruth supplied me with the means of doing so, usually on credit, and every so often I would fiddle the till at the cake shop to pay her off. This was her idea of making friends; she was convinced we were going to be chums for life.

Meanwhile, I was meeting up with Grauman in smoky pubs and greasy cafés where I would push coagulating food around my plate and drink endless cups of coffee. After that first meeting he was sparing with his information, even though I tried to coax him into commenting on some of my theories. I never believed for a moment that he was interested in me personally. I think in his grotesque Teutonic fashion he might have found me diverting, but I kept reminding myself I was only a means to an end. There was no question in my mind he was ruthless, vicious, and entirely without sentiment – and that once I had served my purpose, he would calmly arrange for me to be removed from the face of the earth.

For now, I was determined to spin my usefulness out for as long as possible. Grauman wanted Duncan out of the way and he thought I could help him there. And what was in it for Andreas? I had no idea. He insisted his interest in Violet was neither sexual nor financial. He talked about duty, to sponsors and to heritage, but I could tell that underneath the high-sounding words, it all boiled down to something personal. Grauman and I were very much alike in that way. Naturally, I wondered what it would be like to go to bed with him. The thought of it made me squirm, and not from anything remotely resembling pleasure.

One day, I had just finished rearranging some mushrooms on toast when he made an outrageous suggestion. He'd wolfed down his own food and I'd watched in repelled fascination as he had whipped out a length of dental floss and sawed at the gaps between his teeth. I had witnessed this ritual several times before. He had asked more than once if I realized fewer teeth were lost to decay than to gum disease, had talked at length about plaque and disclosing tablets, had even advised me on what type of toothbrush to buy. Now he finished with the floss and dropped it into the ashtray, then sat back and took a long, cool look at me, a faint smile on his lips, but not in his eyes. I had learned never to trust his smiles.

'You always wear black,' he observed eventually. 'And you skin is unusually pale. Good God, Dora, don't you ever go out in the sun?'

'Not a lot.'

'If I didn't know better, I might think you were like Violet.'

'What? *Me?* A *vampire?*' I laughed.

He laughed too, but his laugh went on long after mine had faded. 'Speaking of which, I should like to ask a small favour. You will be in a certain place, at a certain time. You will not speak. You will do nothing, except take what is offered, and then you will give it to me.'

I glared at him. 'What the hell do you think I am? A messenger service? Do it yourself.'

I could tell he was wondering whether to use threats, but he opted for keeping it sweet. 'But that is impossible. You see, I am too tall, my hair is the wrong colour, and I am also the wrong gender. No one else can do this. Only you.'

The enormity of what he was asking finally dawned on me. 'You expect me to *impersonate Violet.*'

'Not impersonate, don't flatter yourself. No one could ever do that. You will simply be a stand-in, like in the movies.'

'And is she part of this? Does she know?'

After weighing the possibilities, he went for the truth. 'No.'

So it was that, two nights later, I was lurking in the undergrowth outside Violet's basement, dressed in my best black. I knew Grauman wasn't far away, but I could neither see nor hear him. My chief worry was that Violet would make an unprecedented decision to leave Duncan early and I would run slap-bang into her on her own doorstep. It crossed my mind that Grauman might have set the whole thing up specifically in order for this to happen. But then I dismissed my fears; it would have been too elaborate a ruse. He could have delivered me up to her at any time without needing to resort to that sort of baroque subterfuge.

While waiting for the appointed hour I explored the overgrown garden. In summer, any such freedom of movement would have been impossible, but now my path was not quite blocked by false cyprus and rampant ivy. I smoked five cigarettes, one after the other, and was just about to light a sixth when the hinges on the garden gate creaked and the light from the street cast an elongated shadow across my path. My heart skipped a couple of beats; this was going to be more difficult than I had anticipated. The newcomer spotted me standing there and swooped. I melted back into the foliage before he could get too close a look at my face.

But, as he approached, I saw my first impressions had been mistaken. I had been expecting a vampire, but this man was obviously human, and hardly a prime example of the species. It was impossible to be afraid of someone this puny, who had an Adam's apple bobbing up and down with nervousness. With a thrill of excitement I realized he was more frightened of me than I had been of him.

'Hello?' he whispered. 'Miss Westron?' He was clutching an attaché case to his chest as though he thought someone was going to leap out of the shadows and snatch it away.

I followed Grauman's instructions and said nothing.

'Miss Westron,' he repeated, extending a trembling hand for me to shake. I ignored it. 'William Fitch,' he said, nodding like a car mascot. 'I've got the papers you sent for.'

'Oh good,' I said, before remembering I was supposed to be keeping my mouth shut.

'Do you want to go through them now?'

I shook my head and grabbed the case, but he continued to hover. 'Perhaps if I . . .'

I fixed him with what I hoped was a spine-chilling stare, and hissed, 'Go away.' His mouth opened wide, but no words came out, then he turned tail and fled. I watched him go, chuckling delightedly to myself. If this was power, I was already hooked. Being Violet full-time might be fun.

As soon as he was out of sight, I opened the case. It was full of loose pieces of paper and typewritten sheets, and I pulled out a bunch of crumbling yellowish cuttings. The top one was a picture of people milling around a blazing building, cut from an old French newspaper. The man nearest the camera had his mouth wide open and was yelling something. Visible in the background, wrestling with giant snakes and ladders, were harried firemen. My French was rusty but it wasn't hard to decipher the headline – *Eleven Perish in Hotel Inferno*.

I dug around in the case again and drew out a dog-eared black-and-white photograph of people sitting round a table in a restaurant, clinking glasses at the camera: two men, two women. One of the men was familiar; I knew I'd seen that face before somewhere and wondered if it was someone famous. One of the women was slender and chic, a bit like Audrey Hepburn only wispier and blonde. The other woman was a blur; she had moved while the shutter was being pressed and the flash hadn't been fast enough to capture her.

Grauman appeared from nowhere and, no respecter of personal space, started to breathe down the back of my neck. 'I will take those,' he said, easing the cuttings out of my hands so as not to tear them. Reluctantly, I handed him the photograph as well. He said, 'I do not remember giving you permission to examine the goods.'

'And I don't remember you saying I couldn't,' I said,

watching him check the contents of the bag. 'Why can't I look? I played my role perfectly, didn't I?'

He flashed me a grin, unable to keep the smugness out of it. 'Maybe later. Maybe after you do for me another small favour.'

'What are you going to do with those?'

Grauman closed the case and patted it. 'She wants to keep Fender a secret, all to herself, because she knows there are others who would not hesitate to have him killed, if they knew who he was and thought he was getting in the way. She would do anything – *anything* – to protect him.'

'So, what next?'

'I show her these papers. And she will be grateful I was able to stop them falling into the wrong hands. But there will be other envelopes, and other cuttings, and she will be aware of that. She will leave Fender alone, because she fears for his safety.'

'If she's so fond of him, why doesn't she turn him into a vampire? Then she wouldn't have to worry about his life being in danger.'

Grauman stopped being smug. 'It is not so simple,' he snapped.

'I see,' I said, though I didn't. All I knew was that I was going to have to tread very carefully. 'And the favour?'

'Fender's five minutes are up,' Grauman said. 'It is time for him to find out the truth about his lady love. This is where you come in, Dora. You will tell him what she really is.'

I thought it was a bad move, but didn't say so, because Grauman was still in a snappy mood. I had to swallow a lot of pride in order to phone Duncan. I kept telling myself it was worth it; soon I would have him all to myself. But he didn't sound exactly overjoyed to hear me. In fact, he could barely remember who I was — just a vaguely familiar name dredged up from some dim, distant, pre-Violet past.

'Dora,' he echoed.

'*Dora*. You know, from college.'

'Oh yes.'

I said I had to see him, it was urgent. He didn't seem bowled over with enthusiasm. I was tempted to give up, but the thought of admitting my failure to Grauman was more than I could bear. I gave it one last shot, and he grudgingly agreed to meet for lunch the next day, in the cheapest restaurant I could think of.

When I arrived he was already there — slumped in a corner beneath the poster for the peach-flavoured aperitif called Sex Appeal. As a caption, it hardly applied to him, not as he was then. He looked up as I went over and it was obvious he wasn't in the best of health. His eyes were bloodshot, his stubble hadn't seen the edge of a razor for several days, and there were flaky patches on his face. The ashtray in front of him was brimming. It didn't take long to work out that the only way he could stop his hand from shaking was by moving a cigarette up and down like an automaton. Most of the time he forgot to flick off the ash, and it kept falling on to the table.

I said hello, and sat down and stared, searching again for those telltale signs. He wasn't sitting by the window, it was true, but he wasn't turning away from the light, or anything. I asked how he was, but couldn't help answering the question myself. 'You don't look too good.'

'I don't *feel* too good,' he admitted, squinting at me

through a miasma of cigarette smoke. 'But you look great, Dora. Hey, you look terrific.'

I was pleased he'd noticed, and told him I'd stopped eating the buns. We gave our orders to a surly Italian waiter, and I brought him up to date with news from college until the food arrived. The conversation was one-sided, and the food killed it off. We both started picking at our plates. 'How's Violet?' I asked, trying to make the enquiry sound casual.

He shifted uncomfortably. 'Fine. We're both fine.'

I waited, not saying anything. The pause lengthened and grew awkward. Duncan lit up another cigarette – neither of us had got very far with our food – and sighed. Finally, he said, *à propos de* nothing in particular. 'We were thinking of going to Paris.'

I was surprised by an almost physical pain which swept through me. Paris. Oh yes. He had promised to take *me* there. He had promised to show me Père Lachaise. He had promised me lots of things.

If any of this showed in my face, Duncan gave no sign of having noticed. He had more pressing concerns. 'I booked a hotel,' he said. 'I went out and bought tickets, I had it all set up, but then she suddenly decided she wouldn't be able to come after all.'

'What did you do with the tickets?' I blurted, thinking perhaps, even now, I could persuade him to take me.

'Tickets? Oh, I got a refund. But there's something wrong. I don't know why she backed down. I don't know what it is, but there's something she's not telling me.'

I took a deep breath. 'You're right. There is something she's not telling you. That's why I asked you here today. It's something dreadful, Duncan, something you have to know.'

He fixed his red eyes on me. I could see him trying and failing to work out what I knew, and how I knew it. But the effort was too much; he gave up and stared down at his lasagne, which by now had acquired a light sprinkling of ash. 'Don't tell me. She's married.'

I couldn't help it – I laughed. 'Oh, Duncan. What would you do if I said she *was* married? Or if you found out she was having an affair with someone else?'

'I'd kill myself,' he said, smiling so I could see he was joking.

'Don't be silly. If you felt that strongly about it, you should kill *her*.' I smiled so he could see that I too was making a joke. 'But it's academic, because that isn't the problem. It's something much worse.'

He regarded me sceptically. 'What could be worse than that?'

Even though the only other diners in the place were a couple of deadbeats wolfing down plates of cheap spaghetti, I leant over the table towards him, trying to close the gap between us, because I didn't want anyone else to hear what I was going to say. I'd rehearsed it in my head so often, but once it was out in the open it sounded preposterous and lame at the same time. 'Violet is not human. She's a vampire.'

Duncan's reaction was unexpected. I'd been prepared for him to laugh in my face, or blow his top, or just be bewildered. Instead, he dropped his cigarette and clapped his hand over his mouth, scraping his chair back from the table and sitting there with his eyes bulging.

'Are you all right?' I enquired, thinking perhaps he was about to be sick. He responded from deep within his throat;

impossible to tell whether it was yes or no. 'Duncan . .?'

After what seemed an eternity, he took the hand away from his mouth. Even his lips had turned pale. He picked up the cigarette, extinguished it, and immediately lit another. Then he said, much too late, 'I don't believe you.' His voice was steady, probably too steady. He didn't seem to be having a problem with vampires *per se* – just with the idea of Violet being one.

'Yes, she is,' I said.

He shook his head. 'You're wrong. Not her.' And he smiled a secret smile to himself. I had never expected persuasion to be an easy task, but in all my rehearsals of this scene I'd concentrated on the brief history of the species, its nocturnal habits, dietary requirements, recorded sightings et cetera. Now all this information was redundant.

'You know what a vampire is, then,' I said.

'Of course.'

'You *believe* . . .' I began, but he cut in. 'My father did a series of paintings when I was about five or six. I asked him all about them, and he told me. Kids liked scary things, he said.'

'Then you'll know it's true. About Violet, I mean. She only comes out at night.'

'Don't be absurd. You don't know what you're talking about.'

'But I *saw* her!' I blurted out. 'I followed her.'

Duncan's face went from colourless to flushed in an instant. He took a quick look round the room, but no one was showing the slightest interest in our argument. 'Jesus Christ, I don't believe this. You've been *following* her? Jesus Christ, Dora, you're *sick*.'

He scraped his chair back again, even further away from the table, preparing to get up. The finality of the movement and the accompanying screech of wood against lino cast me into despair. I'd blown it, and it was Grauman's fault. Duncan may not have been acknowledging my existence before, but at least I'd had my pride. Now, I had nothing. He was going to stomp off in a huff and I'd never see him again, and if I did see him he would despise me. The future stretched ahead of me like a vast grey nothingness. The idea of it was overwhelming, and I burst into tears.

'Oh, Christ,' said Duncan. He handed me a grubby paper tissue. There was a pause, which I filled with snivelling. 'I'm sorry . . .' he said haltingly. 'I haven't been fair . . .' His voice had lost its harsh edge.

But now I was sobbing convulsively, and his change of heart made it worse. All the pent-up emotions of the past few weeks came bubbling to the surface. I thought about the tickets to Paris, and the unfairness of everything, and great spasms of sorrow welled up and forced their way out of my mouth. Wave after wave, until I no longer cared if people stared.

Duncan paid for the lasagne and coaxed me towards the door. 'Come on,' he said. 'What you need is a nice cup of tea.' I found this protectiveness comforting, and rather seductive. As he led me outside and hailed a taxi, I made an effort to calm myself down, but this led only to a fresh outbreak of sobbing. In the cab, though, a part of my brain was congratulating itself. The crying jag had been a brilliant move. Grauman would have been proud.

FIVE

Duncan's flat wasn't so very different from the last time I had seen it, except that now everything was covered with a thick layer of dust. I sat on the sofa and took nervous sips of tea, wondering how to steer the conversation back to Violet when there wasn't any conversation to begin with.

Duncan was sitting cross-legged on the floor, engrossed in the contents of the ashtray. I tried to kick-start the dialogue. 'Sorry about earlier – about what I said.'

'S'all right.' He was combing abstract designs into the ash with a spent match.

I tried again. 'She sings, does she?'

'Who?' His ears pricked up a bit. 'Oh, all the time. Non-stop. Didn't I tell you she used to be a singer?'

I nodded. 'You also said she'd had her portrait painted by Fernand Khnopff.'

He grunted, not really paying attention.

'*Fernand Khnopff!*' I repeated. 'Fernand Khnopff died in 1921.'

That got through to him. He frowned.

'*1921*,' I said again.

Half a dozen expressions flashed across his face in rapid succession. 'So?' he said at last. 'She's older than me.'

'She'd have to be quite a bit older. *Work it out.*'

Duncan got to his feet and began to prowl up and down. 'For Heaven's sake, what *is* this?' he muttered to himself. 'What does it matter how old she is?'

'She frightens me,' I said. 'You don't know what she can do.'

His face was set in a grimace. I wondered how much time I had before he lost his temper again. For a while he went on pacing, before coming to some sort of decision and parking himself firmly in front of me. 'I can't believe you're saying these things,' he growled. 'She's the sweetest, kindest, nicest person. You'll see.'

'I'm sure she is.' I shuddered at the memory of how close I'd come to meeting her. Perhaps now was the time to fill him in on the details. But he was saying something. I could see his lips moving. I wasn't sure I'd heard correctly, so I asked him to say it again.

'I said, *she'll be here any minute now, you'll be able to see for yourself.*'

'*Jesus!*' Before I knew it, I was on my feet, slamming my mug down so violently that tea slopped over the rim. 'Here? Now?'

He checked his watch. 'Any minute.'

'But . . .' I said the first thing that popped into my head. 'But it's too early, only seven o'clock.'

He snorted. 'What did you think? She only comes out after midnight? Grow up.'

I grabbed my bag. 'I'm off.'

133

'Fine,' he said, but he didn't step aside. For a second or two, we stood there face to face, and he looked genuinely upset to see me go. Under any other circumstances, I would have stayed. But not under these, no way. I went round him.

'Stay if you like,' he said, following me to the door but making no attempt to help as I fumbled with the lock. 'Maybe I should have introduced you before. Then you'd never have worked yourself up into this state.'

'I'm not in a state,' I snapped. 'And there's really no point in me staying, because none of this has anything to do with me, not really.' Finally I managed to pull the door open. I was on the point of stepping out on to the landing, but I didn't, because Violet was standing right there in front of me.

Somebody – probably me – made a small strangled noise.

'Ah,' she said, looking straight at me. 'My little shadow.'

'What?' asked Duncan.

She wafted past. I saw, but didn't feel, her furs brushing against my hand as she swept by. When I looked back, she was standing on tiptoe to kiss Duncan on the cheek. 'How sweet,' she was saying to him. 'You've brought me an audience. Or should we say a *billet-doux*?'

I turned back to the door. Escape was just a step away. The problem was, I couldn't move, not an inch. I was staring hard at my feet, willing them to walk, when I felt a soft voice at my ear.

'*Don't go.*'

It wasn't an entreaty. It was a command. She closed the door and double-locked it right in front of me, and there wasn't a thing I could do about it. She slipped an arm around my waist, like an old chum, and walked me back into the living room.

And then, quite unexpectedly, I realized everything was going to be all right. Suddenly, she was no longer the ice princess, but warm and inviting, and all the tension between us had melted. It was as though we'd known each other for years. She slipped out of her coat, dropped a fur or two on the floor, and arranged herself on the sofa.

'Come, sit next to me,' she said, patting the seat with her tiny gloved hand. I had expected her to talk with a sinister accent, like Rosa Klebb in *From Russia With Love*, but her voice carried not a hint of Eastern Europe.

I sat down next to her. Duncan was left standing awkwardly in front of us. 'Violet,' he said, 'this is Dora.'

'Of course it is,' she purred, and smiled at me as though we were sharing a joke he couldn't possibly understand. Then she stretched out her hand and tapped the teapot. 'Duncan, darling, why don't you run along and brew us some fresh tea?'

Duncan shrugged helplessly as if to say, 'Well, what can you do?', and obediently trotted out to the kitchen with the half-empty pot. Violet adjusted her position so that her arm rested along the back of the sofa. 'Good,' she said. 'Now we can talk.'

'We *can*?'

'Don't look so serious. Please. I'm not going to eat you.' Her expression was so rueful that I burst out laughing. Being eaten was exactly what I'd been afraid of, but now those fears seemed ridiculous. I had been thinking of her in the abstract, as a mindless thirst that required regular quenching. It had never occurred to me that she might be someone I could talk to. It had never occurred to me I might actually *like* her.

'You have many questions to ask,' she said, and there was an intensity in her gaze which made me feel I could have told her anything, anything at all, and she would have understood. I was suddenly convinced we were destined to become the most intimate of friends. I wanted to tell her that, but I couldn't find the right words. Her eyes were bright, brighter than anything else in the room. I could easily have looked away if I'd wanted – it was just that I didn't want to. The past weeks – the blood, the killings, the mausoleum – were a bad dream. And, even if they hadn't been a dream, even if they'd really happened, it was becoming clear to me now that, like everyone else, she had her reasons.

'All a matter of perspective,' she said softly, and for a few tantalizing seconds she allowed me into her mind. The vision there was vast and boundless. I felt certain that, if only I did the right thing, she would allow me to be a part of it. I felt a surge of excitement. If only I played this right, I could live *for ever*.

'So,' she said at last. I wondered if I'd been asleep. Something had just happened and I'd missed it. I was conscious that her arm was now draped across my shoulders – I could feel the weight of it there, and I knew instinctively that I didn't have the strength to remove it. I became aware of the almost absent-minded way in which her velvet-gloved fingers were caressing the back of my neck, and I didn't dare move, it was such a soothing sensation, and I didn't want it to stop, I wanted it to go on and on. Just before I closed my eyes, I saw she had leant forward so her face was inches away from my own, and her lips were very red and slightly parted, she was whispering something but I couldn't quite make out the words as she continued to stroke the back of my neck with one of her hands while the other tugged at my collar, and I wanted to help so I tilted my head back, and listened to the sound of my own breathing, in and out, in and out, and there was no point in resisting, it would have been too much effort, and all for nothing, because it didn't matter, nothing mattered, nothing would ever matter again.

I was just about to drift off into a terminal reverie when there was an ear-splitting crash. I felt a rush of disappointment such as I had never felt before in my life. Everything had been perfect, and now it was spoiled. Reluctantly, I forced my eyes open.

It was Duncan. I'd forgotten all about him. He was yelling. 'What the fuck are you *doing*?' The carpet was steaming, pieces of teapot fanning out around his feet like petals. His face was paper-white, even whiter than it had been in the café. He kept yelling. I didn't like him yelling like that. I'd had enough of it. It really was time for me to go.

I started to get up. Violet, with a casual flick of her wrist, slammed me back down. The impact knocked the breath out of me. I reached out, rather unsteadily, to push myself up again. Perhaps she saw the movement as a threat, or perhaps she was just being playful. My arm was suddenly grabbed, and squeezed, and wrenched so hard I thought it might pop out of its socket.

There was a flash of dazzling white incisor, and a grinding, followed by a crisp snapping sound, like a ginger biscuit being broken in half.

I managed to pull away, or she let me go – I'm not sure which. For a fraction of a second, it didn't hurt at all. I opened my mouth to say something, and then the pain reared up and hit me. For a moment, there was so much pain, I didn't know who I was, or where I was coming from, or what I'd been doing there. It came from my shoulder, my elbow, my hand, all down my left side, all at the same time. The first wave ebbed, but my gasp of relief was cut short when it came roaring back, worse than ever.

I looked at my hand, then away. Then back again. I couldn't believe what I was seeing. The little fingernail had gone. *My little fingernail had gone.* All that was left was a raw stub, and a flappy bit of skin, and something knobbly and white which I didn't want to examine too closely. But it wasn't white for long because while I watched, the whole area filled up with red which spilled over and began to trickle down my wrist. I stared and stared, not wanting to admit that the reason the nail was missing was because the entire top joint of the finger had been bitten off.

It looked painful, but I couldn't quite connect it to the pain I was feeling. After what seemed like an age, I managed to croak, 'My finger.' I tried to glare accusingly at Violet, who was chewing daintily.

Through the pain, I thought I could hear Duncan wailing, 'But it was going to be *me*.' I couldn't work out whether he was wailing at me, or at her. Surely he didn't want *his* finger chewed off. Either way, it didn't matter – I knew I was going to bleed to death, or die from shock, or both. Blood was now dribbling through my fingers, down my arm, and dripping on to the sofa. I knew I had to keep the hand pointing upwards – that way it wouldn't bleed so much – and I had to find something to staunch the flow. With my other hand, I fished around in my bag, only to find I'd used all my Kleenex up on the crying jag.

'Uh, the bathroom,' I mumbled. 'Gotta get something.' It was an effort to form words, and I wasn't sure I was saying them loud enough for anyone to hear, but I managed to totter to my feet.

Violet was twice as quick, and standing in front of me again. 'You are going *nowhere*,' she said. She was still smiling, but she'd given up pretending to be nice. 'You know too much, but you know *nothing*.' She stretched her arms out wide, like a miniature basketball player blocking my route to goal. If I'd been quicker off the mark, I could have dodged around her, but I was thinking and moving in slow motion.

'Here you all are,' she said, 'and you might as well not be there. You are just objects and shadows.' Now she was ranting. She said something else in a language I couldn't even identify, let alone translate. I was in too much pain to care.

'Oh, for God's sake,' said Duncan.

'Help,' I said weakly, but he wasn't even looking at me. My finger was *gone* and the bastard wasn't even looking.

He said, 'Oh, *hell*.'

Violet seemed to have lost interest in me too. 'Remember what I told you,' she said to him. 'Do it.'

'I *can't*.' His voice was much too loud. 'Not *now*.'

'Excuse me,' I whispered, 'I think I'm bleeding to death.'

'Remember what we talked about.' An edge of impatience had crept into Violet's even tone. '*Do it*.'

'I *remember*, for God's sake. Stop treating me like a child.'

'So go ahead,' she said. 'What's your problem?'

I thought he had calmed down, but I was wrong. He suddenly bunched up his fists and started yelling again. He was yelling so hard the veins stood up on his forehead. I couldn't make it all out, but I caught the last part: 'You never *told* me. You never *told* me you were fucking *dykes*. *Both* of you.'

This was too much. I wanted to tell him no, he was wrong, I had *never* liked women, and it had been *Violet's* fault, not mine, and anyway he'd got it all back to front, because after all she *hadn't* been seducing me, she'd gone and bitten off my *finger*, for Christ's sake, and that wasn't my idea of foreplay, not at all, and now look at me, I was bleeding to death. I *wanted* to say all this, but I could barely string two words together.

And then I forgot all about it anyhow, because she laughed at him, and he immediately clouted her hard, across the face.

Time stood still. I even forgot the pain for a second. I held my breath, waiting for her to lunge back at him and take his head off. She could have done it with a single swipe. But she didn't. Her gaze never left his as she slowly wiped her mouth with the back of her hand. Her eyes were glittering dangerously as she said, 'Or maybe you're not up to it, eh?'

'Bitch,' said Duncan, and hit her again. There was a soft scrunch as his fist connected with the bones in her nose. She stepped back in surprise, and her hands flew up to her face. Blood was gushing from her nostrils. Her fingers pushed and probed, as if to inspect the damage. When the gloves came away soaking wet, she studied them calmly for a moment. Then she turned back to Duncan, and smiled and said in a voice that was now slightly nasal, 'You guys, you're all alike.'

When he whacked her again she stumbled, and then he kicked her legs away from under her, and she went down, and there was a loud crack as her head struck the floor, and he immediately started kicking her in the face and stomach, but she kept on laughing and rolling around, as though he were tickling her, as though this were the most fun she'd ever had in her life – which just seemed to make him kick all the harder.

If she'd been human, I might have asked him to stop what he was doing, but it wasn't as though she were one of us. She wasn't human at all, so it didn't count. And besides, she'd *eaten* my little *finger* and now my hand was hurting like hell, so she deserved everything she was getting. But I didn't care for the expression on Duncan's face. It was an expression I'd never seen before – not on anyone. Under any other circumstances, it would have made me feel uneasy. I tried to work out what it was, but my finger was hurting so much, I couldn't think straight, so I sat down and stared. The whole thing was unreal. It was like watching a movie.

Eventually, when her face had been reduced to a bloody pulp, the swelling made it almost impossible for her to laugh. But one of her eyes was swollen shut, so that she seemed instead to be tipping the wink at some huge and incomprehensible joke. Duncan stood over her, only slightly out of breath, and every time she made a noise, he kicked her again. '*You'll have to speak up*,' he said with exaggerated clarity, like someone talking to his deaf grandma. '*We can't understand it when you mumble*.'

She made another noise. Bubbles of blood came out of her mouth and the remains of her noise. To my horror, I realized she was singing. Something from *La Bohème*. It was a thick liquid sound, like someone warbling through an ocean of treacle.

My wounded hand was tucked beneath my right armpit. I had discovered that, if I squeezed hard enough, at the same time rocking back and forth and making small whimpering sounds, I could damp the pain down to an acute throb. But the singing was setting it off again. I wanted to block my ears, but I couldn't – not with only one hand operational. 'Make her stop,' I begged.

Duncan was staring down at the body, muttering, 'Shit, I really killed her.'

'No you didn't,' I gasped, between throbs. 'She's a vampire . . . she was dead already . . . and they call her Mimi . . .'

Duncan appeared to notice me for the first time. 'Dora,' he said. 'You all right?'

'Oh, I'm *fine*,' I said through gritted teeth. 'I'm only bleeding to *death* . . . For God's sake, get me something to wrap this in.'

He went out of the room, and I wished he hadn't left me alone with her. She was staring at me through that one eye, staring at me as though the appetizer had been so finger-lickin' good that she'd developed a taste for the rest of me. I half expected her to fly across the room and fasten her teeth in my throat. I knew I would never feel safe, not ever again. Not unless someone put her completely out of commission.

Duncan came back and wrapped my hand in a dirty teatowel, which he fixed in position with masking tape. It didn't look too hygienic, but the wrapped hand fitted under my armpit even more snugly than before. I went back to my rocking and whimpering routine, pretending not to notice the grubby linen was already turning red.

There was a burbling noise from the bundle on the floor. I said, 'You've got to . . . finish her off . . . you know.'

Duncan gazed at me through red-rimmed eyes and asked, rather sarcastically, 'So what do you suggest?'

'Stake,' I said in what I hoped was a matter-of-fact tone, though it was undermined by a nervous tremor. 'Through the heart.'

He groaned, and it was then I knew he was going to co-operate. 'Stake through the heart. Of course.'

Violet made wet chuckling sounds. It was like listening to someone with a serious speech impediment, but I knew exactly what she was trying to say. She was trying to say we'd gone too far. It was too late for us to turn back now. If we didn't go all the way, we would wind up even deader than she was.

He'd spread newspapers on the floor and rolled her on to them, but the carpet was still getting soaked. What with the both of us bleeding, the room was beginning to look like an abattoir. She lay there winking at him while he wrestled with the cocoon in which she had wrapped herself – layers of leather and cashmere and fur, all the way down to a black silk slip edged in lace and crusted with blood. Even when he'd peeled that off, I was relieved to see there was so much blood and mottled purple bruising that she didn't look naked at all. Nakedness would have made her seem too vulnerable, but the patches of visible skin were so white they were almost luminous, and reminded me of the flesh of the crawling things you sometimes find under stones.

Still, she wasn't as badly hurt as I'd thought – the clothes had obviously absorbed a lot of the punishment.

'She's shamming,' I said.

'No she's not.'

'She *is* shamming. Any minute now, she'll sit up . . . and sink her fangs into you.'

'She wouldn't do that,' said Duncan. 'Maybe to you. Not to me.'

143

'You don't know that.'

'Believe me, she won't sit up. Not when I've finished with her.'

'You knew all along didn't you? That she was a vampire, I mean.'

'There's a lot I didn't know,' he said.

'Oh,' I said, 'and by the way, I am *not* a lesbian.'

Duncan raided his stationery cupboard. The stake wasn't really a stake but an eighteen-inch ruler whittled to a point. He positioned it over her heart and began to bash the other end with a chunky Sellotape dispenser. The point sank in very slowly. He was very calm, as though he were stretching a canvas, or tacking a sketch to the wall. She was calm too; I'd expected her to screech and clutch at her chest, at the very least, like I'd seen in the movies, but all she did was cough up a small amount of claret-coloured blood and belch. When he'd finished she lay there with the ruler sticking out of her, fixing us with her one open eye as she began to hum 'Sola, perduta, abbandonata.'

I hadn't expected this.

Duncan gawped in disbelief. 'What's wrong? Why isn't it working?'

'Mmmnnnn mmmmgggghhh,' sang Violet.

'It's not enough,' I whimpered. 'You'll have to cut her head off.' I was thinking of her as a piece of meat now. I'd gone way beyond the stage of wanting to pass out, but I tried not to look when Duncan fetched a small hacksaw and set to work with it. The teeth kept getting clogged up with bits of gristle, so after a while he switched to a serrated blade designed for carving through frozen meat. It wasn't easy for him because she kept rolling around, spluttering and giggling, while he carved, and the ruler that was sticking out of her chest kept whacking him on the chin.

The head, even when it had been separated from the neck, continued to make noises. This time, I thought I recognized the Humming Chorus from *Madame Butterfly*. She was deliberately choosing well-known pieces to annoy me. I stepped up my whimpering, trying to drown her out.

'Oh for God's sake shut up, the both of you,' snapped Duncan.

Violet continued to hum. I rocked back and forth and tentatively suggested dismemberment.

She had been born into an age when the average human frame was smaller, and her smallness was an advantage to us now. Her ankles were no thicker than my wrists, and it didn't take long for Duncan to hack through them, even though her legs kept dancing around. He did the feet, and the arms, and the hands, and all the pieces continued to wriggle, and the head kept up a contented gurgling interspersed with snatches of melody.

Eventually, Duncan yelled at her to shut the fuck up. The walls of his flat were solid enough, but it was getting late and I didn't want the neighbours getting nosy, so, at my suggestion, he stuffed her mouth full of garlic. She kept trying to spit it out, so he tied my black chiffon scarf around her head to keep the jaw shut. Even then, she kept up an audible insect-like buzzing. Duncan finally lost patience, smothered the head in pages of the *Guardian*, and dropped the whole bundle into a black plastic bag, which he sealed with several yards of electrical tape.

'I've had enough,' he said, collapsing into a stained armchair and covering his face with sticky red hands.

'You haven't finished,' I objected. 'You've got to displace parts of the skeleton and pickle the major organs in holy water.'

'Oh, bugger that. Can't we just put her outside and wait for daylight?'

'Wouldn't work,' I said. 'Not if the stake didn't.' Deep down, I was realizing the books hadn't given the whole picture. Either that, or Violet had been around for so long she was no longer required to play by the rules. She was still singing, for Christ's sake. And we'd need more sunlight than we were likely to get at this time of year. Besides, wherever we dumped the body, Grauman would find it.

Grauman. I'd forgotten about Grauman. The thought of him instantly made me feel twice as sick as I'd already been feeling. This hadn't been part of Grauman's plan, not at all. When he found out what we'd done, he would kill us, no question. I retreated into my rocking, but it wasn't just the pain that was making me whimper now.

The pieces had finally stopped squirming. Duncan settled down to the task of wrapping each one separately in newspaper, and tape, and bin-bags, making a set of neat black plastic parcels. I thought he was being unnecessarily conscientious, but since he was doing all the work I didn't have the right to criticize. All I wanted to do was lie down and go to sleep, but something told me that if I did that, I might never wake up again. I could have murdered a line or two, but I'd left all my drugs at Matt's. I was dying for the night to be over, but I had an uncomfortable feeling the arduous part was just beginning.

I dragged myself over to the window and peered out between the curtains. I knew what I was going to see, but I'd been hoping not to see it, just the same.

Parked just across the street was a battered Cortina. The windows were steamed up, but it didn't take a genius to work out who was inside.

'Oh *God*,' I groaned, collapsing back on to the sofa.

Duncan looked up sharply from his post-dismemberment cigarette. 'What's up?'

Now was the time to tell him about Grauman. But I held back. Once Duncan knew that part of the story, I might not appear quite so innocent in his eyes. In fact, my involvement with Andreas might smack of conspiracy. As though we'd meant for this to happen.

'Feeling any better?' asked Duncan. 'How's the finger?'

He was looking quite concerned about me, almost fraternal. That did it. We were partners in crime now, and I wasn't about to spoil it by telling him things he didn't need to know. With my right hand, I smoked a cigarette, wondering all the time if it was going to be my last.

Duncan sat and stared into space until I told him to take a shower and put on clean clothes. When he looked half-way presentable, I made him pour strong black coffee down his throat until his eyes lit up like a pinball machine. I needed him to drive the car.

It was while he was getting changed that I had my brilliant idea. It was so blindingly obvious I couldn't understand why I hadn't thought of it earlier. Pain had obviously dulled my intellect. Under my breath, I recited a phrase which had

147

popped into my head: 'It is important for all the pieces to be disposed of separately.'

It was then I remembered my Greek mythology.

It was two in the morning when we piled into the car with our baggage. We drove round in circles for about twenty minutes before I summoned the nerve to dispose of the first bag, the one containing the head. I nipped out and dropped it into some roadworks at the junction of Ladbroke Grove and Holland Park Avenue; not a crossroads, but near enough. There was no singing as I let it fall. Her battery must have finally run down.

As we drove off again, I saw the Cortina draw up at the kerb. We left it behind us, but not for long. Duncan caught me looking round. 'What's happening? Don't tell me we're being followed.'

'I think it's an unmarked police car,' I said. 'Try shaking it off.' Duncan threw a sharp left, and the Cortina carried on up the road.

Bag Number Two contained the torso. I weighted it with stones and heaved it into the canal. It sank out of sight immediately, leaving a few sluggish bubbles to float up to the surface and burst.

The Cortina rolled up again as we pulled out. Duncan was looking in the opposite direction and didn't see it, but I allowed myself to relax slightly. The water of the canal was murky and brown; Grauman would be forced to wade in and grope around. It could be hours before he struck lucky. This time, we had gained ourselves an unassailable head-start.

The West End was surprisingly busy, so we headed south

to Kennington and left Bag Number Three in a communal rubbish container outside a block of council flats. Bag Number Four went into roadworks on Clapham Common. In Battersea, Duncan managed to pry open a manhole; Bag Number Five went down there.

I was still jumpy. I thought I glimpsed the Cortina again, but a long way behind us, so I made Duncan take a roundabout route into Fulham – all around the back roads and over Hammersmith Bridge. We buried Bag Number Six beneath some bushes in a small churchyard. As we scrabbled in the dirt with our makeshift spades (me one-handed with an empty yogurt carton, Duncan with a piece of broken slate), an east wind blew up and riffled the tops of some nearby poplars. I thought I saw the bag move as it lay in the hole we had made, waiting to be covered with dirt, but by now I was desperate for sleep and there was a slight rippling at the edges of my vision.

In Shepherd's Bush, while we were stopped at a red light, I stumbled out of the car and stuffed Bags Number Seven and Eight into some cartons of rubbish awaiting collection outside an Indian restaurant. Bag Number Nine went behind a pile of rubble on a small patch of wasteland in White City; by that stage we were too tired even to dig a hole. Relief washed over me as we drove away. Grauman would have his work cut out. He would be too busy to think about having us tortured and mutilated. And he'd be wet.

Violet was history. Not even her Hatman could put her back together again now.

Neither of us wanted to go back to Duncan's that night. And, although I knew he hadn't been keeping count, I had no intention of letting him spend the rest of that night with me. I wanted to get home with Bag Number Ten before he found out it was still in my possession.

I tapped him for cash, left him on the sofa at Matt's place, and staggered to the nearest mini-cab office. In the car, on the way, I dozed off. At Camden Town, the driver woke me, and leered suggestively, and said I looked as though I'd enjoyed the party, and maybe I'd like to go to another one. Then he saw the bloodstained teatowel and asked if I'd hurt my hand. I said yes, I'd hurt it punching a mini-cab driver in the face.

I let myself into my room and collapsed into bed. My hand was still throbbing, but I gulped down a couple of Valium and slept for nine solid hours. There were nightmares, strange shadows which moved through the deepest parts of the forest, but by the time I woke up, the details had faded. I made myself a cup of tea, and then I spread an old news-paper over my bed and opened Bag Number Ten. For a long time, I gazed at the wizened, waxy object which looked like something you might find suspended from a hook in the window of a Chinese restaurant. The crimson nail varnish was chipped and messy, though not as messy as the scraps of muscle and ligament at the wrist. I peeled the teatowel away from my own left hand and compared them. Mine was bigger, but I thought it every bit as elegant as Violet's. My nails were better shaped, even though at that moment they were caked with blood and dirt. A good bath and an even better buffing would see them right. But there wasn't much I could do about the little finger. That really spoiled things.

Later that day, I dropped into the out-patient department of my local hospital. I told them I'd been chopping paper the night before, and had caught my finger in the guillotine. They ticked me off for not having rushed to them immediately with the missing joint – they could have sewn that back on, they said – but they cleaned up the gooey mess that was left, gave me some antibiotics to clear the infection that had set in, and dressed it without asking too many awkward questions about why the guillotine had left me with a chewed-up stump instead of a nice clean slice.

For the next few days, I carried Matt's Teddy boy flick-knife around with me, just in case. I did a lot of looking over my shoulder, but after a while I started to believe we really had got away with it. We really had rubbed her out. Grauman didn't come after us, though I dreamt once or twice that he did. I phoned his hotel and was told he had checked out. He hadn't left a forwarding address, the receptionist said, but she remembered him ordering a taxi to Heathrow. She remembered his departure because there had been a lot of luggage, and he'd been in an enormous hurry, but he'd been generous with his tips.

I went into college and acted as if nothing had happened, though Ruth kept giving me funny looks, and once or twice provided me with free drugs and hinted I could confide in her any time I wanted. I didn't want, of course. She was curious about the big dressing on my little finger, and even more curious when at last it was taken off and she saw the joint was missing. I told her I had shut it in a car door, and she seemed to accept that, although on several occasions afterwards I caught her staring at the stump with a sort of thrilled fascination.

Meanwhile, I kept Violet's hand wrapped up in my room. On the first day, I sketched it. On the second day, I was drawing it again when I thought I saw the fingers move. On the third day, I came home and found the bag empty. After a nervous search, I finally found it clinging to the back of the curtains, fingers gripping the fabric so tightly the knuckles had gone shiny with tension. I prised it loose, wrapped it in a dozen layers of polythene, and put it in an old biscuit tin, sealing the lid with Sellotape, masking tape, electrical tape, and any other tape I could find. That night I lay on my bed, trying to sleep but unable to do anything but lie in the darkness, listening to the muted metallic *tunka-tunk* of soft but persistent rapping from the inside of the tin.

My nerve cracked. I couldn't live with this *thing* any longer. The next day, I took it into college and late in the afternoon, when all but the most dedicated students had abandoned their easels, went up to the deserted etching department – setting of that first historic glimpse of my late rival and consequently, I thought, an appropriate place in which to dispose of her last remnants. I opened the tin and found the hand nestling on a cushion of shredded polythene. For ten minutes I sat and stared at it, but it didn't move a muscle. I began to wonder if I'd ever seen it moving in the first place; perhaps I was hallucinating after all the sleepless nights. But I wasn't going to take any chances. I didn't fancy waking up to find those fingernails doing to my face what they'd done to the polythene.

Carefully, with tongs, I lowered it into the etching bath. I'd always wanted to see what hydrochloric acid would do to human flesh. Inhuman flesh was the next best thing, but the immediate effect was disappointing – not, as I'd imagined, like a shoal of piranhas latching on to a chunk of meat. There was no thrashing at all. It was nothing more than a lump of dead matter covered in tiny bubbles. But, after an hour or so, I saw that the outline was less distinct, that the bubbles were eating into it. I didn't dare go home and leave it, so I turned the lights off and lay low until the night watchman had done his rounds.

It took most of the night. By first light, the flesh had dissolved, but the bones were still resisting. I dried them off, wrapped them in a shoebox, and mailed them to the Smithsonian Institute. I didn't bother marking the parcel with a return address.

As for Duncan and me, things didn't exactly turn out the way I'd planned. He seemed fine for a couple of days — friendly enough, though neither of us made any reference to what had happened, and he avoided catching my eye. But after that he did a U-turn and started sinking. He'd been off college a lot after meeting Violet, but now he stopped attending altogether. A rumour began to circulate that he'd either dropped out of — or been dropped from — the course. I tried to reach him on the phone once or twice. When I hadn't seen him in a fortnight, I had a bad feeling and went round to the flat. He was there, and he let me in, but I could tell he was on a downward spiral. There was nothing I could do about it; I was feeling rather peculiar myself, and I didn't want him dragging me down. I wasn't even sure I fancied him any more, not when he was like this. It wasn't the discoloured teeth that put me off, nor the scraggy beard he'd sprouted because he could no longer be bothered to shave. It was the smile I didn't like. It was the smile of someone who had lost his grip.

There was nowhere to sit because he had thrown out most of his furniture. The floor was spread with dust-sheets, and he had started to repaint some of the walls, but sloppily. He didn't talk much, and when he did, he mumbled, so it was difficult to catch what he was going on about. His gaze kept flicking past my shoulder, to something that wasn't there.

'It wasn't murder, you know,' I said. 'She wasn't human.' It was the first time I'd brought the subject up.

'I'd rather not talk about it.'

I found that I didn't want to talk about it either. So that was that. He said he wanted to be left alone for a while, and by the time I popped back, a few days later, he'd gone. There was someone else in the flat — a short, stocky man with a sand-coloured moustache, who told me Duncan was in Scotland. 'Edinburgh, I think. I'm not sure.'

This was the first I'd heard of it. 'When will he be back?'

The man with the moustache shrugged. 'Haven't a clue. He said I could stay here as long as I wanted.'

Had he left a forwarding address? No, he hadn't. Any idea how I might get in touch? No, none at all. I thought about travelling up to Scotland after him, but I didn't think about it for very long. I wasn't sure I had enough money for train fare, let alone for food or a hotel, and I had no idea how long it might take to track him down.

In the end, I had to admit I was relieved he was out of the way. Now he could have his breakdown, or whatever it was he was having, hundreds of miles away from the scene of the crime, and I wouldn't have to endure the spectacle of him cracking up. I knew he would come back to me, eventually. He was mine now. He would always be mine. The tip of a finger was a small price to pay.

PART THREE

ONE

I caught the Bakerloo line from Lambeth North to Oxford Circus, and I went shopping. This is what I bought: one pair of silver crucifix earrings; two gold charm bracelets with assorted attachments in the shape of tiny football boots, piglets, and crucifixes; one diamanté crucifix; one black plastic crucifix with a hologram of Jesus Christ on it; one black plastic rosary. On the way home, I stopped off at the supermarket and bought three dozen heads of garlic, a couple of jars of garlic salt, and some packets of dried garlic slices. I also stopped off at the timber merchants and snapped up all their dowelling offcuts for a knock-down price. I even remembered to stock up with some replacement blades for my Stanley knife.

Back at the flat, I launched into a frenzy of activity: sprinkling garlic salt around the doors and windows, peeling cloves and hiding them at strategic points, digging out my old crucifixes and hanging them on the walls. I decked myself out in some of my brand-new knick-knacks and offered a silent prayer to Madonna Louise Ciccone for achievements in popularizing the crucifix as an acceptable fashion item. I would be attracting curious glances in the days to come, but only because my choice of accessory was now considered a little *passé*. This whole business would very likely end up ruining my reputation as a person with her finger on the pulse of fashion.

There were one or two things which continued to puzzle me. I couldn't understand why Violet had gone to so much trouble over Patricia Rice, of all people. What was the point of prolonging such a wretched existence? Why hadn't she just ripped out the jugular and got it over with? The idea of an undead Patricia made me come over all shivery. Worse, I realized I was envious. Why her and not me? What had she got that I hadn't? But I knew the answer to that. She had her name on the Multiglom hit list, and I'd been the one to put it there.

I'd almost forgotten about Duncan. It was nearly midnight when he phoned. He sounded out of breath. 'Did you get my messages?'

'No.' I looked down at the counter on my answering machine. I'd been so busy, I hadn't thought to check it. There were four messages, and all of them turned out to be from Duncan.

'Dora, she's still not back.'

There was a tingling in my missing fingertip. 'She hasn't rung?'

'No, and it's not like her to go all *incommunicado* like this. Do you think I should call the police?'

'She's probably pissed off at you for getting drunk and staying out all night. Did you ring Multiglom?'

'I tried. They were all at lunch.'

'When was that?'

'Three o'clock, and again at four and five.'

'Some lunch,' I said. I had already decided not to tell him what I'd seen that morning. There was no point in worrying him unnecessarily.

'Christ,' he said. 'If only we hadn't got arseholed, I would have got home in time to stop her. I could have shown her the negs.'

'Negs? What negs?'

'The ones you half-inched from our friend Francine. I printed them up.'

I'd forgotten all about Dino's negs. I'd left the envelope in the car. 'And?'

'I think you should you come round and take a look.'

'Can't it wait till tomorrow?'

'No, this is urgent.'

I sighed loudly enough for him to hear. I didn't feel like going out, especially after having spent half the day making my flat secure.

'*Please*, Dora . . .'

'All *right*.' I would just have to hope Violet wasn't out on the razzle in W11. I prepared as best I could and set out into the night, stinking of garlic and jingling with junk jewellery. There were plenty of people around, but they weren't the sort of people you wanted to bump into at that time of night. Just off Westbourne Grove, I saw a small mob moving with a great deal of laughter and shouting along the opposite pavement. One or two heads swivelled in my direction, and somebody shouted, 'Hey little girl!', but I pretended to ignore them and they swept along the street. A little further on, I heard the sound of bottles being smashed,

159

and screaming, but I didn't think it was the same crowd; the noise seemed to be coming from the opposite direction. Fights were nothing unusual – not in that area – but I clutched my crucifix and walked faster.

Duncan let me in, reeling back in mock shock as he smelled my breath. 'Blimey. You've been picking up social tips from Francine.'

'Garlic for supper,' I said. *He* could talk, I thought. Put a match to the alcohol on his breath and he'd go up like a Christmas pudding.

He looked at me and laughed. 'Sure you're wearing enough jewellery?'

It's true I was clanking like a suit of armour; I'd dug out my entire collection. 'Just to be on the safe side. Can't be too careful.'

His smile vanished. 'Something's happened, hasn't it? What's going on?'

I said nothing had happened. I told him to show me the blasted photos.

Lulu had been gone three days and already the living room looked as though a bomb had hit it. Duncan poured me a large brandy, poured himself another even larger one, and showed me into his office. He was drunk, but not the way he'd been drunk before. Now he was dogged and forceful; he was going to hammer away until I said exactly what he wanted to hear. I hadn't seen him this animated for years. It was as though he was waking up after a deep sleep. He was getting all manic and obsessive again, and it was frightening me, but it was kind of exciting as well.

'Here we are,' he said, and flung down a pile of black and white prints. I sifted through them; these photographs didn't seem to be part of a regular assignment, they were more a record of an important social occasion. The setting was the same in each; a large room cluttered with antique furniture and a carved mantelpiece, heavy and a little oppressive – not the sort of place likely to be featured in *Home Beautiful*, let alone *Bellini*. People were standing around with champagne flutes in their hands, proposing toasts and generally looking rather jovial. One or two had noticed the photographer but were pretending they hadn't; others were mugging shamelessly for the camera. In one picture, a balding businessman was licking the ear of a pouty blonde young enough to be his granddaughter.

Most of the people in the pictures were smiling, and some appeared to be laughing out loud. This was the bit I didn't like. The worst photos were those in which I could see their teeth, because they forced me, finally, to face up to the truth. We were not dealing with a single vampire here. We were dealing with a pack of them.

I was shocked into silence. This put a whole new slant on things. It might not have been Violet who had dropped in on Patricia after all – it could have been any one of the people here.

'Look,' said Duncan, jabbing at the pictures with his finger. 'Here, here, and *here*. Just *look* at them, will you. Look at this fat guy – what's this in his mouth?'

'Maybe it's a Twiglet,' I suggested.

Duncan jabbed again. 'And what about the shape on the sofa?'

'What about it?' He pointed, and I looked. In the background of some of the prints was a couch with two women on it. They could have been twins, each with the same blank face and slicked-back hair, each clutching a wineglass, and perched stiffly, head cocked as if listening to her master's voice. I'd seen both of them before – behind the reception desk at Multiglom Tower.

There was space between them, and in that space a blur. 'Yes, well, that's definitely someone moving,' I said, shuffling through the blow-ups. In each of the pictures in which the couch was visible, the space between the blank-faced women was occupied by that same blur. You could see there was someone there, but you couldn't make out arms, or legs, or facial features.

'Try this one,' Duncan said, handing me another print – an enlargement of the blur on the couch, blown up so it almost filled the paper. The image was nearly lost in the grain, but you could see it was a woman, and that she had long dark hair.

Duncan helped himself to one of my cigarettes and lit up. He ran his free hand through his hair, leaving it sticking out at odd angles. His spectacles were perched half-way down his nose and he looked completely mad. 'She never did like having her picture taken,' he said.

'Who?' Now I was deliberately being dense. Duncan rolled his eyeballs. He pulled open one of the drawers in his filing cabinet, extracted a folder, and handed it to me. The photographs inside were printed on bromide, not on the modern resin-coated stuff, and the edges had never quite lost their curl. I recognized the locations: Kensal Rise, Highgate, Abney Park. The old cemetery circuit. All night-time views, all taken after dark, with flash.

'You did these at college?' Duncan nodded. There were stone angels, and Grecian urns, and Latin inscriptions, and crumbling dogs, and weeping women, and egg-timers with wings. And in each of the pictures, sometimes flitting through the trees in the background, but occasionally to one side at the front of the frame, I saw the blurred shape of someone who had shifted at the precise instant the shutter had been pressed.

'I could never catch her off-guard. She always moved, every bloody time. She always knew – even with a wide-angle lens, even at 1/125th of a second. She never, ever let me take her picture.'

I felt a sharp pang in my chest, like the bite of a scalpel. He had taken photos of all of them, of Lulu and Alicia and all the ex-girlfriends whose names I didn't know. Jesus, he had even tried to take photos of Violet. *But he had never taken photos of me*. In his files, I didn't exist.

'Oh boy,' I said. 'You really *want* me to say she's come back for you, don't you? You're not going to rest until you've got me to say it.'

'I just want you to confirm it's not all in my head.'

I'd had enough. 'OK, she's back. She's definitely back, Duncan. No question about it, she's back. *And she's going to rip your head off*. Happy now?'

He smiled and nodded courteously. 'Thank you.' He pulled the darkroom door open and slipped into the shadows on the far side, and I could hear him throwing up in the sink. I wondered if there were any prints in the wash there. If so, he would have to rewash them.

I didn't feel too good myself. Into my head floated a picture I'd been trying to suppress for so long – small, fetid packages wrapped in leaking black plastic. I tried to distract myself by going through Dino's photos again. I hadn't recognized Andreas Grauman at first. He looked strange in a tuxedo, with his hair tied back, but the sight of him still gave me the creeps. In fact, it was making me feel ill. My skin went hot, then cold, then hot again, and there was a roaring like motorbikes in my ears, and a faint chirrupping noise as well. I put my head down between my knees, until the chirrupping noise had died away and been replaced by the sound of a tinkling mountain stream. After a while, I realized the water wasn't some New Vague soundtrack in my head, but was coming from the darkroom next door. I sat up as Duncan came back, blowing his nose on a paper towel.

I made small talk, trying to hide my discomfort. 'Rotten photographer, Dino. Did you find out when these were taken?'

'Six weeks ago.' He was explaining about the filing code scratched into the emulsion when the chirrupping started up again. Duncan tensed and swore and hurled himself through the door. Belatedly, I recognized the sound of the telephone, and followed. He was too late; the answering machine had already clicked on, and the caller hung up without leaving a message.

'Shit,' he said, looking devastated. Both of us had the same thought – that it could have been Lulu. 'Shit, shit, shit.'

'Maybe it was her who rang before. While you were throwing up.'

Duncan pressed the replay button. There was a whirring, and a pause, then the familiar little-girl voice. 'Duncan, are you there? Dunc? I guess not . . . Well, I'm having a great time earning pots of money. And don't worry, I'm not doing anything you wouldn't want me to do. I'll call you tomorrow. Take care. Bye now.'

'What the fuck does she mean by that?' asked Duncan.

We listened to the tape again. I was disappointed and relieved at the same time. 'You heard her,' I said to him. 'She's not doing anything you wouldn't want her to do.' It was an odd thing for her to say, but I wasn't going to lose any sleep over it, especially since she had given no indication of wanting to come home.

We inspected the photographs again and then, over another drink, discussed what to do. I thought we should take them to the *Sunday Times* or the *Observer*. Duncan thought we should give them to Jack, whose magazine was small but ideologically sound. We eventually decided that Duncan should print up as many as he could, and we would send them to all the publications we could think of. I wasn't sure what good it would do, but people needed to be made aware of what was going on. There was bound to be an outcry. Someone, somewhere, would settle Murasaki's hash.

Duncan went back into the darkroom to churn out some more prints while he still had the chemicals mixed. While he did that, I went through the Yellow Pages and made lists. Then, just to be on the safe side, I went round the flat leaving cloves of garlic on window-ledges and around door-frames, in the bed and on the dressing-table. After all this and a night cap, I was too tired to walk home. Duncan offered to call me a cab, but I said I preferred not to go out in the dark *at all*, and not after the photographs. I told him I was too scared to sleep on my own, so we ended up in the same bed. He was drunk, but not as drunk as he'd been after our night on the town. It wasn't a very good erection, but it was better than nothing and I exploited it to the hilt.

TWO

I woke with the smell of bacon fat in my nostrils. Duncan was already up and beavering away in the kitchen. I stumbled in, searching for Paracetamol, and before I knew what was happening he'd got me sitting in front of a plate of fried food. He'd already polished off one of his own. Lulu would have hit the roof; she kept a close watch on his cholesterol intake. Breakfast, for Lulu, was muesli or nothing. He was really living it up behind her back.

'I *can't*.' I stared at the egg, and it stared back, unblinking.

'Nonsense,' he said briskly, shovelling a dripping slice of fried bread on to the plate. 'Eat up. We have a busy day ahead of us.'

'We have?'

He sat down next to me and poured a generous slug of brandy into his mug of tea. 'Want a pick-me-up?'

I shook my head and pushed the food around my plate with my fork, leaving a trail of coagulating grease and dark speckled bits. It reminded me of the places I used to go to with Grauman.

Duncan explained he still had some printing to do if we were to have enough copies of the photographs to hand around. In the mean time, I should set out some of our suspicions in a letter. He frowned. 'I don't know. Vampires sound a bit far-fetched, don't you think?'

'We can play down the paranormal side and pump up the conspiracy angle. Maybe we can tie it in with AIDS. Blood sucking spreads diseases.'

'Don't give too much away. Let them phone for the juicy details.'

'Hang on a bit,' I said slowly. 'Let me get this straight. You think we should give them your telephone number? You think we should give them *our names and addresses*?' I was thinking of Patricia Rice.

'Why not?'

He took a lot of persuading, but eventually I convinced him we should preserve our anonymity. 'Even with Jack's mag?' he asked. I hadn't made up my mind about that, but since Jack's magazine was a weekly and we'd missed the deadline, the decision could be postponed for another few days.

There was one other factor we hadn't considered. We considered it now. Once all this stuff about Violet came out, someone was bound to start digging around in her past. They might find more than they bargained for. They might find . . . *us*. It may not have been murder, but some people were going to have trouble understanding that.

'If only she hadn't moved when Dino pressed the shutter,' Duncan said. 'Then we would have had *proof* that Violet

Westron is alive and well and living in ... where is it? Molasses Wharf?'

I struggled through breakfast and half a dozen cups of tea and eventually felt human enough to sit down at a typewriter and compose the letter. It went like this:

Dear Sir or Madam,

We feel you may be interested in the enclosed photographs showing a gathering of executives from the well-known Multiglom corporation. As you can see, these people hold orgies in which the participants wear plastic fangs. We have stumbled across important data which suggests these activities are not quite as harmless as they appear. Some of these people are involved in sadomasochistic pursuits which include biting and the shedding of blood – blood which is not necessarily that of consenting adults but frequently extracted from the veins of innocent children and teenage runaways who have been lured into a career of vice and licentiousness. In these days of viruses communicable via exchange of body fluids, we would suggest that such behaviour is at best irresponsible, at worst a danger to public health. We also have reason to believe there are bogus social workers involved, as well as at least one prominent Tory MP. Perhaps you might care to investigate further, starting with Rose Murasaki, editor of *Bellini* magazine, which is based in Multiglom Tower at Molasses Wharf. This is not, repeat not, a crank letter.

Yours sincerely,
    Concerned of Kensington.

PS. The man who took these photographs has since gone mad and set fire to a building.

I was pleased with this, but especially proud of the bogus social worker angle. I popped out to the local newsagents to make Xerox copies. It was raining again, so Duncan lent me one of Lulu's raincoats. It was see-through pink plastic and I felt a bit like a walking condom, but there weren't enough people around to point at me and laugh. The wind picked up sheets of wet newsprint and whirled them through the air, but I didn't mind the rubbish any more. I felt pretty good. After all these years, Duncan and I were together again. He had cooked me breakfast. We were working towards a common goal. And it was *fun*. I was hoping like mad that Lulu wouldn't suddenly come back and spoil the party.

As Duncan had predicted, the rest of that day was hard work. We had decided to address our hot little envelopes to the respective news desks, but Fleet Street was a thing of the past; now all the newspaper offices were scattered around, everywhere from Battersea to Wapping, and though we split the workload into two it took the best part of an afternoon to deliver them by hand. I parted with my last envelope just as darkness was falling. Night-time made me nervous, especially in the vicinity of the East End, so I caught a cab and headed straight back to Duncan's. He made fettucini with mushroom sauce, and we ate it in front of the television. We drank two bottles of white wine and half a bottle of brandy and then we went to bed. For the first time in my life, I felt like half of a couple. It was a comfortable feeling, and I liked it. I had waited long enough.

Next day, Duncan had to set off early for a fashion shoot. He pecked me on the cheek, just like a husband going off to the office. Alone in the flat, I took the opportunity to poke around, but didn't find much I hadn't uncovered a couple of months earlier, when he and Lulu had gone off to Barbados and left me with a set of keys so I could water the plants.

Around lunchtime I strolled home, stopping off at the newsagents to buy a load of papers and magazines. There was no sign of Dino's photographs in any of them, but it was early days. Give them time, I thought. They would undoubtedly want to do some investigating of their own. Then it would be a case of sit back and watch the fireworks.

I settled down to a spot of work – a completely spurious account of what teenagers thought about violence on TV – when the Krankzeits came in from one of their shopping expeditions and slammed the front door so hard that my unfinished Visible Woman leapt from her shelf on to the floor, where her detachable foetus detached itself, and her liver and kidneys fell out through the gap. My neighbours thundered up the stairs in what I took to be hob-nailed boots, then there was a double-barrelled crash as they flung open the door to their flat and let it slam behind them.

Much later, at about seven o'clock, they had a major argument. I could hear him calling her a 'fucking stupid cow' and her calling him a 'fucking stupid Nazi'. This was unusual; normally they yelled terms of endearment at each other. The crash-bang-wallop went on for so long I wondered if he were knocking her around. I hoped so, though I also hoped she would be giving as good as she got. In the best of all possible worlds, they would be beating each other to a pulp.

Unfortunately, Christine Krankzeit stormed out of the flat before it got that far. She pounded down the stairs so heavily that my crucifixes were still vibrating five minutes later. I thought I could hear her sobbing, so I peeped through' my curtains, hoping to see Gunter storm down after her and start some sort of ruckus in the street. But he didn't. A little later on I peeped out again and saw her standing perfectly still on the pavement outside, her face tilted upward and her gaze fixed on the floor above. Her skin had taken on a greenish cast in the lamplight, which was strange, because the street lighting was orange. I blinked, and saw that it wasn't Christine at all, it was Patricia Rice.

I blinked again. How could I have been so stupid? Of course it was Christine. Who else could it have been? But she was staring up at the front of the building with an other-worldly expression on her face. I shuddered and drew the curtains tightly to shut out the sight. Half an hour later, when I forced myself to look again, she was gone. But I made sure my front door was double-locked.

That glimpse of Christine had shaken me up more than it should have done. I tried to blot out the memory with lamebrained television, and then, somewhere between the end of a documentary about drug abuse on council estates in South London and the beginning of a new sitcom about Vietnam veterans trying to fit back into small-town American society, I noticed someone showing lots of cleavage. I didn't twig at first; I just saw this figure, dressed in black, stalking down a neon-lit street in ridiculously high heels. The other pedestrians, all male, were going ape-shit. The first gulped down a lethal dose of strychnine – you knew it was strychnine because it said so on the bottle. The second threw himself under the wheels of a Ferrari. The third plunged a knife into his belly, and the fourth was so traumatized that his head exploded. Then Lulu (for it was she) turned to the camera, an enigmatic smile playing on and around her lips, and a disembodied voice whispered, 'Kuroi. They'll *die* for the woman who's wearing it.' Then Lulu's face faded into an elegant orchid-shaped chunk of black glass, and the voice whispered, 'Kuroi. By Murasaki.'

It was a grand excuse to phone Duncan. 'Lu's on telly,' I said. He wanted to know which channel. I heard him switch his set on, but it was too late; all he got were bursts of canned laughter and the gatta-gatta of automatic gunfire. 'Maybe it'll come up in the next break,' he said. 'What was it for? *Bellini*?'

'Perfume. *By Murasaki*. Multiglom strikes again. They didn't waste any time, did they?'

'Who?'

'The admen. When do you reckon they filmed it? Two days ago?'

I could sense him considering this at the other end of the line. 'Less than a week, you're right. They must know something we don't know.' He paused, then asked if I wanted to go round and see him that evening. He offered to drive over and pick me up, which suited me fine, because it wasn't just Violet I had to worry about now – it was Grauman, Patricia Rice, and the rest of the crew as well.

Duncan did the cooking again, but I could tell the novelty of it was already wearing off for him. He served linguini with a ready-made tomato and basil sauce from the delicatessen down the road, and then he fried up some bread to boost the meal's cholesterol-packing potential. We ate in silence, trying and failing to stick to mineral water and staring at the television in case Lulu's ad should come on again. It didn't. The news was full of the takeover of three British companies by a single foreign consortium which already owned four national newspapers and a satellite channel. Questions had been raised in the Commons by Her Majesty's Opposition, and the Monopolies Commission was preparing a report, but the consensus was that there wasn't a damn thing anyone could do about it. It was all very dull.

Shortly after we'd finished eating the phone rang. Duncan snatched the receiver up excitedly, but I could see by the disappointment on his face that it wasn't Lulu. He listened uninterestedly for a while, saying 'yes' and 'no' and 'OK, yeah', but then he heard something which made him sit up straight. He talked a bit more animatedly after that, said 'cheerio' and hung up.

'Weinstein,' he said. 'She's having a party tomorrow.'

Ruth's party had completely slipped my mind. 'Just what the world needs right now,' I said. 'One of Ruthie's shindigs.'

Duncan said, 'I'm going.'

'You *are*?' I was taken aback. Duncan disliked Ruth, everyone knew that. He despised her dilettantism and the way she always protested she had no money, even though she was probably the wealthiest person we knew. Her father had bought her the house where she and Charlie now lived, and then he had also bought her an art gallery in Westbourne Park under the pretext of it being a birthday present, though it was more likely some sort of tax dodge. I usually tried to avoid walking past it in case Ruth was there and spotted me, even though she treated the business like a hobby and left most of the day-to-day running of the place to badly paid underlings.

Duncan said, 'Lulu's going to be there.'

'Lulu?' Impossible, I thought. 'You don't know that.'

'Ruth saw her the other day, at Gnashers.'

Ruth had such a bloody big nose. For the love of Jesus, why couldn't she keep it out of other people's business? I wanted to ask Duncan why he wanted to see Lulu so badly, since she obviously wasn't in a tearing rush to come back and see him, but I didn't. Instead, I said, 'Maybe I will come along after all.'

'OK.' And with that, he wrapped himself in his own thoughts and hardly said another word to me. We had a few more drinks, and pretended to watch a late-night film, but all the sparkle had gone out of the evening. He stared at the screen and didn't seem to hear when I asked him questions. A barrier had gone up between us. I felt like an idiot, perched on the sofa in my jingling silver trinkets while Duncan acted as though I was invisible. I felt my recent *joie de vivre* giving way to gloom. The prospect of seeing Lulu again had brought home to me how much, how *very* much, I'd been enjoying her absence.

THREE

Saturday morning got off to a bad start when I suggested to Duncan that we meet up somewhere before going on to Ruth's party together. He started making excuses. He had to work all afternoon. He had no idea what time he'd be finished. I cottoned on fast. 'You don't want Lulu to see us together, is that it? Hell, you don't want *anyone* to see us together.'

'I thought you realized, Dora. Our affair could never be anything other than clandestine.'

'Clandestine? *Clandestine?* What's *that* supposed to mean?'

'We must keep it secret. No one must know.'

'I *know* what it means,' I snarled. 'It means I've served my purpose and now you're going to put me back in the cupboard.'

'It's not like that at all . . .'

'Like *what*? Like *this*, you mean?' I had scarcely touched my egg and bacon, which were swimming in even greater quantities of grease than usual. I picked up the plate and upended it over his lap. The bacon dropped immediately. For a few tantalizing seconds the egg clung on by vacuum suction, then slowly peeled off under its own weight. Duncan opened his mouth to say something, then changed his mind and shut it again. He was wearing his resigned look. I knew what he was thinking. He was thinking it was that time of the month again. Jesus Christ, it *always* seemed to be that time of the month.

There was a large dark stain around his groin. Grease dripped glutinously on to the floor. 'See you later, scumbag,' I said, and stalked off.

The name of Multiglom figured prominently in the day's newspapers, but only in the business pages, not a breath of scandal. Later, while I was flicking through the arts section of *The Times*, I found myself face to face with Lulu, the last person I'd ever expected to see in a quality broadsheet. It was a full-page black and white photo; she had that carefully-made-up-to-look-like-no-make-up look, and there was a roguish glint in her eye that had never been there before; I wondered whether it had been airbrushed in. She looked good, almost not like Lulu at all.

The picture was accompanied by a message in tiny, tiny print – a public plea to shareholders, urging them not to block some takeover or other and outlining why they should be voting so-and-so on to the board of directors. It listed all the advantages a newer, more powerful Multiglom could bring to the economy in general, and to shareholders' pockets in particular. It even outlined the ways in which the corporation's waste products were environmentally sound, neither polluting the rivers into which they were poured, nor threatening the ozone layer and admitting harmful ultraviolet rays. I couldn't see Lulu's relevance; she was simply a means of catching the attention of jaded eyes as they scanned pages of dry, bimbo-free print in a fruitless search for titbits. I searched, and searched, and I found pictures of Lulu in some of the other papers too. She was definitely flavour of the month.

It took me a long time to get ready for Ruth's party. Determined not to dress in the black I knew everyone else would be wearing, I opted for a red dress and then spent the next hour trying to hide as much red as I could beneath a big black belt, big black scarf, big black leather jacket, and lots and lots of crucifixes. I set out early with my pockets full of garlic and headed for the tube station, pushing past the beggars who clustered around the entrance, waving their grubby babies and clamouring for fifty pence pieces. The escalators were still out of order. It was business as usual.

Lulu was in the underground. She was hovering over the tracks on a big black and white *Kuroi* poster, and someone had already braved the electric rail to give her red teeth and horns and a speech-bubble which read, 'I like porking'. I had plenty of time to stare at her. Over the tinny loudspeakers there was a garbled announcement informing us that trains were running late 'due to delays'. There had been signal failures at Mile End, and a suicide on the track at Barking. I knew how the suicide had felt.

When the train finally rolled up, there was a prolonged session of sardines-on-wheels, with lots of stopping in the tunnels. I changed lines at Tottenham Court Road and made it as far as Camden Town, where the train suddenly developed faulty doors and was taken out of active service. Northbound passengers shook their fists and yelled, but it was no good. I gave up and made the rest of the journey by cab.

Despite the delays, I arrived even earlier than I'd intended, but at least I arrived. Ruth opened the door of her Georgian terrace house, squealed 'Dora!', and insisted on performing that complicated kissing manoeuvre in which you miss the other person's lips but bang each other's noses and end up with their lipstick smeared down your cheek.

It would have been pointless and cruel to describe Ruth as dumpy, but she was one of the few people in the world who made me feel long-legged. Perhaps this was why I still tolerated her company. These days, her hair was an incredibly artificial colour which reminded me of baked conkers. She was dressed – yes – in black. No doubt it was a pricey little number, like the rest of the items in her wardrobe, but I was pleased to see it still couldn't prevent her legs from looking like yams.

'Dora, Dora, *Dora*!' she gushed as I wiped her lipstick from my face. 'Haven't seen you for *ages*. How have you *been*?'

Not so good, I said. I started to tell her all about the shellfish allergy I had developed after a dodgy bowl of bouillabaisse, but her attention began to wander and she didn't seem terribly interested in how I had been, after all. We had a little tug-o'-war over my jacket – I wanted to keep it on because I was loath to reveal too much red – and then I gave her my bottle of champagne and she thanked me and put it in one of the kitchen cupboards, and I knew that would be the last I'd see of it all evening if I didn't watch out. Ruth had hired a professional butler to serve cheap wine, but I ignored him, and when no one was looking retrieved my bottle from the cupboard and hid it under my jacket.

I wandered through into the main reception area. Ruth rematerialized at my side. 'So how *are* you?' she asked, as I eyed up the four people who had arrived even earlier than me. I guessed she didn't much want to hear about my shellfish allergy again. Instead, I said, 'Fine thanks. How are *you*?' I looked at her properly for the first time and did a double-take. 'You're looking . . . *terrific*. Good Lord, Ruth, you look really . . . *different*.'

Ruth did indeed look different. She'd had a nose job. I tried to remember her previous nose, but it hadn't been terribly memorable. I hadn't even realized she had been self-conscious about it. I floundered. Was one supposed to pretend that nothing had happened, or offer congratulations, or enquire about the cost, or the pain, or what? I ended up asking, 'Hey, where did you get the nose?' which wasn't what I had intended at all. Ruth stared fixedly over my shoulder and pretended she hadn't heard.

'Oh well,' I said, changing the subject. 'How's the art world?'

This time, she responded with enthusiasm, describing a recent trip to New York in brain-numbing detail and dropping a lot of names which meant less than nothing to me. Then she started babbling on about a brilliant young Australian performance artist who sewed his own eyelids shut and dangled for hours, stark naked, from meathooks. I was saved from having to hear more by Charlie, who wandered up looking anxious.

'Anyone seen Clive?'

'Hasn't arrived,' said Ruth.

'He was bringing the tapes.'

'Doesn't matter,' said Ruth. 'We can play some of ours.'

'No, we can't,' said Charlie. 'Hi, Dora. How are you?'

'Dreadful,' I said.

'Anyway, we don't need music,' said Ruth. 'Not just yet. No one wants to dance.' She and Charlie went on discussing party arrangements, so I wandered away. I didn't know any of the other guests; there were a half-dozen of them now, all gathered in a knot, all dressed in black and looking pale and rather uninteresting. One of them was saying, '. . . I saw him at Gnashers . . .' and another was saying, '. . . I'm so fed up with Gnashers . . .' and a third was saying, '. . . what's wrong with Gnashers anyway . . . ?'

Gnasher chat bored me rigid, so I perched on the sofa and smoked a cigarette, dropping the ash into a potted palm since there weren't any ashtrays. Half a dozen more people arrived. My heart sank as Charlie noticed I was on my own and came barrelling over to talk. Charlie was a film critic who wrote reviews for provincial listings magazines and specialist publications with minuscule circulations. I didn't like talking to him about cinema, because he always prattled on about French films in which the characters sat around in rooms and talked, or Russian films in which the characters went into Forbidden Zones and wandered around for a bit before coming out again. Charlie based most of his opinions on the writing in *Cahiers de Cinéma* or, when he was in a particularly jocular mood, *The New Yorker*. He strongly disapproved of movies in which horrible American teenagers went on panty-raids and got carved up by maniacs in hockey masks.

He opened with his favourite gambit. 'Seen any good movies lately?' I shook my head. 'Neither have I,' he whined. 'Nobody's making them any more. All these bloody sequels and remakes. Where's the originality? What about artistic vision? All we get are big budgets and special effects. The only good films these days are being made by the small independents. Small is beautiful, I always say.'

'In that case,' I yawned, '*you* should be all right.'

He chuckled and patted me on the head. 'I knew I could rely on you to put the case for the drive-in mentality.' Before I could stir myself sufficiently to respond, he added, 'Seen Duncan and Lulu lately?'

'Sort of,' I said.

'I hear Lulu's struck lucky.'

'I saw her in the tube just now. On a poster.'

'Yeah,' said Charlie. 'I saw that too.' He leaned towards me in a conspiratorial manner. 'Is it true about her and Duncan?'

I had the feeling he rather fancied his chances with Lulu. As *if*. 'Is what true?' I asked.

'They split up?'

'How should I know? Why don't you ask her? Isn't she supposed to be honouring us with her presence tonight?'

Charlie shrugged, and just then someone thought it amusing to sneak up behind me and clamp their hands over my eyes. I jabbed my elbow back and felt it connect with something soft; there was a grunt and the hands unclamped themselves. I turned round, half-expecting to see Andreas Grauman, but it was only Jack, thank God. He was clutching his abdomen.

'Jesus, that hurt,' he said. He was exaggerating, of course.

'How was I supposed to know? You could have been a mugger, or a rapist.'

'Oh, he's both,' said Charlie, 'aren't you, Jack my boy?'

'Where's Alicia?' I demanded.

'At home,' Jack said, still rubbing his ribs.

I looked across the room and immediately spotted Roxy, talking to Ruth. 'Oh I see,' I said.

Jack followed my gaze. 'We take it in turns,' he protested. 'I stayed in with Abigail a couple of days ago.'

'I'll bet you did,' I said. 'Someone has to babysit while Alicia shops for groceries.'

'Well, excuse *me*. *You're* in a friendly mood today.'

'Sorry,' I said, holding out my bottle as a peace-offering. 'Have some champagne.'

Jack went in search of a glass. 'You're being a bit hard on him, aren't you?' asked Charlie. 'He's a good father.'

'But a rotten, lousy husband,' I said. 'Poor old Alicia.'

'Oh, I don't know,' said Charlie. 'Alicia's not doing anything she doesn't want to do.'

The line sounded familiar from somewhere. I was still trying to remember where, when Ruth came over to tell Charlie that Clive had arrived with the tapes.

FOUR

I sat to one side of the room, smoking and drinking and occasionally chatting to passing acquaintances, but mostly keeping my eyes peeled so I would spot Duncan or Lulu as soon as either of them arrived. Every so often, someone would interpret my solitude as an invitation and buttonhole me with an in-depth monologue on modern architecture or the state of the nation. I'd escape by saying I had to refill my glass or go and powder my nose, but as often as not, as soon as I'd settled down on my own again, I would be cornered by someone else, and my eyes would be glazing over and I would be thinking about a movie I'd seen or about someone I used to know or about Docklands and Multiglom. Ah yes, Multiglom. I could hear someone droning on about it now. The name hauled me back on to full alert.

'Say that again,' I said. The person who had been doing the talking was a thick-set youth with a Yorkshire accent and big stubble like Desperate Dan. He yelled into my ear. 'I *said*, funny about this Multiglom business, *isn't it?*' He had to yell, because Charlie was playing Clive's trendy samba tapes at maximum volume.

I yelled back, 'What Multiglom business?'

'I *said*, they're taking over the world.'

My blood froze. *'Multiglom?'*

The Yorkshireman allowed himself a patronizing smile. 'No, no.' I heaved a sigh of relief. For a horrible moment there, my paranoia had sprouted wings and been cleared for take-off.

'I'm talking about this Euro-consortium – Dragosh Inc.,' he said.

'Really?' My attention was on the wane again.

'Buying all those publishing companies, and the breweries, and the high-street stores.'

'Breweries? High-street stores?'

'Who hasn't been reading her FT, then?' he smirked. 'High-street stores. Pharmatech, Berkamart, et cetera, et cetera.'

'Wait a sec,' I said. 'I think there was something on the telly last night. Bagwash, was it? Dragosh?' The name rang a couple of distant chimes, but they faded into nothingness before I could match them up. 'Isn't there a law against it? Monopolies and mergers?'

'Loopholes. Did you know they've put in a bid for the country's third largest cinema chain? We heard that at the office today. It probably won't be in the papers for another week, but we sometimes get advance information on these things.'

'A chain of *cinemas*? That's really throwing money down the toilet. They'll never make any profit on that.'

He shrugged. 'They've never made a loss yet.'

'Who? Dragosh?'

'No, *Multiglom*,' said the Yorkshireman, fast losing patience.

'I thought you said it *wasn't* Multiglom.'

He sighed and rolled his eyeballs. 'Multiglom is just the *media arm*,' he explained as though he was talking to a five-year-old. 'Multiglom is a *part* of Dragosh. The nerve centre.'

'But I thought you said . . .'

I was ready to grill him further, but he mumbled something about having to get a refill and swiftly moved off in the direction of the butler. It was the first time I had ever been abandoned by a party bore, and I didn't much care for the feeling. I was wondering whether to tag along with him anyway when I saw Duncan. He was standing, or rather leaning, with one arm draped across the padded shoulders of an all too familiar figure – Francine. I went up and said hello, I could see he'd been working really hard all afternoon.

'Hi, Dora,' he said. 'Dora, this is Francine.'

'I know who it is,' I said. Francine smiled sweetly at me. I smiled sweetly back. 'Where's Lulu?' I asked him.

'Who's Lulu?' asked Francine. As soon as she opened her mouth I was hit by a blast; she'd been at the garlic again. It was overkill. I'd stopped scoffing the stuff after Duncan had complained, and now I kept it ready peeled in my pocket. But I didn't see him whingeing about Francine's breath the way he'd whinged about mine, and that really pissed me off.

'I don't know,' said Duncan, who appeared to be having some difficulty understanding what people were saying to him. He removed his arm from Francine's shoulders and regarded her gravely. 'Do *you* know where Lulu is?' he asked. Francine shook her head.

'Are you sure she's coming?' I asked.

'S'what Ruthie said.' He peered around exaggeratedly. 'Where is Weinstein anyway? Can you see her?'

'Weinstein?' asked Francine, igniting like a Roman

Candle. 'Weinstein Galleries? Maybe I should introduce myself.'

Duncan swayed gently, to and fro. Red wine slopped dangerously near the rim of his glass. 'Where's Lulu?' he repeated.

'Should I know Lulu?' asked Francine. 'Is she famous?'

'She is now,' I said. 'Francine, honey, why don't you . . . run along and talk to Ruth. There she is over there, the one with the perfect nose and podgy calves.'

'No, no,' said Duncan, putting his arm back around Francine's shoulders. 'I think Francine should stay with me. Francine is telling me all about Dino and his latest scheme. It's very interesting, isn't it Francine?'

Francine touched his lips with her finger and made a noise like a soda syphon. 'He's had a bit too much to drink,' she explained, as though I was deaf, dumb, and blind. I was about to ask about Dino and his 'scheme' when I noticed that Duncan, in light-hearted mood, was trying to slide his hand down the front of her little black dress. Her resistance was less than token. I couldn't stand to watch any more. He just wasn't worth the effort. I'd left my cigarettes on a table across the room and went back to reclaim them; no one owned up to smoking any more, so the packet was exactly where I'd left it. I was just lighting up, looking forward to a spot of peaceful isolation, when Ruth bore down on me with that stiff-legged trot which meant business. Her expression was not at all appropriate to a party occasion; it was grim.

'I've been meaning to talk to you,' she said.

'Again?' I said.

'No,' said Ruth, 'I mean *properly*. You never let me talk to you *properly*, Dora. You always change the subject, or turn it into a joke. Now I have something important to say, and I want you to shut up and *listen*.'

'Sure,' I said, not sure at all. I was thinking she was going to tick me off about the cigarettes.

'Not here,' she said, looking around apprehensively. 'Upstairs.' I followed as she headed back through the crowd towards the staircase. One or two people were dancing, but a bit too energetically, as if to prove they had no inhibitions. Someone cannoned into me and I nearly lost my balance. There was a lot of high-pitched laughter and hysterical shrieking. I hadn't realized everyone had been getting quite so intoxicated. Ruth's parties were usually rather sedate.

She led me up to a spare room where the bed was half-buried beneath a mound of coats, and perched on the window-ledge while I flopped on to someone's fake fur and finished my cigarette. 'Give us one,' Ruth begged. I held out the packet, but grudgingly. This was typical; Ruth said she was a non-smoker, but she was always cadging from other people. She took a couple of shallow but showy puffs and asked, 'What's going on?'

'How should *I* know? It's your party.'

'Don't tell me you haven't noticed. Something's happening.'

'Like what?' I laughed, but she didn't laugh back – she puffed on her cigarette and looked anxious. This wasn't like Ruth at all.

She chose her words carefully. 'Everyone is sort of . . . highly strung,' she said. 'It's like the week before Christmas, when everyone's desperate to have a good time, and the harder they try, the worse it gets.' She kept fiddling with her fringe, brushing it forward and then back from her face.

There were surprisingly deep lines etched into her forehead. 'You know what my grandad says? He says it reminds him of the Weimar Republic.'

I'd met Ruth's grandfather once. He had struck me as a senile old codger, but before the war, apparently, he had been something of a mover and shaker in artistic circles. Then the Blackshirts had come along and put a stop to his career by smashing both his Stradivarius and most of the bones in his right hand. Friends and colleagues had urged him to leave Germany, and so he had, but he had not gone far enough. He had survived, but only just; his wife, parents, sister, and three out of four of his children had not been so fortunate.

I didn't like the turn our conversation was taking. 'What do you mean, highly strung?'

Ruth continued to play with her hair. 'You know what I mean. You always know a lot more than you let on, Dora. People are changing.'

'Like who?'

'Like Lulu. When I saw her the other night, she acted like she hardly knew me. It was like she was a different person.'

'Maybe she'd had her nose done.'

This was a low blow, and Ruth ignored it. 'She was sort of . . . blank.'

I relaxed. 'Well, *that's* nothing new. Lulu's always been a bit of a bungalow, in case you hadn't noticed. Not an awful lot upstairs there.'

'No, it wasn't like that *at all*,' Ruth said. I realized she was blinking back tears, and for a horrible moment I thought she was going to cry on my shoulder. Ruth snivelling all over me was the last thing I needed. But she shook it off and got a grip on herself. 'Some of the people here tonight are good friends, people I've known for *years*, but they're different, too. Like they're all caught up in something exciting, and they're not telling me about it.'

'*Invasion of the Body Snatchers*,' I cackled. 'It's the Pod People!'

Ruth suddenly looked very cunning. It was the expression she wore whenever she was about to get someone else to pay for the cab they'd been sharing. 'I think you know more than you're letting on again. I think maybe it's not *entirely* unconnected with what happened to you and Duncan when we were at college.' She looked meaningfully at my little finger. 'You never did tell me how you lost that.'

'Yes I did,' I sighed. Ruth had tried this ploy on a number of occasions. Normally I didn't rise to it, but now I was getting impatient. 'I *told* you, I was chopping paper.'

'Ha!' Ruth exclaimed. 'That wasn't what you said *at all*. You told me you'd shut it in a car door. And you told Jack you'd caught it in the spokes of someone's motorbike. You told someone else it was an accident with a blender, and only last year you were telling Maureen it was a genetic defect common to descendants of an ancient Cornish tribe. You've got a different story for every occasion, haven't you, Dora?'

I didn't much care for the idea of them all comparing notes behind my back. 'Ruth,' I said, 'have you any idea how *boring* it is to get asked the same bloody question over and over again? *Oooh, what happened to your little finger?* It drives me *nuts*.'

'I know it does. That's why I stopped asking about it. But I'm asking you now – what *really* happened?'

'You wouldn't believe me if I told you.'

'Try me. It was Duncan, wasn't it? What did he do to you?'

She'd missed the target completely.

'I know you both changed,' she persisted. 'Something happened, something really big. Duncan went to pieces, he just dropped out. And you . . . you went all religious.' She paused and stared at me. 'Like now. You've gone religious again, haven't you? I really like your *earrings*, Dora. And what about all that junk around your neck?'

I looked down and saw I'd been threading a rosary between my fingers, winding it round and round, like a set of worry beads. 'This is a fashion statement,' I said. 'I'm going through one of my neo-Gothic phases.'

'Like hell you are.'

I took a deep breath. 'All right, I admit it. Duncan and I had an affair.'

'Oh, we *all* know that,' cried Ruth. 'Tell me something I don't already know.' She slid the window open, threw what was left of her cigarette into the street, and then, without asking, helped herself to another.

'Let me tell you about my grandfather,' she said, settling down again with a *Once upon a time* sort of voice. 'He used to be a ladies' man, he used to be *very* romantic. I've seen photos, he was quite good looking. And during the twenties, he fell in love with this movie actress (this was silent movies, of course). She was never very nice to him, in fact I think she was rather a bitch, but he was nuts about her, and later on, after the war, when he was on his own, he hired some detectives to track her down. He thought maybe she'd gone to America and changed her name. I think perhaps he was hoping they would get married or something, that she would

finally recognize him as her soulmate and fall into his arms.
Anyway, he paid for all these investigators, and do you know
what they found out?'

'I have no idea.' I tried to suppress a yawn. This was
turning into a mini-series.

'Nothing!' exclaimed Ruth. 'He stopped looking for her.
I think he'd resigned himself to never seeing her again, he
thought she was dead, but then one day – completely by
accident – he ran into her. In Paris.'

'Well!' I said, glancing at my watch and wondering when
she was going to get to the point. I wanted to go back
downstairs and check on Duncan. 'It's a small world.'

'But, the funny thing was,' said Ruth, 'it *couldn't* have
been the same woman, because she looked *exactly* the same,
even after all those years. Or perhaps it was her daughter or
something, because when Grandpa introduced himself, she
froze him out. Said she'd never heard of him.'

'So he made a mistake.'

Ruth shook her head. 'Grandpa didn't think so. He
thought it was the same woman.'

'Yes, but that was ... what? Twenty-five, thirty years
later? He's an old man. The war messed up his head.'

I wondered where all this was leading. Then Ruth said
something which made me sit up and pay attention. 'The
thing is,' she said, 'he had film of her.'

'He *did*?'

'He was besotted. Just one reel – he stole it from the
studio. And after the war, he tried tracking down the rest,
but it was all lost or destroyed.'

'So what was the movie?' I asked, trying not to sound
too interested.

'Oh, nothing famous. It wasn't even finished – she had

an argument with the director. The same guy who did *Pandora's Box* – have you heard of that?'

I said yes, I'd heard of *Pandora's Box*. Quite a lot of people had.

'Well,' she said, 'he wanted her for the main role in that too, but she was still mad at him, so he hired that American actress instead, the one with the hair. Anyway, the reel Grandpa stole was from this film called *Rotnacht*.'

'*Rotnacht*,' I repeated, trying to stop my face from taking on a lean and hungry look.

Ruth was observing me closely. 'Heard of it?'

'Never.'

'Neither had Charlie. If there was anything to know, he'd be the one to know it. Anyway, Grandpa said this lookalike was hanging around in Paris with an American woman.' She looked at me as though I ought to know what she was talking about. I shrugged and shook my head.

'She was blonde,' she said, still looking at me in that strange way. 'And very beautiful. Her name was Marguerite.'

I shrugged again. 'I've no idea. You tell me.'

'I'm talking about Duncan's mother.'

This was not what I'd been expecting. 'You're kidding.'

'*Marguerite Pearson Fender*. That was her name. I've still got the cuttings somewhere.'

'What the hell is this? You've kept a file? On Duncan?'

'No, but he keeps cropping up in all these other dossiers. Or his parents do. Grandpa collects things. Some of it on suspected war criminals. Other stuff on . . . this woman.'

'I see. Your grandfather is really Simon Wiesenthal. And this woman is Martin Bormann in drag.'

'No, of course not,' Ruth said crossly.

'Anyway, I thought Duncan's father was a painter.'

Ruth squinted at me. 'Don't pretend you don't know.'

'I *don't* know,' I protested. 'This is all news to me, and I'm not sure what you're getting at. What about this film – does your grandfather still have it?'

Ruth said no, he didn't have it any more. 'It disintegrated. The pieces turned to dust.'

'God, I'd have given anything to see it.' The words slipped out – I hadn't intended to sound quite so bursting with curiosity.

'You *do* know something, don't you? Come on, Dora, tell me what happened with you and Duncan.'

'Nothing happened. Except we bust up.'

'It was this woman again, wasn't it? This Clara Weill? Grandpa used to call her *Veilchen*. And he used to tell me stories, like this one by Gogol, called *The Viy*, and he said Gogol had known her too and had written this story about her. It used to scare the shit out of me. Do you know what I'm talking about?'

'No,' I lied. The story was in my *Roger Vadim's Book of Bloodsuckers*. 'The Russians were never on my reading list. What's it got to do with anything?'

'You never met Duncan's parents, did you? No one did. They died when he was little. Tell me, how much do you actually *know* about Duncan?'

This was ridiculous. 'I know a damn sight more about him than you do,' I said, feeling a sudden surge of anxiety. I wanted to get back downstairs so I could pick up Duncan and take him as far away from that house as possible. 'I've had enough of this,' I said, getting to my feet.

'Wait, don't go,' she said, but I turned my back on her and stomped downstairs.

The room was so packed that it seemed to have a living,

breathing life of its own, everyone except me part of a homogenous whole which was throbbing along to its own irresistible rhythm. All the non-smokers had suddenly produced packets of cigarettes, and the air was thick with fog and loud voices. Whenever I tried to move one way, the tightly packed mob would propel me in the opposite direction, until I grew dizzy with frustration. I searched in vain for Jack or Charlie or another familiar face, and eventually I spotted Duncan. He had scarcely moved since we'd last spoken, except that Francine had disappeared and been replaced by another woman. Duncan was squinting at her, as if that were the only way he could see one girl instead of two.

I began to elbow my way towards him, and the tide changed and I suddenly found myself pressed up too close and unable to step back. 'Hey,' I said in his ear, 'I think we should go home now.'

The woman twisted round to look at me and smiled. 'Don't go,' she said. 'Things are just warming up.'

'It's too hot for me already,' I said. 'Duncan?'

'I'm waiting for Lulu,' he said bullishly.

'Lulu's not coming,' I said. 'Ruth was telling porky pies.'

He looked outraged. The woman wrinkled her nose as if I smelled bad, and said to Duncan, 'You should stay, you know. We'll have a really good time later on.'

'He's got a headache,' I said, grabbing his arm. For a moment, the woman looked as if she were going to step between us and sink her teeth into me, but I waggled my crucifix at her and she didn't flinch. So she wasn't a vampire. At least, not yet.

'Who do you think you are?' she sneered. 'The Pope?'

'We can't go home,' wailed Duncan.

'Yes we can,' I said. 'I don't think we should stay another

minute. Honestly, I *really* think we should go.' I had an irresistible urge to get him as far away as possible from Ruth. He was too far gone to raise any further objections as I led him in the direction of the front door. Someone whispered, 'Shall we dance?' and two or three people tried to detain us and start tedious drunken conversations. I managed to squirm free, but Duncan kept stopping to chat, and needed constant prodding and pulling. I looked around one last time for Jack, hoping he might offer us a lift to W11, but neither he nor Roxy were anywhere to be seen.

At the very last minute, Ruth materialized out of nowhere and stood guardian-like in front of the door. 'You're leaving?'

'Looks like it.'

She tried stalling us. 'Have you seen Charlie?'

'He was messing around with the tapes.'

'Not any more,' she said. 'He's gone.'

Duncan snapped out of his daze. 'You told me Lulu would be here.'

'She *said* she would come,' Ruth said. 'It's not my fault she hasn't turned up.' She checked her watch, and I thought she was going to say it was early days yet, there was still plenty of time for Lulu to arrive. But she didn't.

'Charlie must be somewhere around,' I said. 'Look, Ruthie, we have to rush. I'll call you.'

'Please, Dora. Call me *tomorrow*. There are things we've *got* to talk about.'

'Yeah, yeah,' I said. 'Bye now.' I yanked the door open and booted Duncan out into the night.

'OK,' she said, seeming to shrink back into the room. The party noises swelled, and then the door closed and the sound was instantly reduced to a muffled wassail.

We walked down the road, our breath turning to vapour

in the cold night air. Duncan was concentrating hard on placing one foot in front of the other. The roads were busy, but this part of the world was strangely empty of pedestrians, not like Notting Hill at all, though we heard what sounded like the distant howling of teenage jerks on the rampage, animal noises echoing through the underpass. As we trudged down the Archway Road, the wind at our backs, there was a sudden screech of tyres, followed by a loud metallic crunch on the road behind us, but we didn't stop. We kept on going till we spotted a cab.

FIVE

Duncan annoyed me by babbling about Lulu all the way home. Why hadn't she turned up? Hadn't Ruth said she'd be there? Why hadn't she phoned? Everyone liked the ads on TV, but wasn't Multiglom exploiting her, driving her too hard? He was worried, really he was. No one had seen or heard of her for days. 'Ruth saw her in Gnashers,' I reminded him, and then I told a tiny lie. 'Ruth says she was fine.'

Duncan sat bolt upright. 'Gnashers? Hey, let's go there *right this minute*.' He leaned forward to speak to the cab driver, but I pulled him back. 'No,' I said firmly. 'You've had quite enough wild socializing for one night.'

'But what if she's there?'

'She won't be. Not now. Models have to take care of their skin, otherwise they start looking ropy. No late nights, no boozing, no drugs. Lulu's too old to get away with anything like that.'

'But she's only twenty-five. Only a baby.'

'Old for a *model*,' I said. 'Your place or mine?'

We went, as usual, to his place, which had soundproof walls and floors. That way I avoided the Krankzeits and got something approaching a good night's sleep, give or take a drunken groping session.

I sensed there was something missing as soon as I walked in. Duncan went to the bathroom while I prowled around, trying to figure out what it was. And then it hit me. Or rather, it didn't hit me like it should have done. 'What have you done with the garlic?' I asked him when he came back.

'Ooh, I chucked it away,' he said innocently. 'It was stinking the whole place out.'

'No, it wasn't. And that was your *protection*. I put it there *specially*. You can't just *throw it out*.'

'There's some in the kitchen.'

I stared at him in disbelief. 'You threw it out because you thought Lulu would be coming back with you tonight, didn't you? And you didn't want her thinking you'd lost your marbles.'

'Maybe.' He shrugged and got out the half-full bottle of VSOP and poured himself a large measure. He didn't ask if I wanted one, so I went over to pour my own.

'You're a fool,' I said. 'I bet you're not even carrying the crucifix I gave you.'

'So?'

'What happens if you run into Violet or one of her chums? What then? You'll be dog meat, for Godsake.'

'Now who's the paranoid one?' he taunted. 'I thought the bloody vampires were supposed to be confined to Multiglom.'

'That's only the *headquarters*.' The crucifix earrings were heavy; I took them off and massaged my aching lobes. 'This thing is getting out of hand. It's getting *big*.'

'What are you talking about?'

'Only that she's building a fucking empire. *Bellini*'s just the beginning. What we're talking about here is a multi-national corporation with fingers in hundreds of different pies: publishing, drug companies, breweries, God knows what else. She's running *industries*.'

He looked at me sceptically. 'She couldn't do that. Not Violet. Not on her own.'

Fragments of all those conversations I'd had with Grauman thirteen years ago reared up on their hind legs to taunt me. 'But that's just it. She's *not* on her own. We're not talking Bram Stoker any more, we're talking *Vampire City*.' I was aching with exhaustion, but I didn't want to go to sleep because everything was suddenly falling into place. It was so obvious, I couldn't understand why I hadn't seen it before. The Multiglom floor guide with its list of names: Micromart, Pharmatex, Deforest . . . Satellite broadcasting, architects, design groups. I wondered whether there were also banks, lawyers, estate agents . . .

'What would she want with a brewery?' asked Duncan. 'She never drank beer.' He saw I was shivering. 'Are you cold? Want the fire on?'

'I'm OK,' I said, then I decided I wasn't OK after all. I was covered with goose pimples and my teeth were chattering. Duncan put his drink down and took one of my hands between both of his, rubbing it briskly to get the circulation going. 'You're like ice. Do you want to borrow a jumper? No, tell you what, why don't you have a long hot bath? Then afterwards I'll make some cocoa.'

'I'll have a bath if you'll have a bath with me.'

The suggestion amused him.

'And we have to talk about Multiglom in the morning,' I said.

'Yes, yes,' he said, and went into the bathroom to start the hot water. I went into the bedroom to get undressed. I put on Lulu's pink towelling bathrobe and wiped my make-up off with some of her cleansing lotion.

'You look better without make-up,' Duncan said as I went back into the living room. Men always said that; they liked the natural look, though they didn't seem to care if it was achieved by unnatural means. I leaned over to kiss the back of his neck. 'Your lips are chilly,' he said. 'Come round here.' He sat me down on his lap and slipped his hands beneath the bathrobe to massage my skin. I was starting to feel deliciously warm and cosy when the entryphone made a noise like a sick sheep.

'Bugger,' he said.

'Don't answer.'

'Have to,' he said, tipping me off his lap. He went out into the hallway and said something into the intercom.

Lulu's reply came over loud and clear. 'Hi, it's me.'

My spirits plummeted. It was all over. Through the doorway I saw Duncan's face light up, then it was suddenly transformed into a mask of guilt, like a schoolboy caught smoking behind the bike sheds. 'Shit, shit, shit,' he said, racing back to me. 'Quickly, into the bathroom.'

'*What?*' I couldn't believe I was hearing this.

'You know what she'll think if she catches you here. She's possessive as hell.'

'This is ridiculous, like a French farce. Can't we sit down and discuss it like civilized people?'

'*Please*,' he said, flapping his arms. 'I'll make it up to you, Dora, I *promise*.'

There was another buzz from the entryphone. Duncan threw himself back at the intercom, pressed the button so we could both hear her saying, 'Oh Lord, I left my keys behind. Duncan, let me in.'

Duncan went wild. He fled into the bedroom and came back with my clothes all in a bunch, and pressed them into my arms.

I said, 'I don't know if . . .'

He turned very stern and forceful. I wished he was like that more often – I would have done anything he'd wanted. 'Now listen, your hot water heater's bust, someone spilled red wine all over you at Ruth's, and you've come round to take a bath. Now get in there *right now*.'

I slouched into the bathroom just as he was releasing the lock on the front door. I heard him say, 'Hey Lu, come on up,' and then I shut myself in. I dropped the clothes and kicked them as they fell. The black chiffon scarf somehow floated loose and drifted into the bath. I left it swirling in the water. How dared he treat me like this? I picked up a can of shaving foam and squirted FUCK across the steamed-up mirror.

The bath was a large Victorian one with legs, and barely a quarter full, and the water was scalding hot, so I started to run the cold as well. I paced up and down, tweezed my eyebrows, clipped my nails, cleaned out my ears with cotton buds. The everyday bathroom activities helped me to simmer down. I was half expecting Lulu to knock on the door at any second and demand to know what I was doing, but I couldn't hear anything over the noise of the running water. I wondered if they were arguing about me, so I opened the bathroom door a crack, just so I could hear what they were saying.

They weren't saying anything. I opened the door a bit

wider and peeped out. Duncan was sitting in his favourite spot on the sofa. Lulu had her back to me, and she was sitting on his lap, exactly where I'd been before she'd shown up. She had her arms around him, and they were kissing, really getting into it. I couldn't believe it. This was too much. Duncan had swapped one girl for another – as though we were different makes of car or something. He was acting as though nothing had changed, everything was back to normal.

Only it wasn't. Not quite. There was something off-kilter about the scene, only I couldn't work out what it was, not until I felt a draught and started shivering again, more violently this time. I drew Lulu's pink bathrobe more tightly around my chest, and it was then I realized what was wrong. Lulu always wore pink. Pink or red, everybody knew that. But she wasn't wearing pink now. She was wearing black.

I stood there, blinking, trying to absorb this information. It was significant, I knew that much, but I was so tired and drunk I couldn't even begin to work out why. I don't know how long I was standing there. It might have been a few seconds, or it might have been a couple of centuries. Then I must have made a noise. Either that, or it was the cloud of steam leaking out of the bathroom which made her look up. No, *look up* is wrong; she didn't so much turn her head as whip it round.

The black didn't make her look sallow, as she'd always feared, but she seemed paler than usual, powdery white, and the contrast with her skin made her mouth appear luscious and red. At first I thought it was lipstick. Then she licked her lips, and I saw she'd had her teeth done, but the dentist had made a hash of it; some of them were too sharp. There was a small red bead clinging to her chin, and even from where

I was standing I could see minute flecks of white powder suspended on the curved surface. I stared very hard, but I had a feeling I was concentrating on all the wrong things.

'Dora,' she said. 'How nice.'

She rose and came towards me. She'd always been tall – five nine, bumped up to five ten or eleven for professional purposes – but I'd never felt her towering over me quite as much as she did now. Her feet were touching the ground, but she wasn't walking so much as *gliding*, I couldn't actually *see* her taking the steps, no matter how hard I stared. She was getting nearer, and I realized I'd been standing there for ages, staring, when I should have been doing something else, such as making a run for the front door, or shutting myself in the bathroom. But I was no longer sure where the bathroom was. I'd been thinking it was right behind me, but somehow I must have been moving away from it without realizing because now I was standing right in the middle of the living-room floor, staring into the big mirror on the opposite wall. I couldn't see Lulu there, but I could see myself. At least I assumed that's who it was, because it didn't look like me at all; this unfamiliar-looking person had the expression of a rabbit gazing into the headlights of an oncoming truck.

I might have stared for ever if the ancient springs of the sofa hadn't creaked. I tore my gaze away from the mirror and saw Duncan was still where she'd left him. I said his name once or twice, but my voice was very tiny and there was no reply. He was sitting in an unnaturally stiff position, still clutching his brandy glass. The collar and most of the upper part of his shirt were a deep red. Tie-dyed, I thought. It crossed my mind that he might be dead.

I thought, *Oh fuck*.

It wasn't fair. I wanted to wind the tape back and start again. I'd always been so careful and now here I was, half-naked and defenceless, no garlic, no crucifix, no nothing. Lulu opened and closed her mouth like a guppy – it should have been comical, but it wasn't. She was making a strange whistling noise through her teeth. She hadn't yet grown accustomed to them, and the thought filled me with disproportionate relief, as though it made any difference from where *I* was standing. Then she said, in a conversational tone, 'Honestly, Dora. You can't leave him alone for one minute, can you?'

'I was just having a bath,' I said with an embarrassed giggle. 'My Ascot broke.' Even to me it sounded pathetic.

She threw back her head and laughed too, but throatily, not like her normal little-girl giggling. Now she was closer, she didn't look quite so good. The make-up was thick, but not thick enough to conceal the state of her skin, which was dry and flaky, dull and lifeless. She hadn't been taking those early nights, after all.

'And you always pretended to be my *friend*,' she was saying. 'I was always so *nice* to you. And now here you are, trying to steal him away as soon as my back is turned. I always *knew* there was another woman. I just didn't realize it was you, Dora.'

'*But it wasn't me*,' I murmured, trying to remember what I'd done with my crucifixes. There was garlic in the kitchen, but Lulu was standing between me and the kitchen door. There was garlic in the pocket of my jacket, but that was somewhere on the bathroom floor. At least, I *hoped* it was somewhere on the bathroom floor. I tried to remember whether the jacket had been part of the bundle of clothes which Duncan had shoved into my arms, or whether I'd left it hanging in the hall.

'... and you're wearing my *bathrobe*,' she said in an outraged tone. 'You think you can waltz right in and steal my boyfriend and wear my *bathrobe*. But you can't. You look terrible in pink, Dora. It doesn't suit you at all. You should wear black, like everyone else.'

All this time I was edging backwards, and as soon as I found I'd backed into the bathroom doorway, I scuttled inside and slammed the door, shooting the bolt across, but even as I shot it I saw how flimsy a bolt it was. The door shuddered as something crashed against the other side – it sounded much too heavy to be Lulu – and there was a loud splintering as the bolt casing began to part company with the frame. I scrabbled around amongst the clothes on the floor, trying to find garlic, crucifixes, anything. I finally found my jacket, but the only things in the pockets were an old receipt and a couple of mangy paper tissues.

There was a second juddering blow, and the bolt casing flew across the room, and the door was hurled open with such force it swung free from one of its hinges. 'Look what you made me do,' said Lulu.

I started to gabble. 'We saw your picture in the paper. You looked great.' I thought if I could keep her talking, perhaps she wouldn't get a chance to do anything else with that big red mouth of hers. 'How do you manage to put your make-up on without a mirror?'

'I don't need mirrors any more.' She raised one of her hands and ran it through her hair in a parody of one of her favourite model-girl gestures. 'Mirrors and I have parted company. I'm *beyond* the world of mirrors now.'

'But you don't eat meat,' I said hopefully.

205

She smiled and for the first time I had an unrestricted view of her brand-new teeth, which were pearly white and ferocious looking. 'Bugger that vegetarian lark,' she said. 'This is the first time they've let me out on my own, and I'm *starving.*'

'What about Duncan? You came for *him*, not me. You could finish *him* off, and let me go.'

She shook her head. 'You don't know *anything*. Duncan's special. They said I could come here, as a present. I wasn't supposed to kiss him, not yet, but I was so pleased to see him I got carried away.'

'*What* was a present? *They* said? *Who* said? Violet?'

'Violet? No, no, I'm talking about Rose. She said Duncan would know exactly what to do. Because he's done it before.'

'Done *what*?' Lulu's teeth and dietary habits may have changed, but she was as stupid as ever. 'But Rose *is* Violet, you fool. And if *she* sent you, she had a reason. I *know* what I'm talking about, Lu. See this?' I held up my left hand and waggled what remained of my little finger at her. It was hardly a threatening gesture. 'I've been here before.'

A faintly perplexed look skittered across her face, as though an ancient race memory had stirred somewhere in her head, but then it vanished and she was stretching out towards me. 'I'm *so* tired of talking,' she sighed. 'And I'm *so* bloody hungry. Now are you going to come to me or do I have to come and get you?'

'Oh hell,' I said. 'Come and get me.'

She stopped being Lulu and started being something else.

She tried to overwhelm me with her eyes, but she had a few hundred years to go before she mastered that technique, and I was wise to it. I concentrated on the teeth and the soft red flesh of her lips. I was groping around the basin, trying to find something – anything – to use as a weapon, but Duncan's electric razor wasn't much use, nor was his after-shave. I threw a can of hairspray and it bounced uselessly off her arm. Lulu feinted playfully, and I jumped, and my elbow sent a clutch of toiletries crashing to the floor. The plastic bottles bounced and rolled, a couple of glass ones smashed. The air was suddenly fragrant with vetivert, and aquamarine jelly oozed out over the shiny white tiles. She advanced purposefully through the wreckage, heels making a crunching, squelching sound, and carefully stepped from the shiny white tiles on to the fluffy white bathmat. As she did so I ducked and grabbed the edge of the mat and tugged it up as hard as I could.

If she'd been wearing sensible footwear she would have regained her balance easily. But this was *Lulu*, and she was wearing flamboyant fuck-me shoes with lizard-skin trimming and four-inch spikes. So when the earth moved beneath her feet she teetered back and forth in a dainty cha-cha move-ment, one arm windmilling into the bathroom cabinet; one corner of it came away from the wall and sent more jars and bottles crashing across the room. The smell of vetivert was now mingling with verbena and bergamot and Rive Gauche. I put my head down and butted her, and she fell backwards with a surprised grunt, and the rim of the bath caught her behind the knees and she landed in the water with her legs in the air.

For one brief blissful moment, I thought that was it, I thought she was going to lie there quietly, and it would all be over. I was standing there thinking that when she came up screeching and clawing. I pushed her back again but her fingers fastened on to the sleeve of the bathrobe and pulled me down with her. For a few seconds our faces were only inches apart. Her teeth gnashed shut, just missing the tip of my nose, but I managed to push her under the gushing tap, and she twisted her head from side to side and made an enraged burbling sound, letting go of the bathrobe and scrabbling at my forearms so that fine threads of blood dribbled into the water and uncoiled there, turning it pink like dentist's mouthwash. I tried to hold her down, but she was too hot and slippery. My nose and mouth were filled with fragrant steam, but I caught a whiff of something spicy and unpleasant lurking beneath the overlay of perfume. Lulu's face was coming out in large shiny blisters which burst, one after the other. She sat up suddenly, shaking her head so that drops of water flew in all directions, and shaking me off as well. It caught me off guard and I felt myself tumbling backwards.

My feet were cold. I couldn't work out what I was doing on the bathroom floor, but it would have been comfortable enough had it not been for the cold feet and the nagging thought there was some other matter to which I should have been attending. I tried to get up but everything tilted. I slapped my hand down to steady myself, and felt broken glass sink into the palm. I said, very crossly, 'Oh, *shit*,' as it started to sting. My hand wasn't the only part of me which was hurting; the back of my head was throbbing where I'd cracked it against something, and now everything was going hazy, and the steam and the smoke swirled up and made it even hazier. Through the haze, I saw someone stand up in the bath, and her black dress was clinging to her figure and

I recognized Lulu, even though her face was red and shiny. She didn't seem to mind about the mess her face was in – she was laughing as if this were the most fun she had ever had in her life. It was all so *déjà vu* that I *knew* I had to be dreaming.

'Dora Dora get up Dora . . .' Someone was saying my name over and over again. I tried to pull myself up, and then the clouds rolled back and I saw that Duncan wasn't dead after all. He was prancing around like Errol Flynn, holding my biggest crucifix back to front, like a dagger. Lulu snarled, and swiped at him, trying to knock it out of his grasp, but as the metal touched her flesh there was a hissing noise like an iron on a damp shirt, and she jumped back with a howl, pawing at the steaming red mark on her hand. Duncan stepped back and held himself on guard, and glanced at the crucifix in surprise, as though he hadn't really expected it to have had such a drastic effect. Then he lunged and yelled '*Touché!*' as he struck her just above the left breast. This time nothing happened – her skin was protected by the fabric of her dress – and both of them looked rather taken aback. Duncan shrugged it off and lunged again. She dodged, but the metal brushed against her chin and left it sizzling, and she squawked and lashed out with her fingernails. He stepped aside and started casually to cut and thrust at her face. He was treating it as a game, and Lulu appeared to be going along with it, as though they'd rehearsed this many times before, but her retaliatory swiping was getting wilder and he was barely having to sidestep now, and scoring more and more hits, each one followed by a gratifying amount of hissing and yelping. So entrancing was this spectacle, I almost forgot what I was watching until I heard him saying, 'Suck on this, you vampire slut,' in an eminently reasonable voice. Then he half-turned and said over his shoulder in a business-like manner, 'Don't just sit there, Dora, go and get something.'

I tried to reply in an equally businesslike manner, but all that came out of my mouth was a feeble croak. How come I always seemed to be on the critical list when things got lively? Duncan was having all the fun again. I pushed myself up with my uninjured hand, and immediately got broken glass in that one too. I staggered as far as the kitchen, and it wasn't until I sat down to rest that I remembered what I was there for, because I found myself sitting on the wobbly chair. I tugged at the loose leg but it wouldn't come off, so I rocked the chair violently backwards and forwards until the wood split down the middle with a sharp crack, so now I had a useless three-legged chair and a useful chair-leg with an uneven point. I was tidying up the splinters with a vege-table knife when I heard someone shouting, 'Dora! What the *fuck* are you doing?' so I shambled back to the bathroom.

Duncan had tired of his *Captain Blood* routine. Now they were lying in the bath together. Lulu was gargling and kicking her legs and the water was slapping rhythmically. If I hadn't known better I might have thought they were hump-ing. Duncan had somehow got hold of my chiffon scarf and had wound it around her head and was holding her under the water with it. I tapped him on the shoulder and handed him the chair-leg. As he loosened his grip and rocked back on his haunches, she sat up and started to scream, and he said 'Oh, for God's sake, shut up,' and jabbed her with the stick. The point sank in about half an inch and snagged on her ribcage, and they both stared at it in surprise and then looked at each other. They were still looking at each other when he tried again. This time it slid between the ribs and her eyes opened wide, and she made a sort of 'oof' sound, and fell straight back into the water like a toppled tree. He put one knee on her stomach and worked the chair-leg free. As it came out it made an obscene sucking sound, and a lot of dark blood came out with it and turned the water an even darker red. He stuck the stick into her again, several times. The chiffon scarf floated up and away, and half her face seemed to come away with it.

'It's not enough,' I said. 'We have to cut her into little pieces, before she starts singing *Madame Butterfly*.'

'She's not going to sing,' Duncan said, hauling himself out over the side of the bath. 'She's not like Violet.'

'They're all the same,' I said. 'They all wind up with stakes through their hearts.'

'Cut it out.'

I peered down into the bath. The water wasn't running any more; it was thick and stagnant, and there was a lot of red froth on the surface. She was under it with her hair floating like seaweed and the chair-leg sticking out of what looked like a gallon of blackcurrant jelly spread all over the middle of her chest. Her face was almost unrecognizable. Duncan took a hand towel from the rail and let it drop over her head; it floated for a moment and then the water weighed it down and it sank around what remained of her features.

I didn't want to look any more. I looked down at the floor instead, and spotted a diamanté crucifix gleaming in the middle of a lot of broken glass, so I picked it up and watched the light glint off it in all kinds of crazy directions, and decided it was the prettiest thing I had ever seen.

'You OK?'

'We need black bags,' I said, trying to be practical. 'We have to dispose of all the pieces separately.'

'Honestly, I don't think that's necessary.'

'Did you get it right this time?'

He looked at me coldly and said, 'No.' I limped towards the doorway and my knees buckled and gave way. He stopped me falling. 'You're not OK at all, are you?'

'Yes,' I said. 'I mean, no. To be honest, I'm not sure.' Then I felt myself going all floppy, and told him, 'I think I banged my head.'

When I woke up I was no longer wearing the soggy pink bathrobe but wrapped in a large quilt, on the bed, surrounded by damp towels and bloodstained tissues, and my hands were stinging like crazy. Duncan had one of them wedged between his knees and was peering closely at it through his spectacles, picking the glass out with tweezers. The sensation of the steel tips foraging under the skin made my eyes water. By the time he'd finished, my palms looked as though they'd been flayed. He applied TCP and wrapped them in bandages. They didn't hurt so badly after that, so long as I kept my fingers bent.

He lay down beside me. I closed my eyes and breathed in the smell of salt and blood and perfume. The first thing I saw when I opened them again was the bite on his neck. The skin was broken in two places, and the wounds were moist and leaking. 'What about this,' I said, prodding it with a bent finger.

He winced. 'It's OK. I'm fine.'

I wasn't so sure. 'You might turn into one of *them*.'

He sighed and sat up and gingerly probed the wound. 'It's sore.'

'It's all puffy,' I observed.

'It'll take more than one lousy bite to turn *me* into a vampire.'

This was true, but there was no need to take chances. 'We should put something on it. Salt? Alcohol?'

We looked at each other. 'How about the Lord's own logo?' he suggested, and fetched a glass of brandy and dunked my cross in it.

'Here, let me,' I said, making him lie back with his head to one side. Then I knelt over him and pressed the crucifix against the bite. There was a sizzling noise, and he tensed and said 'Ouch.' I thought of the way Lulu's skin had hissed whenever the metal had touched it, and perhaps he was thinking of it too, because I could feel him getting stiff. It was the best erection he'd had of late, so I parted my bathrobe and worked myself down on to it, trying not to use my hands, so that it reminded me of those pass-the-banana party games. Then we bounced around for a bit, trying and utterly failing to synchronize our loin movements. The throbbing behind my eyes diminished, then returned with renewed force until I thought my head was going to explode, like the man in the Kuroi commercial. But it didn't. I collapsed and tried to get my breath back.

After a while Duncan asked if I'd finished. I thought he was talking about the sex and felt vaguely insulted, but then I realized he'd been referring to his neck.

'Let me check.' There were blisters on the skin. This time when I applied the cross there was no sizzling, nor was there another erection, though he said ouch again. He put his arm around me and we stayed like that, not speaking, until I said what I really fancied was the cocoa he'd promised me earlier – light-years ago, it seemed now.

'Me too,' he said. 'I'll do the bathroom in the morning.'

'She'll crumble in the daylight,' I said. 'No problem, never had a chance to toughen up, not like Violet. The older ones are trickier.'

I hadn't meant to be insensitive, but there was an acerbic edge to his voice as he said, 'Don't I know it.'

'Duncan . . .'

'Yes?'

'She said you'd know what to do.'

'Who said?'

'Lulu. She was told that *you* would know what to do when she got here. So what do you suppose that was all about?'

'Well, we all *know* what I did,' he said bitterly. 'I stuck it to her real good.'

'Maybe that's it.'

'What?'

I shook my head. 'Sorry.'

'Yeah,' he said. 'I should never have let her go.' He made a feeble joke about how he ended up murdering all his girlfriends. I laughed and said I trusted him not to murder me. 'Well *you* should be all right,' he said, 'since you're not my girlfriend.' Had I not been so exhausted, the remark would have stung almost as badly as the broken glass.

I fell asleep while he was in the kitchen preparing the cocoa, and woke later to find a mug of cold pale liquid stagnating on the floor. I stayed awake long enough to notice the other half of the bed was empty. Duncan was sitting in the wicker chair by the window, gazing out at the first streaks of daylight in the east. Before I drifted back to sleep, I thought I could hear him snuffling very softly to himself. But I might have been mistaken.

SIX

It was nearly lunchtime when I woke up. Duncan had already popped out to buy the Sunday papers. We sat on the bed and went through them. Nothing, not the slightest hint of our story in any of them except the *Sunday Sport*, which had plastered the headline LONDON SHAKEN BY VAMPIRE EPIDEMIC across its front page, with a fuzzy reproduction of one of Dino's photographs dwarfed by a large colour shot of a busty blonde with fangs. 'Great,' I said. 'Now we'll never get anyone to take us seriously. What on earth possessed you to send the photos to the *Sport*?'

'I didn't,' Duncan said testily. 'I thought it was you.'

'Well, we're screwed now anyway,' I said, holding up the business section from one of the broadsheets. There was a big announcement at the top of the page, MULTIGLOM BID FOR ICI, and further down a photograph of two men shaking hands. One was fat and balding and horribly familiar; he was smiling at the camera and showing his teeth but this time there was nothing unorthodox about his dental work. Out loud I read, 'Under the new chairmanship of Mr

215

Ferdinand Drax, the Multiglom takeover looks set to win additional support from the upper echelons of the business community.'

The whisper of a suspicion tiptoed into my mind. I riffled through the rest of the newspaper until I found the letters page and checked the address at the top. Readers were instructed to send their letters to Multiglom Tower. In all, we found three readers' letters pages with the same address.

'I think we may be too late with the newspapers,' I said.

The bathroom was a mess. Duncan had left the window wide open and drained the water away and the body in the bath now resembled the remains of a large Chinese takeaway regurgitated by a team of drunken rugby players. It smelled almost as bad, but at least it had decomposed so thoroughly there was nothing left to remind us of Lulu. This was just bad meat.

'What now?' I asked, one of my hands clamped over my nose to block out the stench. 'Can you just flush it down the plughole?'

Duncan made a face. 'I'll wait. It's coming apart quite nicely.' We had made an unspoken pact to refer to the corpse as 'it'. Vampires were things, not people, and it would have been dangerous for either of us to start thinking otherwise.

My head still ached, and there was a small soft lump on the temple where I'd banged it. I felt hungover and bloated and extremely depressed. It was past two when I finally summoned the willpower to get up and get dressed. Duncan said he'd put my red dress in the washing-machine because it was all trampled and stained, so I helped myself to the contents of Lulu's wardrobe. She wouldn't be needing them now.

I wondered what would happen between Duncan and me, now she was gone for good. Everything might have been perfect if it hadn't been for the hovering presence of Violet. But then again, if it hadn't been for Violet, Lulu would still have been with us, and I would still have been confined to the outskirts of Duncan's life. There were pros and cons whichever way you looked at it.

When I had dressed, I went into the living room and found him rooting through an expensive-looking handbag, black leather with lizard-skin trimming. 'Lulu's bag,' he said – quite unnecessarily, because I knew it wasn't mine.

I curled up on the sofa next to him. 'Anything interesting?'

'Make-up. Hairbrush. Filofax. Tissues. I don't know, I've never gone through a woman's bag before. I guess it's all the usual junk.'

'Let's look at the Filofax.' He handed it over and I went through it. The pockets were stuffed with old receipts, Lulu's driving licence, and credit cards. The diary section was almost blank, apart from the occasional bit of cryptic scrawl: *dentist 2pm, Jack & Alicia, phone Katy*. The latest entry was for the previous Tuesday, and it read, *RM/Multiglom Tower/ Malassus Warf / 10am*. 'Nothing we don't already know,' I said, handing it back and noticing that Duncan was half-sitting on a plain white envelope, trying so hard not to draw my attention to it that it became impossible to ignore. 'What's that?'

'Nothing,' he said. 'An invoice.'

'From the bag?'

'Of course not,' he said, sounding annoyed. 'It just came in the post.' He upended the bag and shook it so that various bits and pieces came tumbling out: hair grips, hand lotion, a packet of mints. When it was empty he held it out to me. 'You want this?'

'Sure,' I said. 'Thanks. It's really nice.' Then I told him I was going home, though I didn't tell him the reason – that I was dying for the bath I'd never had the night before. I waited for him to suggest I come back to see him later on, but he didn't. I then dropped a strong hint that he should come round to see me at my place, Krankzeits or no Krankzeits, but he didn't pick up on that either. 'So what are we going to do?' I asked finally. 'About Multiglom, I mean.'

'I guess I'll have to talk to her.'

'Talk to *Violet*? Are you *mad*?'

'It's me she's after. She's not interested in you.'

This was true, and I couldn't work out why it should make me feel so aggrieved. He was almost making it sound as though I were irrelevant to the entire business.

'There's not much else we can do,' he said.

'We can do some serious damage. Put her out of the running.'

'We tried that before, and look where it got us. No, this has gone on long enough. It's time I faced up to her.'

'She'll kill you,' I said. But what *really* worried me was that I didn't think she would kill him at all. As soon as Duncan and Violet connected, it would all be over, one way or another. It was essential they be kept apart. 'Listen,' I said. 'Before you do anything rash . . . Tomorrow's the fourteenth, isn't it? Well, that's my appointment with Murasaki.'

'You can't be serious. You're not thinking of going.'

'Why not?' I said, sounding more optimistic than I felt. 'I've been there before. I know my way around. I'll take precautions.'

'I won't let you go. Christ, this is like Lulu all over again.'

'I'm not Lulu. I can look after myself.' I was touched by his concern, but a little worried in case he insisted on accompanying me. The varnish on my nails was chipped; I worried at it with my teeth until another strip peeled off, and told him, 'I think I've got an idea.'

Duncan said it was the stupidest idea he had ever heard, but couldn't come up with a better one. It wasn't as risky as he thought, because of course I'd done this sort of thing before, though he wasn't aware of that. And I had an ace up my sleeve, or at least a high-ranking card which might be mistaken for an ace in a bad light. And the light was all bad around here.

Just as I was preparing to set off homewards, the phone rang. Duncan answered and poked the receiver into my ribs. 'Weinstein. For you.'

'Hello, Ruth,' I said. 'Thank you so much for the wonderful party.'

'Dora, it was *awful*. At least you took off before it got really bad. Sara had one of her fits, and we had to get an ambulance, and I kept getting calls from her sister, only I couldn't find out which hospital they'd taken her to, and no one knows where she is. And Charlie disappeared, I still don't know where he got to, and I couldn't find Jack either, and then everything fell apart, and somebody got beaten up, and somebody else fell through a window and cut their head open, and there was blood *everywhere*. And then all these gatecrashers turned up, and . . .'

'Sounds great,' I said.

'Oh, and Lulu arrived just after you went, and she was *furious* when I said Duncan had already left. I've never seen her like that before, she was *spitting poison*. Did she catch up with you in the end?'

'In the end,' I said.

'Listen, you remember what I was talking about last night? Well, there's a meeting this evening. Can you make it?'

'You've got to be kidding. I am *not* schlepping all the way up to Archway again.'

'No, no, you don't have to. You know the gallery? Well, in the offices upstairs. Just round the corner from you.'

'Matt's old office? After all these years? Good Lord.'

'Matt? Oh, you mean Matthew. Yes, he'll be there as well. Nine o'clock. We'll have drinks and things.' I told her it sounded perfectly lovely, and hung up. I had no intention of letting myself in for another question and answer session with Ruth.

Duncan emerged from the bathroom wearing pink washing-up gloves and carrying a bottle of Liquid Gumption. 'What did Weinstein want?'

'She's throwing another party. Tonight. Want to come?'

'One dose of Ruth per weekend is quite sufficient.'

He saw me to the front door without taking his rubber gloves off. On the doorstep he asked, 'What are you doing tonight, I mean after the private view?' At last. I'd thought he was never going to ask.

'This and that,' I replied non-committally.

'Well, be very careful. Especially if you're out after dark. Don't take those earrings off again.'

This wasn't what I'd been expecting to hear. 'So what are *you* up to? How about getting together?'

'Dora, you *know* what happened last night,' he said reproachfully. 'It's something I'll have to come to terms with. I need to spend time on my own.'

As I was walking away, I replayed his words in my head. They seemed ominous. I wondered what had been in the white envelope; perhaps Lulu had written him a letter, or perhaps it really had been an invoice. I vaguely remembered him saying he'd got it in the morning mail. But he must have been confused, because there were no postal deliveries on Sundays.

On the way home, I took a slight detour and found myself in the crescent where Jack and Alicia lived. The curtains were still drawn in their first-floor windows. I wondered whether Jack had made it back from the party in one piece, and – on an impulse – rang their bell to find out. The entryphone speaker crackled, and a woman's voice said, 'Yes?'

'Alicia. It's Dora.'

I waited for the sound of the lock being released, but there was silence. I pressed the bell again. There was a long pause, then Alicia said, 'You can't come in. Go away.'

'Alicia? It's *me*. *Dora*. Is Jack there? Let me in.' There was another pause, then a click as the lock was released. I barged in before she changed her mind.

She was peering down over the banisters, face pinched and anxious. 'Sorry, Dora. Are you all right?'

'I'm fine,' I said, climbing the stairs towards her. 'Why shouldn't I be?' I was surprised to find her wearing a dressing-gown over dance tights and a naff T-shirt with the *Mona Lisa* on it. Her hair was scraped back into an elastic band. Alicia was normally very finickety about the way she looked.

'Jack phoned this morning,' she said, as though it was quite normal for husbands to phone their wives in order to say things to them. 'He told me not to let anyone into the flat, though I can't believe he meant people we know, like you.'

We went into the living room. There was just enough light filtering through the closed curtains for me to see it was unusually messy – old newspapers and unwashed cups all over the place, and a slightly rancid smell I couldn't identify. Abigail's cot was in the middle of the room, and Alicia's knitting lay on the table, next to a half-finished mug of tea. She asked if I wanted some, and disappeared into the kitchen to pour me a cup. When she handed it over I took a sip and almost choked. It was stone cold.

'Where did Jack call from?' I asked casually.

'Don't know,' she said. 'He sounded funny when I spoke to him. Not like Jack at all.'

I was wondering whether he'd been phoning from Roxy's, and whether it wasn't time someone told Alicia what was going on, when all of a sudden she began to snivel. I looked on, embarrassed, as she wiped her nose with her sleeve. The small bundle of grubby pink blankets in the cot began to whimper in sympathy, and Alicia stared at me accusingly. 'Shit. Now you've gone and woken Abby.'

'Wait a minute,' I said, but she turned to scoop up the baby, and as she did so I caught a glimpse of Abigail's face. It was grey, and the eyes seemed unnaturally black and beady.

It stopped crying for a moment, breathing in with a sort of whiffling noise before opening its mouth for another bawl. 'Christ,' I said. 'It's got a lot of teeth already.'

'*She*,' said Alicia. 'She's not a *thing*. And she's got a *name*, Dora. She's called *Abigail*.'

I didn't really blame Alicia for being tetchy. I would have been tetchy too, if my husband had forbidden me to talk to anyone before buggering off for a dirty weekend with his personal assistant. Then I saw she was rucking up her T-shirt and preparing to feed the baby. I tried not to imagine what might happen when those sharp little teeth fastened on to one of her swollen nipples, but an image of Lulu in the bath popped unbidden into my brain and I began to feel light-headed. 'Don't you think you should give her a bottle or something?' I said. 'I wouldn't breastfeed, if I were you – it's too dangerous.'

Alicia looked amazed and exasperated at the same time. 'Don't be *stupid*,' she said, quite vehemently. 'It's been proved time and again that mother's milk is better than the bottled stuff.'

'I didn't mean it would be dangerous for the *baby*.'

But she had stopped listening. I eyed Abigail doubtfully, and Abigail stared back – rather maliciously I thought. The little beast had stopped crying; now she was licking her lips.

I tried once more. 'Don't do it, Alicia.'

'Oh, for Christ's *sake*!' she yelled. 'You're getting on my nerves, Dora. Why don't you get out of here? You think you can come round and cause trouble. Well, *fuck off*!'

Never before had I known Alicia to lose her temper and swear. Hearing those words from her, of all people, shocked me almost as much as anything else that had happened that weekend. I had no desire to hang around and watch Abigail's feeding time. I left the stone-cold tea on the table, and fled.

SEVEN

I went to Ruth's 'meeting' after all. I had nothing better to do that evening – except stare at the phone, wondering whether I dared interrupt Duncan's orgy of introspection. I went past the gallery, which was showing a wide selection of what appeared to be carpet underlay, and knocked at the door leading up to Matt's office. It was opened by a teenager wearing a black beret and cradling a machine-gun. I wondered if it had been Ruth's father who had provided the hardware.

He looked me up and down. 'Who you, babe?' He wasn't wasting any syllables. I gave my name, and he consulted a small notebook. I was apparently on the guest-list, because he nodded and stepped aside.

'Strict door policy you've got here,' I said, keeping an eye on the barrel of the gun as I squeezed past. 'That won't be a whole lot of use, by the way. Bullets don't stop them.'

'Yeah, they do,' he said. 'Shoot their feet off and the fuckers can't walk.'

The place I'd used as an HQ all those years ago had been

transformed. The threadbare carpets had been replaced by sanded-down floorboards and a couple of plush oriental rugs. Someone had knocked a hole in the roof and inserted a large fanlight, and this, together with an excess of greenery, gave the place the look and feel of a conservatory. It was a clear night; if you looked straight up, you could see the stars. There were stars on the walls as well: signed portraits of pop singers, and a couple of certificates. It seemed that my erstwhile friend Matt was now an important and much sought after director of pop promo videos.

'Dora!' exclaimed Ruth, detaching herself from a bunch of people who were sipping wine and laughing at their own jokes. 'You made it!'

'Well,' I said. 'Look at you.' Yesterday's chic black frock had been replaced by a flak jacket, lumpy army-surplus trousers gathered around the ankles by drawstrings, and a samurai headband printed with some Chinese characters and a red sun motif. I saw her puckering her lips, ready to perform the kissing manoeuvre, and swerved to avoid it.

'Have a drink.' Her eyes fell on my bandages. 'Good Lord, what have you done to your hands?'

'An allergy.'

'Allergy? What kind of allergy?'

I told her I was allergic to broken glass. She made a sympathetic face. 'Poor Dora, you're always doing horrible things to your hands. Oh well, mingle and enjoy yourself. Dino'll be here any minute.'

'*Dino?* You're kidding.'

She shook her head solemnly. 'Our most valuable asset. Our *main man.*' I cringed, but she had already waddled off to greet another arrival. I endeavoured to chat with the other guests, surprised at how much information they had gathered. None of the obvious conclusions had been drawn, but Duncan and I were evidently not alone in our efforts to hold the fort against the rampaging hordes of night's black agents.

I ran into Desperate Dan, who had acquired an additional twenty-two hours' worth of stubble since our last meeting. He reeled off a list of industries which had fallen under Multiglom control in the mean time, Sunday or no Sunday. I talked to a TV presenter who had lost her job after refusing to swap her day shift for a night one, and to an editor of consumer affairs who had been sacked for resisting the drive towards intensive, non-critical coverage of Multiglom-linked products.

I talked to a computer buff who had hacked his way into the Multiglom files and been horrified by what he'd found there – a sort of hit list, he said, with some pretty famous names on it, though he refused to elaborate further. I talked to an advertising copy-writer, and to the sales manager with a firm of kitchenware manufacturers, and to an intense-looking man with a beard who said he was a film director; this last fellow had subjected me to ten minutes of unmitigated boredom before I recognized him.

'Matt,' I said. 'It's Dora.'

He did a double-take. 'I *thought* I'd seen you somewhere before. How long has it been?'

'Thirteen years,' I said, wondering how such a charming young hophead could have turned into this overfed entrepreneur.

'This is really wild, isn't it,' said Matt, or Matthew as I found out he now preferred to be known. He had once changed his surname to Paint, but the age of flippancy was long gone.

I was thankful when our desultory conversation was

interrupted by Ruth, who hollered and waved her arms like a cattle-driver. 'Ssh, everyone. Dino's here. Why don't you fill your glasses and take a seat.'

There was a mad rush to the bar, followed by aimless milling around the half-dozen or so chairs. Most people hunkered down on the floor. Finally, two people were left standing. One was Francine, still in her party frock and looking slightly the worse for wear. The other was a short, bullet-headed individual in a camouflage jacket. Even before he'd scratched his crotch and introduced himself, I guessed who it was.

'We all know what's happening,' Dino began, glaring fiercely at the assembled company. 'And we know what we have to do. We're all British here, so none of us have actually lived under an oppressive Fascist regime. But I've been conferring with the Weinsteins – Ruth's father and *his* father – and, believe me, these are guys who know what they're talking about. *They* lived through the Holocaust. And the way things are going, they reckon this country is turning into something that'll make Nazi Germany seem like a vicar's tea-party. The only way we can stop this happening is if we stand up and fight. We've got to do it, and we've got to do it *now*.'

He paused, possibly for applause that wasn't forthcoming, and went on: 'Me, I've always been a pacifist, but maybe that's because we've never had a cause worth fighting for. Until now. Now, our customs, our traditions, our *way of life* are being threatened by inhuman invaders who will stop at nothing to impose their vile regime. We *must* stand firm – not only for our own sake and the sake of our children, but for the sake of *mankind*. Now – are we going to lie down and let these scumbags walk all over us? Or are we going to stand up and *fight*?'

There was a hubbub of approval. I didn't join in – I was thinking about a dream I'd once had, and wondering whether to keep mum or pipe up. Dino's smarmy expression helped me make up my mind. As soon as the noise died down, I raised my hand.

'You don't have to put your hand up, Dora,' said Ruth.

'Well,' I said, feeling everyone's eyes on me and almost wishing I'd kept my mouth shut, 'it seems to me that you've missed the point.'

Dino was frowning. 'What point? What are you talking about?'

'I don't know whether you can compare all this to Nazi Germany,' I said. 'I think if you *must* use an analogy, it's more like the situation in the Middle East.' There was a ripple of unease, but I pressed on regardless. 'Look at it this way. All down the ages, vampires have been hunted down and persecuted, just because of what they are. Now they've had enough. They've decided to create a haven where they can live and hunt in safety. No more torch-wielding villagers, no more stake-happy vigilantes – just a smoothly run econ-omy and specialized catering facilities. Business goes on as usual, the only difference being that it goes on at night. There wouldn't be a problem if it weren't for *us*. We're in their way, you see. *We're* the Palestinians.'

Suddenly, everyone was yelling at once. Ruth had gone purple with rage and was jabbing a finger in my direction, but I couldn't hear what she was saying because of the racket. Dino looked extremely pissed off at having lost the limelight. I'd had enough of being yelled at, so I tried to direct attention back to him. I said, 'Francine gave us some of your negatives.'

Everyone looked at Francine, who blushed and stared at her shoes.

Dino snarled, 'Who's *us*? You and the PLO?'

Ruth butted in. 'She's talking about *Duncan*. Duncan *Fender*, aren't you, Dora? So why isn't *he* here tonight?'

'Yeah, why isn't *he* here?' asked Dino. 'And why the hell did you give him those negs, you silly bitch?'

'He was a *photographer*,' Francine protested. 'I thought he'd know what to do with them.'

'We sent photos to all the newspapers,' I said, adding lamely, 'No one ran them. Except the *Sunday Sport*.'

Dino slapped his forehead in exasperation. He didn't seem too thrilled about his work appearing in something so downmarket.

'Why should we believe you?' asked Ruth, who was still looking quite flushed. 'You *know* who Duncan is. Why would *he* want to have those photos made public?'

'No, I *don't* know who Duncan is,' I snapped back. 'Or rather I *do* know, but I don't know why you keep going on about it as though all this is his fault.'

They were still staring at me, so I let them have it. 'OK, so he used to go out with a vampire. But as soon as he found out what she was, he put a stop to her. He did, you know. If it weren't for him, all this would have happened thirteen years ago, and we wouldn't be in a position to stand around discussing it.'

There was another uproar. I wasn't sure what had upset them this time. I had assumed that Ruth, at least, would have worked out the connection between Duncan and Violet by now. She was saying something, and she had to repeat herself several times. I finally managed to read her lips. '*Ask him*,' she was saying.

'Ask him *what*?' I mouthed back.

Then I heard her say, quite clearly, 'He doesn't give a fuck *what* she was. He just likes beating the crap out of people.'

'Don't be ridiculous,' I said.

'He's a known sadist,' said Dino, his lip curling.

'Lulu had a shiner only the other week,' Ruth said. 'No wonder she left him.'

'Don't be silly,' I said. 'That wasn't Duncan. She banged into someone at her dance class.'

'Oh *yeah*,' said Dino.

'Pull the other one,' said Ruth.

I was about to protest again, but the meeting was on the verge of fragmenting into petty squabbling. Dino called for order with a sergeant-major roar. The bickering petered out. 'Perhaps Miss Vale would be so kind as to return my negatives as soon as possible,' he said sarcastically. 'But in the mean time, I think we are all in agreement that we are on the same side. If we're to survive, we must stick together. Now, I don't know how many of you know about *Rotnacht* . . .'

Someone volunteered the information that it was a little-known German expressionist film.

'No, no,' said someone else. 'It's a type of soft cheese.'

'Stop it!' snapped Ruth. 'This isn't *funny*. Now, are you going to be serious, or not? Because if not, we might as well forget the whole thing. We're *history*.' She drained her glass and stomped across the room for a refill. My little remark about Palestinians had ruined her entire evening.

Dino took over again. 'If we're not prepared to take this seriously, we'll end up dead, or changed into one of *them*, or worse.'

231

'What could be worse than being one of *them*?' asked the TV presenter. 'The idea of drinking blood makes me feel *sick*.'

'Is it true they never grow old and die?' someone asked. 'Do they ever get ill?'

'Great,' said someone else. 'I could cut out my BUPA payments.'

'Couldn't we give them AIDS?'

'Nuke them!'

'I know, let's emigrate.'

Dino called for silence again. '*Rotnacht*, basically, is the night when the decks are cleared for action, when all opposition is wiped out in one fell swoop, when the garbage is disposed of, for keeps, with extreme prejudice. And when I say garbage — let's not be coy about this — I mean *us*. *Rotnacht* is the night *our* number comes up. That is, if we're not prepared to take a stand and do something about it.'

There was a shout from the back of the room; it might have been Desperate Dan. 'How come *you* know so much?'

This was Dino's cue. He smiled bitterly and said in his best Method actor voice, 'I used to be a part of it. I was part of the original Multiglom set-up. When I saw what they were up to, I got the hell out. They've been on my case ever since.'

He'd seen too many Marlon Brando movies, but I had the feeling he wasn't all bullshit. I wondered how close he'd got to Violet, and I wondered what had made him draw the line and opt out. Had it really been his choice, or was he just trying to save face? One thing was for sure; Dino was not playing at being a freedom fighter for lofty moral reasons. This was personal. He was getting his own back on someone. Just like the rest of us.

Ruth was beaming again, with only the faintest tinge of pink in her cheeks to suggest she had ever blown her top. 'What we really need is to know when *Rotnacht* is planned for. So we can warn everyone.'

Someone asked Dino how come *he* didn't know, since he seemed to know everything else. 'They didn't fix the date until after I left,' he said, with that shifty look you get when someone isn't giving you the whole picture. He stood there a bit listlessly, as though he'd run out of things to say, but Ruth was already gesticulating in my direction. 'Tell us what *you* know, Dora,' she pleaded.

'Not a lot,' I said. 'All the usual stuff. Don't invite anyone into your home. You know about the garlic, and some of you are already wearing crucifixes. Swot up on your Stoker. Watch some Christopher Lee. I would have advised everyone to wear black, so you don't stand out in a crowd, but I see most of you are dressed in black anyway.'

There were a few chuckles at this. Someone asked, 'Why black?'

I shrugged, but everyone was looking at me as though *I* was the expert. I realized I probably was. 'Something to do with absorbing the sun's rays? I don't know. I don't have a degree in biophysics.'

'What do you know about *Rotnacht*?' asked Ruth.

'I'm no wiser than you,' I said.

'But you're closer,' said Dino. No one was paying him much attention now, and he wasn't looking very friendly. 'You're in with the vampire's boyfriend.'

'Oh, for Heaven's sake,' I sighed. 'He *isn't* the vampire's boyfriend, not any more. He *hates* vampires.' I paused, and decided I might as well spill the beans. I couldn't have them

233

thinking Duncan was a traitor to his race. 'As a matter of fact, we staked one only last night.'

There was a shocked hush, followed by an awestruck murmuring. I felt proud of Duncan. For all the fine talk here, no one had yet seen action the way he had.

'Lulu,' Ruth said quietly.

'Let's go get 'em all!' someone yelled.

'Where is this Duncan? We should raise our glasses to him.'

'It's no good plunging straight in without a plan,' said Dino, trying to regain the goodwill he could feel had shifted towards the absent stake-wielder. 'They'll just pick us off one by one. We've *got* to get ourselves organized.'

'It's quite simple,' I said, with a withering look. 'But bloody hard work. You track them down in the daylight, while they're asleep, and you hammer stakes through their hearts. In most cases, that should be enough, but if you want to be on the safe side you give them the garlic treatment as well, cloves up the nose to short-circuit their sense of smell, and then if you *really* want to be on the safe side you drag them into the open and let the sun finish them off.'

'Stake 'em, stun 'em, and sun 'em,' said the copy-writer.

'But what if they've taken over the whole of Multiglom Tower?' asked the computer buff. 'It's a massive place. That'll take for ever.'

'Well, yes, I told you it would be hard work,' I said. 'Perhaps you can suggest a better method.'

'We could negotiate,' someone piped up.

Dino whirled on the speaker. 'Negotiate? With *murderers*? Not only would that be immoral, it would also be extremely dim-witted. We're not talking about the MCC here. This is not cricket, this is *war*.'

'Not yet, it isn't,' said Ruth. 'If we can just find out about *Rotnacht*, we can nip the whole thing in the bud.'

I said, 'I might be able to find out something.'

'You can?'

'I *might*. Give me a couple of days. Can't promise, though.'

'Of course you can find out,' sneered Dino. 'Just ask Fender.'

'Leave Duncan out of this,' I snapped back, and then I remembered something. 'Hey, I was snooping around in the Multiglom Tower,' I said, 'and I found your name and address on the computer.'

Dino looked embarrassed. He glanced sideways to see how many people were still listening. 'So? I told you I used to work there.'

'When your name came up, so did the word *Rotnacht*.'

Dino's face went a pale green colour which toned almost perfectly with his T-shirt.

The meeting broke up. As people began to drift towards the door, Ruth barred their way and shouted for quiet. 'Now you know what we're trying to achieve, perhaps you could persuade some of your friends to come to Tuesday's meeting. The more the merrier. Same time, same place.'

A few minutes later, as I was trying to slip past without her noticing, she caught my arm. 'I've got something for you,' she said, pressing a small paper packet into my bandaged palm. 'For old times' sake.'

'What is it?' I asked, realizing what the packet contained as soon as the words were out of my mouth. 'Thanks,' I said, intending to throw the drugs away as soon as I got outside. 'Oh, and may I make a suggestion?'

'Of *course* you can, Dora.'

'Why not hold your meetings during daylight hours? It would make things so much simpler.'

I left her at the top of the stairs, staring after me with her mouth open.

I made myself a nest of garlic and slept soundly in it, even though the Krankzeits had a visitor and made a great deal of noise overhead. But I was so tired I managed to stay asleep and incorporate all their usual thudding and shouting into my dreams, which for some reason were about Patricia Rice and involved a lot of chasing around. At one point, I woke up and peered out through the curtains and saw her standing perfectly still on the pavement outside, face tilted upward and her gaze fixed on the floor above. I blinked, and then I saw it wasn't Patricia Rice at all, it was Lulu. And then I knew without a doubt that I was still dreaming. Because Lulu was dead.

PART FOUR

ONE

A ll those years, I'd kept my black leather jacket. It was distressed enough to be not really black any more, but it was black enough. I dug out a crumpled black dress which reeked of a perfume I'd stopped wearing ten years ago, and ironed out most of the deep-seated wrinkles and tacked up the hem. But I didn't have any black stockings. I had to go out to the shops and buy some, so while I was there I bought a tube of hair gel and one or two extra items of make-up. I also bought a bottle of the loudest scent I could find – something called Fleur de Paris – and splashed great quantities around while I was getting dressed. It was a vile chemical blend of apples and roses, but I wasn't wearing it to smell sweet. I was wearing it to blot out the aroma of *me*. For the same reason, I had stocked up with twice the usual number of packets of cigarettes. This was going to be the sort of occasion on which my health might depend on chain-smoking.

I didn't normally wear a great deal of make-up, but now

I trowelled on the foundation until my face looked dry and flaky, dull and *very* lifeless, though it still didn't look nearly as bad as Lulu's had done. I carefully painted my mouth in a scarlet bow, and slicked my hair back from my face, and it was only then I began to believe that the plan I had outlined to Duncan might have a fighting chance of working.

I unwound my bandages. The blood had dried and stuck to the dressings, and pulling them off made my eyes water. The palms were still raw. I dabbed at them with TCP and pulled on a pair of black gloves.

I was reluctant to venture out without pockets full of garlic, but the smell was too distinctive, and this was one occasion on which I wouldn't want to stand out from the crowd. I half solved the problem by wrapping some cloves in several layers of kitchen foil and hiding the small package in my make-up case; at least it was there if I needed it. I selected a single rosary and enfolded it in tissue paper before placing it in an old cigar tin which I then buried right at the bottom of Lulu's lizard-trimmed bag. I had a vague notion that the vampire sense of smell was something like the X-ray machine at Heathrow – unable to penetrate metal.

I took one long last look at myself in the full-length mirror in my room. Dora Rosamond Vale, vampire. I thought I looked quite good. I wondered if I would be the same person when I came back. I wondered if I would ever come back at all.

Not liking the idea of being caught half-way across town when the sun went down, I set out early for Molasses Wharf. By the time I got there, it was late afternoon. I marched

straight into Multiglom Tower and announced myself to the
po-faced receptionist. She checked her watch. 'You're four
hours early.'

'I know,' I said. 'But I don't mind waiting.'

She shook her head. 'You can't wait. There's nowhere to
sit.'

'You needn't worry about me.'

'You can't wait here,' she said, this time more emphati-
cally, and I saw her trying to catch the eye of one of the
doormen.

'OK, OK,' I said, 'I'll come back later.'

There was only one place to go.

I crossed the road to the Bar Nouveau.

The oil paintings had been replaced by out-of-focus photographs of cats and dogs, but otherwise the Bar Nouveau was
exactly the same, and once again I was its sole customer.
When I ordered a Perrier, the barman did a double-take. I
thought for a moment he had recognized me, then I realized
it was more likely he was just surprised to see someone up
and about so early.

'How are you, Mr Renfield?' I asked. He squinted at me
suspiciously. I nodded and smiled before taking a seat by
the window and watching as Multiglom Tower reflected the
gathering night, windows glinting pink and navy blue as they
shifted into unfathomable dark. The barman sauntered over
to the jukebox and fed it with a handful of coins. The first
record was a load of scratchy white noise overlaid with a
bored female voice droning on about suicide, but I cheered
up as soon as the needle hit the second platter and Roxy

Music started up. It was just like old times. I hummed along under my breath. '*All I want is the real thing. And a night that lasts for years.*' Then Marc Bolan sang, '*Girl, I'm just a jeepster for your love*', but that was as good as it got. The rest was rinky-dink synthesizer stuff.

Might as well work up a fug in here, I thought, and lit the first of my cigarettes. At about six o'clock a man and a woman came out of the Multiglom Tower and made their way across the street. They were both dressed in black. I steeled myself for the big test. Would they take one look at me and *know*? Or would it be assumed I was one of them? I was clothed not so very differently from the woman. She was yawning as they came in, but her teeth seemed as regular as mine. The man delved into his pocket and slapped some money down on the bar and I heard him say, 'Two halves of Special.' As far as I could see, his teeth were normal too.

The barman muttered something. The man shook his head and was presented with some change and a couple of large Bloody Marys.

Other people drifted in, all of them dressed in black, with pasty faces. All the women and even some of the men were wearing an excessive amount of make-up, but other than that there was nothing unusual about them. Not one of them had an excess in the ivory department, and all could have mingled with a regular night-club crowd without attracting undue attention. One or two of them inhaled deeply, rolling the air around their olfactories and looking a little perplexed as if they'd picked up the suggestion of an unaccounted-for scent, but no one looked twice at me. I was counting on their inexperience, on their not having learned to sniff the difference between bottled claret and haemoglobin on the hoof.

They were all neophytes, I could tell, all new to this game and therefore easier to hoodwink. An old hand like Violet would never have fallen for it.

But they were all drinking 'Bloody Marys', every last one of them. And I knew that if I wanted to blend in, I had to drink one too. My glass of mineral water stuck out like a colourless beacon. I went up to the bar for another drink. I was just going to ask for a Bloody Mary, when I saw the barman looking curiously at me again, so I changed my mind and asked for a half of Special.

The barman stared straight at me and asked, 'Vintage?'

I held my ground and stared straight back. 'What have you got?'

He reeled them off in a bored monotone. 'Ruby Regular. Profondo Rosso. Premier Cruor. Take your pick.'

'Regular.'

'You go easy now,' he said. 'You don't want to drink it all at once.' And he winked at me.

If this was some kind of trap, I wasn't going to fall into it. I didn't even blink, just went on staring with what I trusted was a stony expression. I saw the label on the bottle as he poured it out. A rosy-cheeked infant in diapers beamed out from beneath a date-stamp which vouched that the contents were only six months old and guaranteed free from contamination. I wondered whether the six months referred to the liquid or to the age of the donor.

Back at my table, I gazed at the stuff for a long, long time. The red froth reminded me of Lulu lying in the bath with half her face missing. I tried to convince myself that what I had in front of me was vodka and tomato juice, and after about ten minutes' contemplation I took a tiny sip. The taste was quite unexpected. I had thought it was going to be vile, but it wasn't, not so long as I swallowed straight down without letting too much of it come into contact with the tip of my tongue. Just so long as I pretended it was tomato juice.

I began to relax. I was doing what they were doing. Was there any difference between us? But I could make a single Bloody Mary last for ever. I smoked and, very occasionally, held my breath and sipped. Outside, the street had come alive and was swarming with people. They were just waking up, and it was breakfast time. Some headed uptown, others jumped into taxis and cars and roared off God knows where. Others wandered into the Bar Nouveau for some sustenance to set them up for the long night ahead. The place was hotting up – I had the feeling I would soon be forced to share my table. Sure enough, two men and a woman came up and asked if the seats were being saved. I said no, and they sat down. At first their proximity was unsettling, but once seated they barely glanced in my direction, concentrating on yattering amongst themselves. I tried to keep aloof, but couldn't help eavesdropping. One of the men worked for the advertising department of a magazine. The woman was in publishing. I couldn't catch what the other man did because he had a bad stammer. *Déjà entendu*. I risked another look. The advertising man was dressed all in black except for his red-framed spectacles, and his girlfriend had Rita Hayworth hair – *she wished*. Dexter, Josette, and friend, last seen saving a table down in the Foxhole.

I had a mild panic attack. Without thinking, I picked up my glass and gulped down a mouthful of Ruby Regular. As soon as the metallic taste hit the back of my throat, I started spluttering, and Dexter, Josette and friend turned to look at

me. I raised my glass at them and managed to cough, 'Libiamo, libiamo.' Obviously they didn't share Violet's taste in
music, because they smiled indulgently and turned away,
giving no sign of having recognized me. Of course I was
safe; they hadn't observed me carefully enough to connect
Duncan's subdued companion then with the white-faced red-
lipped creature sitting next to them now.

As I listened to their talk about accounts and magazines
and salaries and mortgages I couldn't help but be disappointed. Being undead didn't seem to make much difference
– they were still talking about the same tired old topics. The
only difference, as far as I could make out, was the way
everyone kept referring to 'nips'.

'Maybe we could pop into Gnashers for a nip,' Dexter
said, and I assumed he meant a small quantity of alcohol
until Josette started bragging that she'd had three 'nips' the
previous night. I didn't think three small quantities of alcohol
was anything to get worked up about, but then they all
swapped 'nip' stories, each trying to top the others with their
nip-counts. I changed my mind and decided they weren't
talking about alcohol but about Japanese people – it wasn't
so wayward an assumption, what with Murasaki and everything – but at last I couldn't escape the conclusion I'd been
trying to evade all along. 'Nip' was vampire slang for human.

When this information sank in, I felt a bit giddy. The bar
was full of the sort of person I encountered every day in the
course of my career; shallow, boring, trivial. It was a shock
to realize they could no longer be dismissed as mentally
defective but basically harmless. They were nothing like
Violet, they didn't have her skills or her style, but the lack
made them, if anything, even less human than she. It was

disturbing to think just how easily they'd crossed the line. They still had a lot of practical things to learn, but they were taking the ethical shift in their stride. Perhaps this was the first time in history when neophytes had ever been able to embrace the circumstances of their radical new existence with a complete lack of moral scruple. They'd already been half-way there in life, and they weren't so very different now they were dead – they were still cramming into bars and talking too much. I had always despised such people, but now – thanks to one of nature's malicious little pranks – they would be looking on me as just another bloody nip.

Even so, it was hard to take them seriously until the student walked into the bar.

This was not a local boy. He had longish hair and wore shabby blue jeans and a hooded grey sweatshirt with GREEN-PEACE appliquéd to the front, and he was carrying a zippered nylon holdall decorated with a recurring Snoopy motif. God knows what he was doing in Molasses Wharf. Perhaps he'd been trying to find the Tower of London and had boarded the wrong train. But he strolled into the bar, grinning cheer-fully, and, in an accent that might have been Canadian, asked for a pint of Moosehead.

The whole place went quiet. Every head swivelled to stare at the newcomer. The barman leant over and whispered something, but the student shook his head and carried on grinning, waiting for his drink. The barman shrugged and picked up a glass and started to fill it from one of the taps.

The hush gave way to a softly swelling murmur. Dexter said, 'I might have known it, I *thought* I could smell a nip in the air,' and Josette nodded and asked, 'Who's going to have him?' and their friend said, 'I g-g-guess it's first c-c-come, first served,' and I could hear similar things being said all around us. Then one or two drinkers got up and, a little self-consciously, started to sidle up to the bar. The student didn't notice a thing until one of them, a tall woman with a mane of curly black hair, rested a hand on his shoulder. He looked at her and his grin vanished, to be replaced by a look of I-don't-believe-my-luck amazement.

'Hul-*lo*,' he said.

'Hi,' she purred back at him. Her fingers wound themselves around his hair, caressing the back of his neck, weaving a spell.

'And what's your name?' he asked. What did he think this was? A singles bar? I felt I should be warning him, or running for help, or something, but I didn't see how I could do it without giving myself away.

'You can call me Dolores,' she replied, continuing to stroke the back of his neck.

'Dolores by name, Dolores by nature, eh?' What a jerk, I thought, but I was still willing him to pick up his bag and get the hell out of there.

Dolores was joined by an angular man in a black polo-neck and leather jacket and dark glasses. He too began to stroke the student's neck. The student wasn't so keen on this unexpected new development. 'Hey, hang *on* . . .' And then he saw the others moving towards him. 'Hey, what is this? You weirdos or what? I'm not into . . .'

His voice tailed off as Dolores's lips parted in a brilliant smile and he saw her teeth. So did I. I wondered where she'd been hiding them. 'This is a joke, right?' he said. 'This has got to be a joke.'

At last it dawned on him that it wasn't a joke at all. I saw the barman duck down out of sight as though he expected a gang of Mafia hitmen to charge into the room at any second. The student had seen *The Godfather* too, and he suddenly let out a frightened squawk and tried to worm free of Dolores' caress, but she raised her other hand and brought it down again in a flamboyant swooping gesture, like the dropping of a sword to signal the beginning of a cavalry charge, and the student's eyes snapped wide open in shock and disbelief. Her fingernails flashed scarlet. I thought this was a piece of theatre, just for show, until I saw the broad gout of crimson gushing in stops and starts from his ruptured throat.

There was a loud communal *aaahhh* – the sort of noise one associates with a packed cinema audience getting a glimpse of cute babies and animals – and then they were all over him, clustering around in a panic, jostling, trying to position their open mouths beneath the drinking fountain. The student sank beneath their onslaught without another word. I was thankful I couldn't see him any more. What I *could* see was not a pretty sight. Table-manners were shot to hell. Chairs went flying as the smell reached those who had been hanging back, trying to play it cool, and the urge became too strong to resist. Their teeth had suddenly sprouted as if by magic. They scrabbled and grunted, not caring what they drank from, so long as they drank. I saw a grey sweatshirt, shredded and stained, trampled on the floor. Briefly, I glimpsed a trainer with the foot still in it rolling out from beneath the scrum, but it was immediately snatched up. I saw one or two things which looked like giblets held up in the air and sucked dry.

I was watching, hypnotized by the spectacle, when it

occurred to me that I was the only one left sitting down. It was a bad moment. I stood up and meandered, trying to make it look as though I was taking part, though the noises coming from the crowd were making me feel sick. My foot slid and I looked down and recoiled – I had skidded on a stray bloodclot. But then I thought better of it, and dipped down to smear some of it on my chin, trying to make it look as though, like everyone else, I'd had a couple of mouthfuls. No one was paying much attention, but it was better safe than sorry, better red than dead, especially now I'd seen them in full swing. This was a mob in heat; they confirmed all my worst fears about crowds. They made Violet look positively civilized.

It was over as suddenly as it had begun. One minute, mayhem. The next, customers were wiping their small, neat mouths and returning to their chairs and smoothing their hair down and chatting and smoking and retouching lip-gloss, raising halves of Special as though nothing had happened, though here and there one could still see a fine red stipple on their dead white flesh. The barman emerged with a dustpan and brush and began to shovel what was left on the floor into a black plastic bin-bag, but there wasn't an awful lot left to shovel. There were a few bones, and what looked like scraps of desiccated parchment. I tried to work out how far a single student would have gone around the sixty or so people in the bar. Even though he'd been burly, it couldn't have been far. They must each have got only a morsel. But the chat was more animated now, and a dozen people quickly knocked back their drinks and stalked off into the night as though questing for an entrée to back up their bite-sized *hors-d'oeuvre*. Juices were flowing.

There was an aching, empty feeling in the pit of my stomach, and a bitter taste at the back of my throat, all mixed up with the sour tang of Ruby Regular, and I began to wonder what the hell I was doing. I lit a cigarette with a hand which I willed to keep steady, and, as I did so, noticed to my annoyance that one of my gloves was wet. I hadn't intended to get quite so much of the student's blood on me. I was in the process of peeling the glove away from my hand when I heard Josette saying, 'That's funny. I can still smell him.' And then I saw Dexter peering in my direction, gazing at me with an interested but not entirely comprehending expression. I looked down at my hand and saw that the palm was gently but steadily weeping a thin mixture of blood and pus.

I closed it into a fist before Dexter could see.

This was hopeless. It was all going wrong. I'd been imagining it would be like my encounter with Fitch in Violet's garden, but the memory of the power I'd felt then must have turned my head. This was no longer a game. It was me on my own against sixty of them: not good odds.

I got up, straining to appear casual, but evaluating potential escape routes in the turmoil of my mind: (a) from my current position to the main exit was roughly thirty feet, with about five tables and ten standing customers in the way; (b) from my current position to the emergency exit was across a bare stretch of floor in full view of the dozens of customers who were standing at the bar, and after that would be required a great many complicated weaving manoeuvres through the tables nearest the door; (c) from my current position to the Ladies toilet was less than ten feet, and I had to pass only three people directly.

I went for this last option. It was the only door I could
be sure of reaching before my stomach heaved one last heave
and I threw up. Half-way there, I was hit by an attack of the
cramps, but I struggled on to the swing door. Inside was a
sort of small, useless airlock and another door leading
directly into the Ladies. I splashed cold water on my face
and tried to sharpen my wits until, behind me, the outer
door creaked. Just in time, I tucked myself away in the
nearest cubicle. I could hear stiletto heels clattering over
the floor, then there was a crash and a sigh and the sound
of someone in the cubicle next to me. Vampires, it seemed,
had to attend to their routine bodily functions like the rest
of us.

I kept quiet and waited. While I waited. I did what I
usually did in the circumstances – I read. I read the graffiti
on the back of the door, and I read the small print on the
wrappings of the spare toilet-rolls, and I read the instructions
on the Tampax machine.

And as I was reading – insert coin in slot, pull knob, etc
– that sick feeling in my gut returned, but this time I knew
what it was. I'd had sick feelings in my gut many times over
the past few days. It hadn't been so surprising considering
what I'd been through, but now the feeling was much, much
worse. A kind of dull ache, which ebbed and flowed in a
great tidal wave even as I grasped its significance.

I was trapped in the middle of a bar full of vampires who
flew into a feeding frenzy at the smell of fresh blood. And
there was plenty of fresh blood here. The reopened wound
in my hand was pumping, fresh and tasty, come and get it,
but that wasn't the worst of it. My ovaries had always been
regular as clockwork and they weren't about to let me down

now, even though the time of the month had slipped my mind, as it usually did until the cramps weighed in to remind me.

Oh, great. Now I was really for it.

I didn't know how I was going to get out of this one.

My period had started. Bang on time.

TWO

I inserted a twenty-pence piece into the tampon machine and extracted a packet of two. And, because I didn't know what else to do, I stayed where I was and read the small print on the packaging. And that was how I learned the tampons were no longer being manufactured in Havant, Hants; the address was now somewhere near by in Molasses Wharf. I should have been formulating some ruse to extricate myself from this predicament. Instead, I sat there wondering whether female vampires menstruated and, if so, what they did with their used tampons.

It felt as though aeons had passed, but according to my watch I'd been in there only ten minutes. Time itself had slowed to a crawling pace; there was still more than an hour before my appointment. I was beginning to think it might be a good idea to skip it. Perhaps I could hunker down for the night where I was, and take off at dawn in complete safety. In the absence of a better plan, I stuck with this one for a while, but then things started to get a little hairy.

While I sat and gibbered, there was a lot of the coming

and going common to the toilets of all pubs, clubs, and discos. People clip-clopped in and out of cubicles, chattering aimlessly about whether so-and-so was going out with whats-isname, or which lipstick best complemented one's dead-white skin, or whether it was better to go for the jugular or the carotid. There was a fair amount of giggling, and I even thought I detected the telltale tippety-tap of metal on por-celain, the familiar and rather nostalgic sound invariably followed by that porky little snuffle as illegal substances were inhaled.

Every so often, someone would try to open my door and find it locked.

Only now, someone was knocking and asking if I was all right.

'I'm fine,' I said, a bit too quickly.

There was a pause. There was breathing, and clip-clop-ping heels. Then more clip-clops, different ones. The clip-clops mingled. Another voice. 'What's going on?'

'She's been in there ages. I think she's ill.'

'No, I'm not,' I said, but I couldn't think of another excuse for staying cooped up for so long, so I added, 'I'll be all right in a sec.'

'Are you sure?'

'I'll be *fine*. I just need to be on my own for a little while.' Now I was sounding like Duncan. I wondered whether they could smell the blood.

Then the first voice said, 'Are you *sure* you're all right?'

'Absolutely,' I chirrupped. 'No problem.' For God's sake, *go away*, I thought.

'Are you new to this? Are you feeling rough? Would you like me to get you a drink? Ruby? Profondo Rosso?'

The thought of a pint of Profondo Rosso instantly made me want to throw up. 'No,' I groaned. 'Oh, no thanks.'

'She *does* sound ill,' murmured the second voice. 'Is she with someone? Maybe we should get the manager.'

'I *thought* that guy tasted funny. A bit gamey, I thought. Obviously hadn't bathed for weeks – I can still smell him.'

'I'll be out in a minute,' I said quickly, trying to sound perky, but not so perky that I was ready to emerge right that instant. 'I feel better already. Really I do.'

'If you're sure.' There was the noise of two pairs of retreating heels, then the clip-clops parted company and one set paused and came back. 'Look, what you need is a good swig of plasma. It'll make you feel much better. Hang on a bit, and I'll get you some.' She was off again before I could protest. A do-gooding, busy-body, nosey-parker kind of vampire. This was all I needed.

When I was certain she'd gone, I left the cubicle. In the mirror I saw my lipstick was smudged, so I quickly retouched it and squirted another blast of Fleur de Paris all around my neckline. Then I scrunched the bloodied glove under the cold tap and wrung it out and stretched the sodden fabric back over my suppurating palm. It smarted something rotten, as though I'd been rubbing it with sandpaper. The other hand wasn't so bad, but I felt as though I were radiating waves of human scent.

Just then, over the noise of the running tap, my ears picked up a small, neat chopping noise coming from one of the cubicles behind me. I'd thought I was on my own, but now I realized someone else was here, operating under cover of the water. I reckoned she'd be waiting for the coast to clear before she emerged, but I wasn't wasting any more time

– I dug out the cigar tin and unwrapped the rosary and wound it snugly around my bloodied glove and then buried the hand in the pocket of my jacket. I was going to aim straight for the main entrance. With any luck, the cross would be sending out enough anti-vampire vibrations to make them want to steer clear without knowing why.

I snatched one last long look in the mirror, and held it just a few beats longer than I should have done. It was dispiriting to realize how closely I resembled the rest of the clientele. And then I did a double take, and my stomach fell through the floor. Behind me, the cubicle door was opening. And, of course, nobody was coming out. It was just me, alone with my reflection. I made myself turn around, quite slowly, and as I turned I heard a little sniffle, followed by a little sigh.

She looked as if she'd downed a few too many Rubies. Strands of mousy-coloured hair had escaped from her chignon and were spilling over one of her eyes. Her make-up needed reapplying – especially around the nostrils – her nose was running, and her mascara smeared where she'd been rubbing her eyes. And then there were the large, greenish-grey blisters on one side of her face – blisters which even the thick foundation failed to conceal.

Of all the toilets in the world, Patricia Rice had to walk into mine.

And I thought the jig was up until I remembered she wouldn't know me from Eve, because she'd never set eyes on me before, so I gave her my best ring of confidence and headed towards the door. She loped alongside me in a chummy manner until something pulled her up short and she swung into my path. 'Wait a minute,' she said, racking what few brains she had. 'This is very strange. I can see your reflection.'

'Not really,' I said. 'It's this new type of mirror they've just developed in the Pharmasan labs, especially for putting on vampire make-up.'

She frowned, and for a moment I thought I was going to get away with it. No such luck: she was dumb, but not *that* dumb. She squinted at the mirror, then back at me. 'But I can't see *me*,' she said, her voice rising in shrill excitement. 'You're a nip, aren't you? My God, you *are*. You're a nip *spy*.'

There was no time to think, because she grabbed at me. All I did was bring my hand up out of my pocket to fend her off. There was a dull crunch as the knuckles mashed into her cheek, but it wasn't my fist which hurt her so much as the rosary wrapped around it, and the blisters instantly cracked and spurted a greenish liquid. She backed away from me, clawing at her steaming complexion and making a noise like a whistling kettle. I charged through the doors, pausing in the airlock to thrust my fist back into my pocket, and then I took a deep breath and sauntered back into the bar. I felt horribly exposed, but no one was looking. They all went on chattering and drinking and being boring, so I started to pick my way through them. I went past where I'd been sitting and, out of the corner of my eye, glimpsed Dexter and Josette and their friend. I could feel Dexter's eyes boring into the back of my skull; he was trying to put his finger on what it was about me that had piqued his curiosity. I had no intention of hanging around long enough for him to figure it out.

I wasn't thinking far ahead, but I had a vague idea that if only I could reach the Multiglom reception desk, I'd be safe. I was counting on the black clothes, brisk pace, and garlic to see me through the night. The receptionist could call me a cab to take me back to W11. All I had to do was get out of the bar. I squeezed past some standing customers, and wove around some tables, and the Exit sign was there, right in front of me. I was so close I could have stretched out and grasped the door handle. I was so close I could almost have punched a hole through the glass and flexed my fingers in the night air. So close, but not close enough, because at that moment there was an almighty crash. In front of me, the glass door quivered in sympathy, and I knew my number was up. Someone shouted, '*Stop her!*' and then there were other voices, and I couldn't work out whether they were shouting or sighing or gasping, but the sound was elemental, like the ocean trying to rip pebbles off a beach. This was it. This was the beginning of the end. I'd made a complete mess of things, and now I would never see Duncan again.

Even then, there was a residual thought that, if only I wanted to badly enough, I could still make it to the door. And I wanted to very badly indeed. There was an outside chance all that yelling had nothing to do with me, so I pretended not to notice it, and prepared for one last desperate lunge. I might have made it, too, if the slimeball sitting near by hadn't stuck out his leg and tripped me up. As I scrabbled for balance, someone else sank his fingers so hard into the fleshy part of my upper arm that it made me squeak with pain and I brought the rosary back out of my pocket and clouted him with it. He fell back screeching and clutching at his face, just as Patricia Rice had done. I liked the effect, but I didn't get a chance to try it again because I was spun round, and dragged back, and then somebody did something to the nerves in my arm which made my fingers jerk open of their own accord. The rosary dropped to the floor, and someone kicked it away and I couldn't see it any more. The first thing I saw when I looked up was Patricia Rice standing on a table, her legs splayed out like a striptease artiste, hair flying all over the place and half her face mashed into raw hamburger with cucumber relish. She was pointing a finger and shrieking that she'd seen me, *in the mirror*, and she didn't have to stop and explain, because they all *knew*.

Now I was on the receiving end of their attention, they didn't look in the least bit human. How could I ever have imagined I would blend in? They loomed over me, jockeying for position with the points of their elbows, the hunger sharpening their features so they looked like painted demons. I could smell their breath, and it was worse than bad – it was like the gas coming up from a bucketful of pig's entrails left too long in the sun. And their colour was unnatural; under the white lighting their skin was flat and dead, and the make-up made it look like mouldy old dough.

But I got a grip on myself. I told myself sternly I wasn't like the student, I wasn't some hapless nip who had strayed in off the street. And this had obviously thrown them off balance. They couldn't work out what I was doing there, dressed and made up to look like one of them. I glared defiantly, and – I hoped – a little contemptuously. Dead or alive, they were scum and I wanted them to know it. They had led worthless lives and now they were leading equally worthless deaths.

'Let's party,' hissed the man who had made me drop the rosary. Once he had been fat, but death had left him sagging like a perished balloon. He pinched my arm like someone testing an oven-ready chicken and licked his once-plump lips with a rasping sound.

'Wait.' He was held up by a woman with eyes so pale they were almost transparent. 'We should question her. What's she up to?'

'And who else knows about it?' snarled a man with a nose like a vulture's beak. Ex-Lardo rounded on Vulture Man and sneered. 'What does it matter who knows? Nothing can stop us now. *Rotnacht* here we come.' At mention of the R-word, there was an outbreak of shushing. It was some sort of military code, like Operation Sealion or Market Garden, a nip too far, and careless whispers could prove costly.

'Ssshh. Don't even *talk* about you-know-what in front of nips.'

'They might as well know they've got it coming.'

Some of them were bickering now. I felt myself being pushed and shoved and pulled, first one way, then the other, until it started to hurt. So this was how it was going to end. It might have been my imagination, but out of the corner of my eye I thought I saw the barman shrug in resignation and duck out of sight once more.

But no, I wasn't like the student. I wasn't going to stand for this shoddy treatment. If they'd homed straight in, I wouldn't have had a chance, but the squabbling had given me heart. It helped me forget the masks and see them as I'd seen them before – as little people with tiny brains and no imagination, drones who hadn't a hope in hell of doing things properly.

Unfortunately, Ex-Lardo came to a unilateral decision. 'I don't give a toss,' he said to no one in particular, and raised one of my arms to his mouth. His breath warmed the inside of my wrist as he paused to seek the most direct tap into the vein. So disagreeable was this sensation that I started babbling for all I was worth: 'Stop it I wouldn't do that if I were you *Violet* wouldn't like it *Rose Murasaki* wouldn't like it or *Clara Weill* or *Livia* or whatever she's calling herself nowadays.'

This was the trump I'd been holding in reserve, but now I was hoping like mad we were still playing the same game, that the cards hadn't been shuffled and dealt out in a different order while I hadn't been looking. As the words left my mouth, I began to have doubts. What if they'd never heard of her? What if we'd been wrong, and she hadn't come back after all? What if they were so hungry they didn't *care*?

But it did the trick. It was as though my arm had suddenly turned white-hot. Ex-Lardo dropped it and stared, blinking stupidly. There was a hush, broken by a disgruntled muttering.

'Rose Murasaki?'

'Who's Violet?'

'You mean you don't *know*?'

'Murasaki.'

'Better not touch.'

'Rose'll go mad.'

Three of them still had me in their grip, and though they weren't tugging any more, they showed no signs of wanting to let me go. Nobody was quite sure what to do. I avoided looking at any of them directly; I didn't want them to see I was bluffing. Instead, I stared at the floor, concentrating on the footwear – an assortment of brogues, winkle-pickers, cha-cha heels, and satin slippers, patent or suede, but all of them, every last blasted shoe, in black and black and black.

Then, without warning, I felt myself released. I saw the feet shuffle and regroup, making way for other feet which were coming my way. They advanced without the slightest hint of urgency, and it was by his feet that I recognized him, even though the boots had changed. They were a peculiar, pock-marked hide, cut wide and handsome like cowboy boots and stacked up on chunky dirt-digging heels which had been worn down so far on the inside edge that he rolled as he walked, a bit like a landlocked sailor. In any other circumstances, I would have feared for my life. But I was fearing for my life already. And at least these boots weren't black.

I looked up.

'Well, look who's here,' said Grauman. He wasn't smiling.

I asked him what had happened to the snakeskin. 'I am going through an ostrich phase,' he said, looking round. 'I was told there was a disturbance in the farmyard. I had no idea it would be you.' He sighed. 'You had better come along with me, before these people force you to provide them with the next round of drinks.' I tucked in right behind him as he retraced his steps. The vampires fell back, but gracelessly. He had spoiled their fun and they resented his presence. Some of them grumbled rebelliously, but none dared touch.

It was only when we were well out of earshot, when he'd got me outside and had grabbed me by the wrist and dragged me half-way across the road to the Multiglom Tower, that he dipped his head and hissed into my ear, 'This time, you little bitch, I will see you boiled in oil before I let you make a fool out of me.'

I'd gained time, at least, and I didn't really think I was

going to be boiled in oil. The death of a thousand cuts, perhaps, or my spine snapped in a dozen different places, but I couldn't see him resorting to the oil option because it would have been over far too quickly.

We went straight into the Multiglom Tower, and no one lifted a finger to stop us, neither the neo-Nazi guards nor any of the other figures that were flitting around.

'You wanted to get to see Violet,' said Grauman, as the revolving doors propelled us smoothly into the white marble reception. 'You did, didn't you? Well, you will get to see her now.'

THREE

He leaned against the wall of the elevator and looked me up and down. 'Dora Rosamond Vale. Just what do you think you are playing at?'

We were going down – a long way down. Multiglom Tower had hidden depths, like an iceberg. I checked my watch and saw it was a quarter to nine. 'I have an appointment in fifteen minutes.'

'With Murasaki?' For a few seconds there, I thought I'd caught him off guard. 'But of course you know about Murasaki.'

'Of course,' I said. 'It's obvious. *Murasaki* is the Japanese word for *purple*.'

If Grauman was impressed by this demonstration of arcane learning, he showed no sign of it. 'Your watch has stopped,' he said. 'It is now nearly ten o'clock.' He paused, then added, 'And what makes you think she won't drain your veins as soon as she sets eyes on you?'

'Perhaps she will, but I was hoping to play it by ear.'

For the first time he allowed himself to look faintly

amused, but I didn't flatter myself it was anything I'd said. More likely he was imagining how I'd look with my veins drained. 'So you dress up like a Halloween witch? You think you will disarm her like that?'

'Well, *they* fell for it.'

'Sure they did. Oh yes, it certainly looked that way when I arrived.'

'They *did* – until someone saw my reflection in the mirror.'

He chuckled. 'Mirrors! Damned mirrors! We all see things in them that we do not want to see.'

Speak for yourself, I thought, but I didn't dare say it out loud. The thirteen years had left their mark on him. I guessed he would be in his mid-forties, but his hair was the same old straw colour, and now I was certain it was bleached. It was tied back in a ponytail, and he was wearing a scuffed leather jacket instead of the Turkish bazaar number, and straight jeans instead of flares, but there was still something about him which made my flesh crawl.

I asked him whether he was taking me to see Violet. 'If you like.' He shrugged, then put his head on one side and regarded me thoughtfully. 'So you are here as a delegate of Duncan Fender?'

'Not at all. I'm an independent operator.'

He nodded sceptically. 'I would very much like to believe that, but I have learned from experience that I must take everything you say with a pinch of salt.'

The lift stopped and we stepped out into a concrete-lined room upholstered with cream-coloured leather. 'Please take a seat,' Grauman said, and vanished through a door to his left.

I took a seat; there wasn't much else to do. Nothing to look at: no windows, no pictures, no magazines. I was in Multiglom Tower all right, and I wasn't sure if I'd ever be able to find my way out again. I felt as though we'd journeyed to the centre of the earth. The subterranean silence was oppressive, broken only by the creaking of leather whenever I adjusted my position. This was often, because I was still suffering from headaches and stomach cramps. I wished I'd remembered to bring some Paracetamol.

After a few minutes, Grauman reappeared and sat next to me, spreading his knees, the way men do, so that one of his legs was nestling uncomfortably close to my thigh. I tried to wriggle away, but space was limited and I didn't want to show I'd noticed his proximity and was made uncomfortable by it. I hadn't been looking forward to seeing him again, not after what I'd done, but now he was here, it was almost like meeting up with an old friend – an old friend whom you intensely disliked and distrusted, who you knew had every reason to want you dead – or worse.

'Show me your hand,' he said.

My head was still dancing with playing card metaphors, and I didn't respond, so he reached out and took my wrist, wrinkling his nose as he stripped the soggy glove off in a single rapid movement and let it drop to the floor. He lifted my hand the way you might lift a dead animal, and held it up in front of his face, scrutinizing it with interest over the top of his spectacles. He seemed particularly intrigued by the missing joint.

'Well,' he said eventually, 'what a mess you have made,' and he smiled a thin-lipped smile and deliberately jammed his thumb into the palm. I yelped with pain and tried to snatch it away, but he merely tightened his grip.

He glanced sideways at me. 'So, Miss Vale. Which finger would you like me to break first?'

I stared at him aghast. He grinned wolfishly, and I saw the past thirteen years had not been kind to the teeth he had worried about so much. 'Just kidding,' he cackled. 'I like to have fun with you, Dora. I know you have a very peculiar sense of humour. Just like me.' And he carefully replaced the hand in my lap, back where he'd found it. 'I should have that attended to, if I were you. The smell of the blood is very strong, and the streets are full of sharks.'

He got to his feet and walked over to the door. 'Murasaki will see you now,' he said, holding it open. He stayed on the outside.

I went in.

I walked into darkness. The only light was from the doorway, and when Grauman shut that, there was nothing. It was pitch black.

But there was sound. There was music, some sort of tuneless singing in a language I couldn't identify. I had no choice but to stand and listen as it swelled to a climax and tapered away.

After a while, I heard her say, from somewhere in front of me, 'Forgive me, but you were a few minutes early. *Več Makropoulos* by Leoš Janáček. You know it?' The voice was soft, little more than a whisper, but somehow it bypassed my eardrums and penetrated directly into my brain. I shook my head. I assumed she could see me, even if I couldn't see her.

'It is about a woman who is three hundred years old. She has been good, and she has been bad. Now she realizes it makes no difference whether she sings or keeps silent. Life no longer has meaning.' She paused to let her words sink in, though I had understood them perfectly.

After a while, she went on: 'I listen to this piece of music at least twice a day. I would like to take this opportunity of recommending it to you. Then perhaps you will come to see things the way I see them.' The voice was coming from behind me now, even though my ears had picked up no sound of movement.

'I am not what I seem,' she said.

I tried to turn round, but misjudged the manoeuvre badly and nearly toppled over. The darkness had stolen my sense of balance as well as my sense of direction. She waited longer than was necessary before saying, 'But my dear child, what am I thinking of? You can't see a thing. Let me provide you with some illumination.'

There was the swish of rapid movement, followed by the dull click of a switch being pressed. The lamp cast a small pool of light on to the desk-top where it stood, but it didn't do much to brighten the rest of the room. I blinked, trying to accustom my eyes to the contrast between light and shade.

'Sit down if you like.' The voice came from the darkness beyond the desk. 'I am not going to hurt you. At least, not yet.'

I could think of several cute answers to that, but swallowed them all. Now was not the time to be cute. I groped around and found an armchair.

'Now let us get things straight,' the voice continued. 'I know your name is not Patricia Rice. I know who you are. You have grown older, but I remember you, Dora. I still have the taste of your blood in my mouth.'

I held up my left hand with its four and a half fingers. 'Ah yes,' she said. 'And I can see *you* remember *me*.' She sounded genuinely amused. 'Andreas tells me you led him a merry dance, like Medea. He would have killed you, you know, if you hadn't forced him to stop and pick up the pieces.'

'I know. That's why I did it.'

There was a sound which might conceivably have been a chuckle. 'Tell me, do you *like* Andreas?'

The question caught me off guard. I wondered whether to lie, but I had the feeling she would know instantly if I didn't tell her the truth. 'I can't stand the sight of him,' I said.

She emerged from the shadows far enough for me to see her face floating in the darkness like a white mask. The rest of her was black on black. 'You can't stand the sight of him,' she echoed. 'And he can't stand the sight of you. This is an excellent start, don't you think?'

I was immediately on the defensive. 'What do you mean?'

She sighed. 'At one time, I had high hopes for the two of you. That is why I wouldn't let him have you killed, even though there was nothing in the world he wanted more. His pride was damaged, you see. He is only human, after all, with an inclination towards rash action which he may later regret. All these years, you've owed your life to me. How do you feel about that?'

I wasn't sure what to reply. The idea of *me* and *Andreas Grauman* – *together* – was so preposterous I wanted to burst out laughing, but if this was what it took to keep my veins undrained, I certainly wasn't about to pour cold water on it. 'Grateful, I suppose.'

'Poor Andreas.' She sighed again. 'Fate has not been kind to him, and neither have I. I suppose I should feel guilty, but I don't. When you get to my age, you don't feel guilty about anything much. But I should like to see him happy. And I know – better than he knows himself – what will be good for him.' The white mask danced and settled down behind the desk and tilted forward into the pool of light. The lips were very red. The lashes cast long shadows on her cheeks. 'And why are you here? They said you were looking for freelance work. Is this true?'

'In a manner of speaking. I'm always on the lookout for career opportunities.'

'And what is it that you do?'

'Creative consultancy.'

'Oh yes, one of those non-jobs. It means whatever you want it to mean, am I right? Well, in that case I am sure we can find some use for you in the teeming multinational network that is Multiglom.' Her voice had taken on the barest hint of sarcasm. '*Quocunque modo.*'

I sensed the interview was coming to a close, and abruptly leapt in with both feet. 'The truth is,' I said, taking a deep breath, 'we've known for some time that you're back.'

'We?'

I kept quiet. The white mask stared at me impassively, then it said, 'I assume you refer to yourself and Duncan. Tell me, did he receive my *billet-doux*?'

'You mean the note?'

'I mean the note. I mean the girl, as well. You might say she was a love letter also. What was her name? Laura? Louise? I trust Duncan had fun with her.'

The room seemed very cold all of a sudden. I felt my skin prickle. 'Her name was Lulu. Yes, I think he had fun.'

'Like he had fun with me. Though, of course, I had a lot more staying power. No one is capable of providing quite so much fun as I.'

'Of course not,' I agreed.

'Would you like to see what he did?'

'Not really.'

'Well, I am going to show you anyway.' A white hand floated up and peeled back some of the blackness surrounding the mask. She tipped her head back to give me a better view of the neck. It was encircled with a thick line of puckered scar tissue, a scarlet necklace marking the place where the head had been fixed back on to her shoulders.

I said, 'I don't know what to say.'

'I have many such mementoes. Our surgeons wanted to get rid of them. They can do that now, you know, especially in Japan, which is where Andreas took my parts for reassembly. But I wouldn't allow it. Scars are important to me; they are the nearest I will ever get to the creases of old age.'

'Most people try to avoid wrinkles.'

'Most people,' she said, 'are not three hundred years old. Please believe me when I say you can have too much of a good thing. Now I want to ask you a question.'

I nodded. She extended her arms towards me. There was one white hand, and there was the other, which was encased in a black leather glove. She started to peel the glove off, and I wanted to ask her not to, but didn't dare. What was underneath was flesh-coloured, but was not flesh. She flexed the fingers, and I heard the faint mechanical gurgle of an hydraulic apparatus operating beneath the artificial skin.

'You see? I should like to know what happened to the hand.'

In my mind I saw a mass of fizzing bubbles attacking a lump of white marble. 'What do you mean?'

The fingers flexed and gurgled. 'Don't be afraid. You can tell me. What did you do with it? I would simply like to know.'

I eyed the mechanical hand. I didn't want it coming any nearer. I told her what I'd done. The acid, then the parcel.

There was a flicker of a reaction. 'So,' she said. 'A part of my anatomy is on public display in a far country. I guessed it had to be something like that. An eye for an eye. A hand for . . . a fingertip. Not much of a bargain from my point of view, is it?'

There was a silence, and then I plucked up courage to say, 'Perhaps I can ask you a question in return.'

She gazed at me evenly. 'Of course.'

'What are you trying to do here?'

She paused, as if to consider the implications of this, though I hadn't meant it to sound so complicated. 'Here in Molasses Wharf, you mean? Or in this room now? Or here on earth? I am merely looking after . . . other people's interests. I am a figurehead, nothing more.'

'And what do you want from Duncan?'

'Oh, now we're really getting down to it,' she said, suddenly smiling in a way which turned my blood to ice. 'That is more than one question, you know, but I will answer all the same.'

I didn't see how she did it. Not once did I take my eyes off her, nor did I see her move, but one second she was on the far side of the desk, and the next she was right in front of me, blotting out the light so she was no longer black and white, but all shades of darkness, and grasping me by the armpits, hoisting me out of the chair so my feet were dangling in mid-air. I struggled to refill my lungs, but they seemed already to be bursting. Her eyes were so close I couldn't focus on them properly, but I saw enough there to make me try and twist my head away. Her breath was not like that of the vampires in the bar; it was dead, but sweet, and it made me feel weak.

She continued to speak in the same mild, even voice as before. 'You must understand,' she said, 'that Duncan is mine. He always has been mine and he always will be mine. He is the only thing – *the only thing* – I care about in this wretched existence, and if you interfere again I will kill you.'

She dropped me back into the chair and turned away in disgust. 'You smell like a slaughterhouse. If you wish to survive the night, you had better get my Hatman to take you home. Now get out.'

Back in the concrete-lined room, Grauman was sitting with his hands behind his head and ostrich boots up on the leather upholstery. He watched with a disinterested expression as my knees gave way and I collapsed on to the seat opposite and took a number of very slow, very deep breaths, trying to slow down my galloping pulse.

'The headmistress was strict, huh?'

Her last words were still echoing in my head. The journey to W11 stretched in front of me like an endless void and I knew I couldn't make it on my own. 'She said you're to take me home.'

'But of course,' he said, looking at his watch. 'Say in about one hour. Then we can get a lift. I have no wish to negotiate the London Underground. Can you walk?'

I nodded.

'Then perhaps you would care to inspect the penthouse while we wait?' I nodded again, not really listening. He could have broken every single one of my fingers just then and I wouldn't have felt a thing.

He got up and disappeared for a few minutes. I breathed in and out, counting slowly. When he came back he was wearing some kind of shit-eating grin.

As the lift shot upward, I felt the silence of the tomb fall away from my ears. It was replaced by a rapid-fire popping. 'The hospitality suite,' Grauman announced as the door slid open. 'Fiftieth floor.' We stepped out on to a black marble floor which reflected the floor-to-ceiling windows. The city stretched out in all directions, bright lights on a matt black background. 'Hampstead,' said Grauman, waving his arms like a ringmaster. 'Westminster. Crystal Palace.'

'Very impressive,' I said, wishing I could get more worked up about it.

'Let me get you a drink. I mean a real drink, none of that Profondo Rosso, or whatever they call it. You tried it, yes? And it was the vilest thing you have ever tasted, am I right? I too have tried it, and it was completely revolting. Perhaps you have started to wonder how anyone can ever develop a taste for such unpleasant stuff. I ask myself such questions all the time.'

I eyed him warily as he produced a bottle of Bollinger from the refrigerated bar. 'What is there to celebrate?'

'A new era,' he said, removing the wire and easing the cork out with his thumbs. 'A new city – one in which the trains run on time. And a new collaborative spirit. I gather Murasaki offered you a job.'

'Sort of,' I said, still suspicious. He was being too chummy by half.

The cork came out with a gentle *phut* and he filled a

couple of glasses and handed me one. 'To this new job of yours, whatever it turns out to be,' he said, raising his glass. I raised mine back and took a sip and instantly felt a whole lot better. Grauman lowered the bottle into a bucket and packed it with ice. 'Let us sit over here for a while and savour the view,' he said, settling down into a seat by one of the windows and patting the empty place next to him.

I hesitated, feeling manipulated. 'Did Violet tell you to bring me up here?'

He seemed genuinely puzzled. 'Of course not. Why should she?'

'You're being very friendly all of a sudden.'

'That is because I have realized we are no longer enemies, Dora dear. We are on the same side.'

'Uh-huh,' I said. I'd heard that one before. I sat down, but not where he'd suggested. I maintained a safe distance.

'You are going back to Notting Hill Gate tonight?'

I nodded.

'And you will see Duncan Fender?'

'Perhaps.'

Grauman rocked gently back and forth, tapping the glass against his front teeth. After a while he said, 'What I am about to say must go no further. You understand?'

I said I understood.

'You will not be surprised to know that I do not want them to get together. Not again.'

'Yes, I've gathered that.'

He hummed and hahed for a bit, then said, 'And I know that you do not want them to get together either.'

'That's right.'

'So we are wanting the same thing.'

'I suppose so. Same as before.'

He bared his horrible teeth at me. 'But this time you will not double-cross me.'

'Wouldn't dream of it.'

'Good,' he said. 'Have some more champagne.'

I held my glass out and he topped it up. I said, 'Perhaps it would have been better if you'd told me more about what was going on. I don't like feeling like a pawn in someone else's master plan.'

'Of course you don't. And neither do I. So what would you like to know?'

'What's in it for you?'

'Ah,' he said. 'You want to know that? It's a long story.'

'Tell me,' I said. So he did. The way he told it, there were these two women. The first woman was more than three hundred years old. The second woman, by comparison, was a stripling – in her early thirties – but she was very beautiful and very talented. They loved each other very much, these two women – the love that dares not speak its name and so on. The elder had long since grown weary of her endless existence and despaired of ever finding a companion who would rekindle in her breast the fading embers of human feeling. The younger was eager to taste everything that life had to offer. She sensed the elder woman would be able to give her everything, and more. So the elder prepared to initiate her lover into the mysteries of the inhuman condition, but the younger said, 'Wait. First I must have a baby.' And the elder of the women said, 'Where you are going, babies don't matter.' But her protégée was insistent – she *had* to experience this miraculous act of giving birth, before it was too late.

'This is 1947,' Grauman said, 'and we are in Paris. Now you must imagine this cute little baby with curly blond hair. He has lost his mama and papa in the air-raids on Berlin. And the elder of the women thinks, ah ha, I will adopt the cute little orphan baby with the curly blond hair and present her to my protégée, whose mothering instincts will thus be assuaged and she will think no more about becoming pregnant.

'And so she does this. And for a while the cute little boy with the curly blond hair does the trick, and the two women dote on him, and he in turn adores them both. But alas, the younger woman becomes broody once again, and this time she will not be denied. "I *must* have a baby," she cries, "a baby *of my very own*." And so the elder of the two fixes things up once again. This time, she arranges for her protégée to be made pregnant. She had carefully selected the man who will do this; he is feckless, an artist and a notorious womanizer who has already fathered several illegitimate children by different women, and abandoned them all. He is perfect, she thinks. And so, her beautiful, talented young protégée is encouraged to sleep with this man, and so she does, and she even insists on marrying him because she does not wish her child to be illegitimate, and by and by she finds she is indeed pregnant.'

Grauman topped our glasses up with more champagne, lit my cigarette, and continued. 'Unfortunately for Clara, and despite her very great wisdom, she has been too long divorced from the vagaries of human nature, and her plan begins to go wrong. The beautiful Marguerite is now, what? Thirty-six, thirty-seven years old? This is old for a first pregnancy, am I right? And she has a very difficult time – a very difficult time indeed. And the father, who up until now has lived up to his feckless reputation, suddenly becomes very solicitous, for he too has fallen in love with the beautiful, talented Marguerite – as who would not? And now he begins to take an unexpected interest in the welfare of his wife, and in the development of his new-born son, and Marguerite is filled with mother-love, and for the child's sake, she finds herself responding to her husband's overtures.'

'Oh,' I said.

'You can see where this is leading? Oh yes, we have an enormously touching romantic triangle here, with a baby in the middle. The husband gets on well with the elder of the women, though he has not yet found out she is more than just a family friend, and that his wife has at last been initiated, shortly after the birth of their son, into the mysteries of the inhuman condition. When he does find this out, many years later, it will be a disaster, and neither husband nor wife will survive the discovery. These Fenders, you know, they are ugly people, with ugly tempers. And so the elder woman will be left sorrowful and bereaved, and she will have nothing left to live for, even though she knows she must live for ever. And she will naturally turn to the sole surviving child of the union, and in time she will naturally conceive of the idea that the child will one day take his mother's place.'

'Oh,' I said again.

'And what do you suppose has happened in the mean time to the cute little orphan baby with the curly blond hair?'

'I think I can guess.'

'Cheers,' said Grauman, raising his glass once more. He took a mouthful and I heard him sucking the champagne through the gaps in his teeth. He gazed at me with the sort of wide-eyed expression affected by politicians when they are trying to appear sincere. 'He is now the right age. She will shortly be presenting to him everything that has always been due to me. So you understand why I would like him out of the picture.'

'And you can't kill him.'

Grauman breathed in sharply. 'He is the last thing standing between her and eternity, the link to her lost humanity. If I were stupid enough to harm a hair of his head, I would be torn to pieces. At the very least, I would lose everything for which I have been waiting so patiently all these years. However . . .' He fished in his jacket pocket, and came up with a fat envelope. 'This might solve all our problems.'

I took the envelope and opened it. Inside were two air tickets to Orly, and a thick wad of five-hundred-franc notes.

'I've never been to Paris,' I said.

'Well, this is your chance. You will find there is a suite booked in your name at the Crillon. No payment is necessary.'

I examined the tickets carefully, holding them up to the light. The flight was due to leave at eleven o'clock the following night. 'This isn't Heathrow?'

'Heathrow will not be such a great place to be, tomorrow night. Believe me, you will find the City Airport a lot easier. I shall arrange for a limousine to pick you up and take you there. All you need are passports.'

'What if she comes after us?'

'She won't,' said Grauman. 'There is too much at stake – if you will pardon the pun. *Rotnacht* is scheduled to begin at midnight tomorrow, and she will be required to co-ordinate the media coverage. It is very important. She cannot leave. The backers saw her through the last crisis because they needed her, but they will not indulge her weakness a second time.'

I studied the air tickets for some time, trying to work out the downside to this offer, then finally decided that perhaps there wasn't one and slipped them into my bag.

Grauman suddenly reached across and grabbed my hand. This time, though, instead of ramming his thumb into my palm, he stroked it tenderly with his forefinger. The gesture seemed so intimate it was obscene. I pulled away in alarm and embarrassment.

'You must get that seen to,' he said. 'It is dangerous for you to be out on the streets like this. The garlic will not be enough.'

'I'll be all right,' I said, sounding more confident than I felt.

Grauman stared into his drink for a bit, biting his lip, then appeared to make up his mind. He dug deep into an inside pocket and this time produced a small gun with a pearl handle.

I gaped. 'Where did you get that?'

'I have many contacts,' he said. 'I want you to take it, for protection. You know how to fire it? Just squeeze the trigger, like *so*.' The hammer clicked on an empty chamber, which was just as well because the barrel was pointing straight at me. I took it away from him and examined it closely, intrigued. This was the second real gun I'd seen in two days.

'But what's the point?' I said eventually. 'Guns don't make a blind bit of difference to vampires. You can fill them full of lead, and they'll still keep coming at you.'

SUCKERS

'Lead, maybe,' said Grauman. 'But silver bullets . . .' He held his fist out in front of me and opened it, like a magician demonstrating the last stages of a marvellous trick. Nestling in his palm were three acorn-shaped nuggets of silver. He slotted them into a small metal cartridge. 'I have only three,' he said, 'so you must use them carefully.'

I watched him carefully. 'Don't be ridiculous. You've got your monsters mixed up.'

He nudged me playfully on the chin. 'So Dora believes everything she sees in the movies?'

'Silver bullets are for werewolves. Everyone knows that.'

'And Dora believes in . . . *werewolves*?' He was trying to suppress a smile.

I thought about it. If vampires existed, why not werewolves? Why not unicorns, or Martians? 'Probably not,' I said, 'but these days I like to keep an open mind.'

'You will forgive me for saying so, but I know more than you. I have spent a lifetime studying. How can I convince you about this? The werewolf and vampire share the same origins in Eastern Europe. Somewhere along the line, the folk tales split into two. All the things you thought applied to lycanthropes – well, some of them apply to vampires too, and vice versa. Now take this – you may need it. If someone tries to stop you tomorrow . . .'

'You mean if Violet tries . . .'

'*No!*' he said. 'Don't even *think* about that. If you shoot Violet, it will be a disaster for all of us, and you will never reach the airport. But you will not *need* to shoot Violet, because she will not be coming after you. But she may send others – I don't know. And there are the loose cannons, these promiscuous types – they don't care who or what they bite.'

281

A look of revulsion crossed his face. 'There are many changes we must make, once *Rotnacht* has taken place.'

I watched as he slipped the cartridge into the hollow handle of the gun. 'What if I'm not a very good shot?'

'You don't need to be. These are .22 bullets, very small calibre. From a distance they are useless, but with the gun held so . . .' He placed the barrel, very carefully, against the side of my head. I froze, not daring to breathe.

'. . . you will not miss.'

FOUR

It was after midnight when we climbed into the back of the Double Image van, and by then we'd polished off the best part of another bottle of champagne. I felt aggressively optimistic; everything was going to be all right. I couldn't see who was driving, but Grauman said they were going to pick someone up in W11 and it made sense to set me down at the same time. I tried to peer out of the small tinted windows, but we were bouncing around so much it wasn't easy, and Grauman kept distracting me by chatting and offering cigarettes. I caught myself thinking that maybe he wasn't so bad after all – but this was going too far, and I gave myself a mental slap on the wrist.

Around Whitechapel, I caught a glimpse of something burning, and crazy people leaping and dancing around the flames like figures from Hieronymous Bosch. 'Did you see that?' I asked Grauman, but he shook his head, and I began to wonder if I'd imagined it, because I was feeling rather woozy. There were other things, though, and I definitely wasn't imagining those. Near Fleet Street, as a policeman

283

with big fluorescent gloves waved us past a heap of mangled cars, I saw a naked leg poking stiff through the middle of a shattered windscreen. And once, while we were stopped at a red light, I heard someone clambering on to the roof of the van. Whoever it was started jumping up and down, making great booming sounds over our heads, but Grauman rapped on the partition, and our driver moved off so abruptly that whoever or whatever was up there was flung into the path of the car behind us. There was a screech of brakes and a grinding of metal, followed by a banshee wailing. I craned my neck as we accelerated away, but all I could see was a heap of rags and a sparkle of glass.

'I thought *Rotnacht* wasn't until tomorrow,' I said.

'You thought correctly. But try telling those yobs out there.' Grauman sighed and tutted. 'They have no idea, no idea at all.'

'Then why did she bite them?'

'She didn't. She might have bitten someone once, a long time ago. That would have been enough to set the ball rolling. I am not a mathematician, but you could probably work it out. If everyone who has been bitten goes out each night and bites one or two others – well, eventually you will have an epidemic. Some will die from shock. Others may be torn to pieces. But others will develop a taste for blood and darkness, and they will spread it around.'

'I thought it wasn't so easy. Didn't you once tell me it took six or seven days? A long and arduous process, you said.'

'Well,' said Grauman, 'so it is. But what we have here is the difference between hiring a cheap cowboy to erect a flimsy partition, and saving up for a skilled bricklayer who will build a solid wall. The first is only a temporary solution.'

It sounded suspiciously like a final solution to me. It might have worried me more if I'd been sober. 'You mean you're going to get rid of the flimsy partitions, once they've served their purpose? You guys, you're so . . . *democratic*.'

Grauman looked scornful. 'There is no need to get rid of them. They will self-destruct soon enough.'

'Leaving the coast clear for solid walls?'

His gaze grew more distant, almost dreamy. 'Think of it as a game of Chinese Whispers. Each time the message is passed on, if it is not passed on properly, it will become weaker, more distorted. Eventually, you will end up with something that bears no resemblance to the original. And maybe at the end of it there won't be any words left at all. Just meaningless noises.'

This was getting too abstract for me. I lapsed into a not unpleasant stupor, watching the play of red and white light reflecting off the windows as the van bounced on its way, over potholes and up on pavements, over big chunks of things that had been left lying on the road.

'You remember our conversation?' asked Grauman, as we veered right off the Bayswater Road. 'The one we had at the top of the tower?'

I nodded and patted my bag. The small automatic was nestling inside. 'I'm not likely to forget it.'

'The limo will pick you up from Fender's place tomorrow night at eight. Make sure you are ready. Any delay may be dangerous.'

I nodded again. I couldn't believe my luck. I tried to imagine Duncan's face when I showed him the tickets.

'I suggest you give it a couple of months,' Grauman said.

'Once things have cooled off, it will be completely safe to come back. Everything will be back to normal, and you will begin your work with Multiglom in a capacity of your choosing. Day or night, it will be up to you. You are privileged; not many get the choice.' He looked me straight in the eye, and said in a voice that was almost affectionate. 'Be very careful, do as I say, and you might just make it through *Rotnacht* with your blood vessels intact.' I looked straight back at him, for once, and noticed something in his gaze that hadn't been there before.

'I stick my neck out for nobody,' I said.

Grauman grinned. It might have been my imagination, but the grin wasn't quite as wolfish as usual. He said, 'Something tells me this could be the beginning of a beautiful friendship.'

But as we drew near to where I lived, that old caution was reawakened. I didn't want him knowing my address, even now, even though common sense informed me he could have picked up the information easily enough. Instead, just to be on the safe side, I got him to drop me around the corner from Duncan's, just outside Jack and Alicia's. 'You live here?' he asked, peering out at the high building. 'Looks expensive.'

'It is,' I said, climbing out. Half the streetlights were on the blink, and most of the buildings were shrouded in darkness. The pavements were deserted, but the van sat with its engine running until I had climbed the steps to the front door. I couldn't help giggling – this was new-style Grauman in his New Man incarnation, making sure I got home safely. I fished my keys out of my bag, then realized that, of course, they wouldn't fit Jack and Alicia's lock, so for want of something better to do, I turned and waved goodbye. Only when the van had driven off did I realize I had forgotten to ask if it would be safe for Duncan to come back to London at the same time as me. Now I thought about it, it might be better if he were to stay in Paris for a while longer. Perhaps I could persuade him to stay in Paris for ever, out of harm's way, while I commuted between capitals. There would be plenty of photographic work for him in France.

As soon as the van had disappeared round the corner, I backed down the steps and started off towards Duncan's. I had no wish to drop in on Alicia again, especially if my suspicions about the baby had been correct. Thinking about it put the first big dent in my champagne high. I had quite liked Alicia. It wasn't her fault things had turned out badly.

Duncan took a long time to answer the door. I looked back along the road while I was waiting, beginning to feel a little nervous. It might have been my imagination working overtime again, but I thought I saw movement in the shadows beneath the trees. Then the lock clicked and I pushed the door open. It clanged shut behind me as I started up the stairs.

'Sorry,' Duncan said, rubbing his eyes as he poked his head out to greet me. 'I was napping.'

'You should be more careful,' I said, going in and stripping off my jacket. 'You didn't know it was me. It could have been anyone.'

'Oh, I knew it was you,' he yawned. 'Who else would it be, this time of night?'

'It could have been Violet,' I said darkly.

That woke him up. He opened his mouth to say something, then changed his mind and shut it, then opened it again. 'So what happened?' He snapped into focus. 'Christ, Dora, you look awful.'

'Thanks. So do you. How's the neck?'

'Still sore.' He touched the sticking-plaster with his finger, and winced.

'Better put another dressing on it. I'll just wipe some of this slap off my face, if you don't mind.'

'I cleaned up the bathroom.'

'That's OK; I'll go in the bedroom.'

He followed and watched as I spilled some of Lulu's lotion on to a cotton-wool ball and dragged it across my face. There was garlic all over the dressing-table. In the mirror, I saw there was garlic strewn all over the bed. It looked as though he'd been rolling in the stuff. A bit excessive, but I couldn't complain. At least he was taking precautions.

After a while, he asked, 'So did you get to see her?' as though the subject didn't really interest him any more.

'No.'

'A wasted journey.'

'Not quite. I met up with an old acquaintance. *Grauman*.'

'That bastard. And how is Andreas?'

I couldn't keep it to myself any longer. I finished wiping my face, and turned round. 'Slimy as ever. But have I got a surprise for you?'

He shifted his weight uneasily. 'I don't know. Have you?'

I opened my bag and pulled out the package. 'Look.'

'What's this?' He took the envelope and whistled as he saw what was inside. 'Tickets? Money? Hey, where'd you get this?'

'Tickets to *Paris*,' I announced triumphantly. 'Tomorrow night. You and me.'

I waited for him to punch the air with delight. But instead

of being pleased, he was wearing a gutted expression, as though somebody had punched him hard in the stomach. 'I . . . Dora, we . . . can't go. Not tomorrow.'

I couldn't see what the problem was. 'Why on earth not?'

'Work,' he said. 'I've got a whole load of work to finish.'

'This is more important than work. This is *life or death*.'

He shook his head. 'Well, I can't do it. Sorry.'

'I don't believe this.' I followed him as he went back into the living room and lit a cigarette. 'I don't believe it,' I repeated. 'You like Paris, don't you? Why don't you want to go there? Especially now, with all this shit happening. What the hell's the matter with you?'

He didn't reply. 'Or is it me?' I yelled. 'You just don't want to go there with *me*? You don't mind going with Lulu, or Alicia, or Francine. But I'm not *stupid* enough for you, is that it?'

I picked up the warning signs too late. He didn't raise his voice, but it took on a vicious edge. 'Well, maybe I'd have appreciated it if you'd consulted *me* first. Maybe I just don't *want* to go to fucking Paris. I'm fed *up* with you telling me what to *do*, Dora. I'm sick to death of you hanging around, and demanding explanations all the time, and sticking your nose into what doesn't concern you. Years and years of it. For God's sake give me some *space*. Let me get on with my *life*.'

There were some empty wine glasses on the coffee table in front of him. On the word *life* he snatched one up and hurled it across the room. It missed my head by a couple of feet and shattered against the wall behind me. I jumped back, stunned. There was glass all over the place. Everywhere I went these days, there was broken glass.

'Fine,' I said weakly. 'If that's what you want . . .' I

snatched up my bag and jacket, and marched to the door.

As I opened it, he faltered, 'Dora, I'm sorry.' Without turning to look at him, I paused. 'My back's killing me,' he said. 'Look, give me a ring in the morning, OK?'

'Anything you say,' I snapped, stepping outside and slamming the door behind me. I stormed home, and if there were sinister figures lurking in the shadows they sensed my fury and kept their distance. Steam was coming out of my ears. Too late, I wished I hadn't stormed out. I wished I'd had the nerve to stay and yell back at him, but Duncan, when he lost his temper, was scary; I knew that better than anyone, and I didn't want to push my luck.

I wished I'd had the nerve to ask about his mother.

Back in my own flat, I took a long, hot bath, rinsed half a gallon of gel out of my hair, and swabbed my hands with antiseptic. I lay awake in bed, in a nest of garlic and crucifixes. I lay awake and stared at the ceiling, because I could hear the Krankzeits partying with a couple of guests upstairs. I watched the light-fitting sway from side to side, and presently I rounded up all the angry feelings in my head and put them on a shelf out of the way, and then I started to pick away at the edges of the evening, unravelling everything and trying to work out exactly what was bugging me about it. There was something not quite right, and it wasn't easy working out what it was, because the entire evening had been surreal from the very beginning. *Surreal* – that had been Lulu's word. But I ran through it all again, detail by detail, even though there were some things I already wanted to forget. I made myself sit through the Bar Nouveau again, and I relived the meeting with Patricia Rice, and the encounter with the man who had once been fat, and the feeling of his breath against my wrist, and the faces, and Grauman, and Violet, and Grauman, and the journey home, and Duncan. And Duncan. I replayed that last bit again and again.

I had started off drunk, but now I was lying there stone-cold sober. In my excitement over the tickets, I had missed it, but now his words came back to me in their entirety.

'*And how is Andreas?*'

It took a while for the truth to penetrate my thick skull. The truth was this: I had never before mentioned Andreas Grauman in Duncan's presence, not in the entire thirteen years I'd known him. I knew that for certain, because Grauman was a dark secret I'd been keeping to myself. As far as I'd been aware, Duncan had never even *heard* of Andreas Grauman.

My heart did a slow dive into an empty swimming-pool. All of a sudden, I knew why I had been plied with champagne at the top of the Multiglom Tower. Not waiting to be given a lift, but kept there for a preordained amount of time. Not a celebratory toast, but delaying tactics. And I remembered what the Double Image van had been doing in W11. Not just taking me home, but picking someone up. Now I knew why Duncan had taken such a long time to answer the door. He had been busy scattering garlic all over the flat, all over the dressing-table and the bed, replacing what had been removed so I wouldn't suspect anything – he wasn't going to make that mistake again – but overdoing it in the process. In my mind's eye, I replayed the scene of him picking up the empty glass and hurling it across the room. But there had been more than one glass on the table, and the rim of the other one had been stained. With lipstick.

I stared dry-eyed at the ceiling and listened to the Krankzeits until I heard a lot of screaming, and a great deal of thrashing around, and what sounded like heels drumming against the floor over my head. A little later on, I heard footsteps on the stairs outside, and then a voice I recognized shouting, 'Fuck you, Gunter Krankzeit!' Then a door slammed and I heard Patricia Rice go downstairs, and another door slammed as she went out into the street.

Sleep was beyond me. I got up, fitted a new blade into my Stanley knife, and stared out of the window until the darkness lifted.

FIVE

All those nights staring sightlessly at the ceiling, staring mindlessly at the light-fitting as it swayed from side to side, staring into my own soul and not liking what I found there. The slamming doors, the clumping feet, the sour nothings shrieked from one end of their flat to the other, any old hour of the day or night, and never mind who might be trying to get some shut-eye down below.

The Krankzeits were the first to go.

They kept their key exactly where a burglar might expect to find it – on a small ledge over the door. Just because Gunter and Christine had kicked the bucket didn't mean they'd all of a sudden turned Brain of Britain, and the Krankzeits were evidently somewhere near the lower end of the Chinese Whisper chain.

They'd made an effort to reach a safe resting place before the sun came up, but it wasn't nearly enough. It was dark, but I found them couched in a pile of shoes and scarves and bags, at the back of the large cupboard they used as a walk-in wardrobe. Gunter was lying on his back with his mouth open, snoring. His teeth, apart from their unusually high metal content, were unremarkable. His girlfriend was snuggled up to him like a dormouse, fresh puncture wounds seeping on the side of her neck.

I wasn't going to waste precious bullets on these two. I didn't need to. I drew back the curtains and ripped down the black plastic bin-liners they had taped over the windows. Then I dragged first Gunter, then Christine, out of their hidey-hole by the feet.

Even before I staked them, they were charring at the edges, curling slowly away from the light, like phototropism in reverse. Gunter's eyelids flickered as the sharpened point pierced his chest, and I thought I heard him say something German and obscene-sounding as I whacked it further in. The air filled with a fine spray of blood and foul-smelling gas, but all he could muster in the way of retaliation was a reflexive snarl. Christine was even less formidable; she did nothing but squirt gore like a punctured sauce bottle. Luckily I was wearing Lulu's pink plastic raincoat.

For a long while I stood and looked at the blackening bodies, which were twisting into foetal positions around their wooden skewers, like giant shrimps on a big barbie. Time was playing strange tricks; there were peculiar gaps in my memory. I was always cranky for the first few days of my period, but it wasn't just that. I couldn't remember having had breakfast, for instance, even though I was sure I *had* had it, because there were small pieces of muesli lodged between my teeth. Gunter and Christine's flat took on a timeless, watertight quality, like an abandoned railway platform in the middle of nowhere. I wondered whether I'd dreamt the noises in the night; I had expected to find a pile of gnawed bones at the very least. But the only two corpses were my own handiwork. It was just as well they were decomposing; I would have had a hard time explaining them away.

Later, I found myself standing fully-clothed in the Krankzeits' bath with a shower attachment in my hand, hosing down the pink plastic until the water ran in thin red puddles at my feet, spiralling clockwise down the plughole in timehonoured *Psycho* tradition. When the raincoat was lightly streaked as opposed to thickly splattered. I clambered out, sloshing water all over the floor, feeling that surge of energy you sometimes get after an invigorating bout of physical exercise. I would need to consult a dietician about it, but I reckoned that staking vampires would burn off more calories than digging a ditch, swimming twenty lengths, or running a three-minute mile. Staking vampires would no doubt provide benefits of an aerobic nature, would keep you trim around the waist, would firm up the flab at the top of your arms — and would have the not inconsiderable side-effect of doing civilization an enormous favour as well. It had been rigorous physical exercise, but now the tough part was over, I found myself regarding it as *fun*, like squashing greenfly. I squelched downstairs, popped some Feminax, had a big toot of Ruth's sulphate, and wondered who was going to get it next.

Some of Weinstein's urban guerrilla enthusiasm had rubbed itself off on me. I drew the line at samurai headbands, but I dug out a khaki holdall and plundered Gunter's toolbox, which was better equipped than mine. To be honest, mine was little more than a biscuit-tin full of odd fuses and unstrung beads. From Gunter's, I took wirecutters, pliers, a set of screwdrivers, wrench, hacksaw, nails. But I kept my own hammer; I'd chosen it carefully before buying and it was a hefty weight, with a rubber grip, nice and solid, good for driving nails into the wall or shattering the skulls of robbers and rapists. Even better for banging sharpened sticks through vampire ventricles.

Almost as an afterthought, I packed Grauman's gun as well, though there would be little point in wasting precious silver on opponents who were horizontal and *hors de combat*. I had a vague idea it might come in useful after sundown. What with time playing strange tricks, there was always a risk of the darkness sneaking up and catching me off balance. Squeezing the trigger would be easy, so long as I could stop my hands from shaking too much. They weren't shaking now, despite too much caffeine and not enough sleep. I studied them carefully; the skin was waxy, the nail-beds caked with dried blood, and the stump of my little finger was all puckered and dead. I wondered if these really *were* my hands; they could easily have belonged to someone else. It wasn't until I turned them over and saw the mushy palms that I knew for certain they were mine.

Lastly, I packed the envelope containing the air tickets and francs, and tucked my passport in beside it. I had rushed things yesterday. I had lost my head. I wasn't going to make that same mistake again today. Once I had presented Duncan with the *facts*, he was bound to see the light.

My vampire-hunting didn't go quite as smoothly as I'd planned. Next for the chop, I'd decided, would be the couple next door, the ones with a penchant for noisy all-night parties, but it wasn't till I'd forced the lock on their back door that I discovered they were out. Frustrated, I stalked up and down their living room, smashing small ornaments.

There were so many people who deserved to be staked, and I was beginning to realize I couldn't make more than a dent in their number on my own. There was the drug-dealer with the howling Alsatians. A few doors further down, there was the unemployed yob who spent his afternoons and evenings fiddling with the engine of his customized Ford Capri. Then there were all those people who wore leaky headphones on the tube. I didn't care whether they were vampires or not; I hated them all, and they deserved what was coming to them.

But they would have to wait. I headed west through the vegetable market, weaving between the heaps of rotting fruit as the stall-holders chanted their cauliflower bargains and two bundles of rhubarb for the price of one. Quite a few of the shops were boarded up, as though this were the aftermath of a ripping carnival weekend, but otherwise life seemed to be going on as normal, and I couldn't find any more vampires, not after Gunter and Christine. It was something of an anticlimax – all that carefully sharpened dowelling going to waste in my bag – but I couldn't work up much passion for the hunt when it was nothing personal. I'd been thinking it was an epidemic, but maybe they'd all upped and moved to the security of Molasses Wharf. I had no intention of going back there again, not without the protection of a Home Guard of Van Helsings.

I went past the end of Duncan's road. This was where I'd been heading all along, but I was putting off getting there, so I doubled back and tramped up and down the tree-lined crescents which forked off Ladbroke Grove, peering into windows and pressing doorbells willy-nilly. Whenever someone opened the door, I pretended to be a mail-order catalogue salesperson who had got the wrong address. One old lady insisted on taking a look at my catalogue and became quite angry when I confessed I didn't have one, though, unlike some of the other householders, she didn't seem at all perturbed by the streaky stains on my pink plastic raincoat. If no one answered the door, I cased the joint, unless there were bars on the windows or a visible alarm system. I must have broken into three or four basements in all, but they turned out to be a waste of time. No joy in the vampire department, none at all, but I left plenty of garlic strewed in my wake, and a lot of small ornaments got broken.

I kept an eye on the time. Or tried to, in between forgetting who I was and what I was supposed to be doing. The hour hand on my watch slipped nearer the bottom of the dial, and I found myself outside Jack and Alicia's flat. I gazed up at the windows, and saw that the curtains were drawn. Of course they were. I rang the bell, and waited. No answer, of course not, so I pressed all the other bells and said I had a package for Jack Drury, and one of the neighbours released the latch. I climbed up to the first floor and knocked. There was a long silence. I was wondering whether to take out a screwdriver and tackle the lock, when my ears picked up a gentle scuffling on the other side of the door. I rapped again, more insistently this time, and there was more scuffling, then a clunking as bolts were slid back, and the door opened a crack, and the security chain snapped taut across the gap.

Alicia peeped out over the chain. Her face was the colour of flour and there were dark smudges around her eyes. She looked rather like the somnambulist in *The Cabinet of Dr Caligari*, only not as well dressed: she was still wearing her *Mona Lisa* T-shirt and dance tights and grubby dressing-gown. Poor Alicia. First Roxy, and now this. I felt sorry for her.

'Dora,' she said in a flat voice. 'What do you want?'

'I've come to help,' I said in my best soothing voice.

'I don't need help.' Her speech was thick and furry, as though she'd been drinking.

'Come on, let me in.'

She mumbled something I didn't catch. I lost patience and drew out the wirecutters. She looked on uncomprehendingly as the chain fell apart. 'What are you doing?' she asked. I stepped in, shutting the door behind me, and her eyes widened as she spotted the raincoat. 'That's Lulu's.'

'There now,' I said, advancing into the living room. 'That's better.' She was still backing away, trying to fend me off with her skinny forearms, trying to make me disappear. As though I was the vampire. I glanced at my watch. It had stopped again, at a few minutes to six. 'What time do you make it?' I asked. She swivelled to consult the clock on the wall, but I had seen past her shoulder already. It was half-past.

'Half-past six,' she said, turning round to face me again, which was when I shoved her off balance. She crumpled against the table and banged the back of her head, and slithered down until she was sitting on the floor with a puzzled look on her face. 'Dora?' she said. 'I can't see. Where are you?'

'I was hoping I wouldn't have to do this,' I said. And it did turn out to be even more difficult than Gunter and Christine, because I couldn't help remembering all the times Alicia had invited me to dinner, and so it didn't seem like squishing greenfly at all, not this time. I even found myself sniffling a bit, which took me by surprise because I'd never considered myself sentimental. I wished I'd brought Duncan round with me – he would have got on with it without snivelling. Duncan was a natural.

Alicia watched disinterestedly as I positioned the point of the dowelling on the left eye of the Mona Lisa. I hammered it in as gently as I could, apologizing as I did so. 'Whoops, sorry,' I said. 'Sorry Alicia.' There was a soft squelching as the sharpened end sank in, and the Mona Lisa cried real tears of blood. By the time I'd finished, she wasn't smiling any more, and neither was Alicia. She was still looking at me, though, watching as I attempted to clear up some of the mess. I closed her eyelids as best I could.

I turned to go, but then Abigail started to whine. Conscience prevented me from leaving a little orphan vampire on its own, unable to fend for itself when the whole world was about to erupt. The dowelling was too big, but I found the perfect substitute: one of Alicia's wooden knitting needles. I felt guiltier about dropping all those stitches than I did about turning the little nipper into shish-kebab, but then, I was doing it a favour. The baby teeth gnashed uselessly as its travesty of a life fled skywards with a tiny wheeze.

I arranged mother and daughter on the floor and pulled the curtains back. There wasn't even a wisp of steam, but the sky was already dark. The dawn would finish them off, even if *Rotnacht* didn't, but I tried to fix Alicia's hair so it didn't look quite so stringy, then sat down and had a cigarette. At least there was no longer anyone to complain about smoke polluting the baby's airspace. By the time I'd smoked two or three, and snorted the rest of the sulphate, I felt a whole lot better, not wobbly at all. I took off the raincoat, folded it up and slipped it into my bag. There hadn't been so much mess with these two. The baby had hardly bled at all, simply caved in like a dry meringue. My chief regret was that Jack wasn't around. It would have been neater to have nobbled the entire family in one swoop.

SUCKERS

I went downstairs slowly. I had all the time in the world, even though the sun had set, even though my watch had stopped and the limo would be arriving at Duncan's in less than an hour. There was nothing more to be done here. And by morning, we would be hundreds of miles away, in Paris.

I decided I was ready to face him now.

SIX

There seemed to be rather a lot of noise coming from the direction of Ladbroke Grove, so after I'd rung Duncan's doorbell, I had to press my ear right up against the entryphone. At first, there was nothing to hear. Then, at long last, an electronic crackle, followed by Duncan's voice. 'Hello?'

'It's me.'

I waited and waited, but nothing happened, so I pressed the buzzer again. 'Well, aren't you going to ask me in?'

There was a mild spluttering from the entryphone. 'I wasn't expecting you. You said you'd ring.'

'I didn't get a chance. Things have been rather hectic.'

Again, silence. I tapped my foot edgily on the doorstep, casting glances back along the street. There was no one behind me, but I could still hear shouting, and it seemed to be getting closer. After a while, I pressed the buzzer again, long and hard, several times.

'Look,' I said, 'I don't feel safe out here.'

'OK, you can come up for a quick drink.' He sounded pissed off. 'But you can't stay.'

Nothing like a warm welcome, I thought. He buzzed the door open and I started up the stairs. 'Why can't I stay?' I asked as he let me into the flat.

'Because I'm *busy*, Dora,' he said. 'I told you yesterday, I have *work* to do.'

I took a good look around. The blinds were drawn and the room lit only by the flickering light from the television. As far as I could make out, he'd been doing two things before I arrived – drinking, and watching TV. 'Ah yes,' I observed. 'I can see you've been working *really* hard. Just like on Saturday.'

'I was watching the news,' he said, turning off the TV and switching on the table-lamp. 'There's some sort of riot in Tottenham.'

'So what's new,' I said.

His expression didn't change. I was about to say I thought there was something going on in Ladbroke Grove, when he added, 'There's a riot in Dulwich as well.'

'*Dulwich?*'

He opened the whisky. 'Don't ask me what's going on. Like I said, one drink and out you go.'

I planted myself on the sofa. 'Who are you expecting?'

'No one.'

'Then come with me to Paris.'

He laughed awkwardly. 'You've got Paris on the brain. I don't suppose it occurred to you there might be things I have to take care of here.'

I stuck my chin out. 'So what are you waiting for? Throw another glass at me.'

He looked remorseful. 'Sorry about that. I guess I was still upset. About Lu and everything.'

'You and your temper, always taking it out on us girls. Promise you won't lose it again.'

'Cross my heart,' he said, handing me a measure of whisky which barely covered the bottom of the glass.

I swirled it around, but it still looked inadequate. 'Not even if I say something I shouldn't,' I said.

'Something you shouldn't?' He frowned. 'Like what?'

I drained the whisky in two small gulps and held the glass out for a refill. He poured another shot without thinking, and I said, 'There are certain things I think you might have told me.'

His manner, all of a sudden, was icy. 'Oh yes?'

I took a deep breath. 'But come to Paris and I won't even ask, because then it won't matter. I've got the tickets, I've got the money, all you need is your passport. There's a car coming at eight.'

Duncan was staring at me with a tired look on his face. I wished he would sit down. He was making me uncomfortable.

'I never asked for much,' I said.

'Tell you what,' he said, brightening. 'I've got a better idea. Instead of Paris, why don't you go down with Jack and Alicia tomorrow, and I'll join you at the weekend.'

'Go down? What d'you mean? Go down where?'

'Dorset.'

The whisky glass slipped through my fingers and cracked into two neat halves on the carpet.

'Oh, well done,' said Duncan.

'Dorset? With Jack and Alicia?' I couldn't help giggling. 'That's a great idea, Duncan. I can't imagine why I didn't think of it. *Dorset!*' I couldn't stop giggling, even when I tried.

'What's so funny?'

'Nothing,' I said, taking deep hiccuping breaths. 'Nothing at all.' But there must have been something in my face, because he was looking at me warily. I said casually, 'I don't suppose you've seen Jack?'

He stooped to retrieve the two halves of glass. 'Yeah, I was over there earlier.'

I chose my words carefully. 'Then I suppose you saw Alicia? And the baby?'

'I said I went over, didn't I?'

'*How were they?*'

'Not so hot.' He walked over to deposit the broken glass in the waste-paper basket. 'There's some bug going round, and they've both gone down with it. Jack wants to take them down to the country as soon as possible. He reckons it's traffic fumes. Everyone's coming down with bronchitis.'

'*Bronchitis?*' I tried to act naturally, but ended up with the giggles again.

He was losing patience. 'What's the hell's wrong with you?'

I tried like mad to keep a straight face. 'I made a mistake. I thought Jack was one of *them*. Alicia, too.'

'*Jack?* Nah, he's way too smart. You know Jack.'

I didn't want to talk about Jack and Alicia any more. I grabbed at the first thing that came into my head. 'But *Dorset?* You've got to be kidding. What the fuck am I supposed to do in *Dorset?* You don't want to go to Dorset, do you? Not really. You've got better things to do than go there. You've got lots of *work* to do.'

He was playing with the remote control, even though the set was off. 'I hadn't made up my mind. I wanted to hear what you . . .'

'Duncan, can I ask you something?'

'Feel free, ask away.' He wasn't even looking in my direction.

'How long have you been lying to me?'

I wasn't sure that he'd heard. He sat down on the sofa, making sure there was a fair amount of space between us, and placed the remote control on the coffee-table. Then he folded his arms, and looked straight at me. 'I've *never* lied to you, Dora. What makes you think that?'

'Oh, maybe not *technically*, like in a court of law. But you've been *deceiving* me, haven't you? Violet's been coming here, hasn't she? For the last couple of days? Come on, let's have a look at your neck.'

I leant over and tried to pick at one corner of the sticking-plaster, but he pulled back, out of reach, laughing nervously, and said, 'Don't be stupid.'

'Come on, show me.'

'No, I . . .'

'*Show me.*'

He sighed and peeled back one edge of the plaster. Saturday night's blisters had burst once already, and they were ready to burst again. 'There,' he said. 'Satisfied?'

'Not quite.' Before he had time to retreat, I lunged at the dressing and ripped it all the way off. He slapped his hand over the exposed skin, but not before I'd glimpsed the *other* bite: two very small, very neat puncture wounds, just below the blisters.

'That was Lulu,' he said.

'That's not Lulu. That's *fresh*.' I was trying to be angry with him, but all of a sudden there was a lump in my throat. 'Ruth was right. You're one of *them*. Or you will be – because it's not over, is it? How many more sessions? Two? Or three?

306

That's why you won't come to Paris. *That's* why you want me out of the way.'

'You don't know what you're talking about.' But he was unable to suppress a faintly supercilious smile.

It was all coming apart. There was no longer any point in pretending it wasn't. 'Oh, but I do know. I wish I didn't.' I tried to keep my voice steady, but couldn't stop it quavering. 'She's giving you the works, isn't she? You're getting the VIP treatment. Not like all those one-bite wonders roaming the streets. You're right up there – right up at the top of the Chinese Whisper chain.'

'Dora, you're hysterical.'

'*I'm not hysterical!*' I screamed. '*I'm just fucking angry!*' It all seemed so obvious now. 'How old are you now? *That's* what she was waiting for. She wanted you the same age as she used to be. The same age as your mother.'

'My mother's dead. Don't you *dare* bring her into this.'

'I didn't *bring* her in – she was already *there!*'

He made a last-ditch attempt at mollification, but his heart wasn't in it. 'Look,' he said. 'I'm sorry. I never meant any of this to happen.'

I laid into him. 'Like hell you didn't. You've been making a complete fool out of me, all this time, and there I was, thinking . . .'

He shrugged. 'I can't help it if you got the wrong end of the stick.'

'I got the *short* end of the stick,' I said, holding up my little finger. 'As usual.'

'Look, I was going to tell you, eventually. I just didn't want you finding out this way. I didn't want you getting hurt.'

I'd heard that one before. He was so full of shit, I couldn't understand why I hadn't smelled it. 'So tell me,' I sneered. 'What happened thirteen years ago? What was I supposed to be? Some sort of appetiser? Except you went and blew your top, just like you're always blowing it. Is that what happened? Things got a little rough, did they? Things got a little out of hand?'

'You don't know anything. *She* made me do it.'

'Don't talk *crap*!' I shouted. '*You set me up.*'

He shook his head. 'She set *me* up. She said it wouldn't work, and I didn't believe her. But she was right. She wanted me to see for myself. Staking, decapitation, dismemberment – none of it worked. And *nothing* will work. Nothing will ever work again. Just like nothing will work with me.'

'Oh, so it's a *fait accompli*? You're one of *them* already?'

'I'm not even half-way there. This is not like a one-night stand, Dora, this is the real thing. We're going to be together *for ever*.'

I wanted nothing better than to wipe that smug look off his face. 'So what are you going to do now, Duncan? Bite me? Get a foretaste of things to come? Go on, admit it. I was on the menu all along, wasn't I?'

'*Bite* you?' A faint look of distaste crossed his face. 'Bite *you*? No, I would never do that. You must understand it was nothing personal, Dora. None of it had anything to do with you. You just happened to be there.'

I couldn't sit still. I found myself holding the gun, fiddling with the safety catch, turning it this way and that, though I couldn't actually remember taking it out of my bag.

'So all that other stuff didn't work,' I said. 'But there was one thing we didn't try. We didn't try *this*. It was something we didn't know about.'

He glanced at the gun and dismissed it instantly, shaking his head again. 'No way. You know that's useless.'

'But *silver* bullets.'

'Come *on*,' he said. 'Silver bullets are for werewolves.'

'Vampires too,' I said, and lifted the gun and held it against the side of his head and pulled the trigger. I was quite surprised when it went off. The bullet made a much bigger hole than I'd expected, just above his ear. Nothing else happened, not really, he didn't say anything and his expression didn't change, but he slumped forward in his seat, so that his head rested on his knees. After a while, I heard something dripping on to the carpet.

'Fuck you, Duncan,' I said, annoyed I hadn't remembered to say it earlier.

I don't know how long I sat there. It was easiest when I wasn't thinking about anything in particular, so I let my eyes drift out of focus and concentrated on the regular rhythm of the dripping, noting how the sound of it changed as the carpet became more saturated. I counted the drips, slowly from one to ten, and then again. There was an uncomfortable feeling in the pit of my stomach, and it wasn't just period pain. It reminded me of the feeling you get when you go mad with your credit cards and spend a lot of money you haven't got. It was that sort of feeling, only worse.

After a while, I remembered I'd run out of cigarettes, so I helped myself to one from Duncan's packet, and smoked it very slowly and deliberately. Half-way through, I noticed someone sitting in the armchair opposite. I hadn't heard her come in, but that wasn't so surprising because she always moved quietly. She was staring at Duncan without appearing to see him.

'He never even took my photo,' I said. It was that, more than anything, which made me want to cry.

A few minutes later, I asked. 'What are you going to do now?' The room was chilly, and when she looked at me, it became even chillier. There was nothing in those eyes, nothing at all. Not even a spark.

She said something in a language I didn't recognize, in a voice that seemed to come from a long way off. She watched without expression as I ground my cigarette into the ashtray, got to my feet and took two paces forward and, holding the gun steady with both hands, shot her in the chest, round about the place where her heart should have been.

She didn't flinch as the bullet went in. She didn't even look surprised. She sat perfectly still, and I thought perhaps she was dead after all, until she moved her head to look down at her left breast. I couldn't see the hole I'd made, because the room was too dark, and of course she was dressed in black, but she prodded with the fingers of her right hand, the white one, and then her finger and thumb worked their way inside and dug around for a bit. There was a small wet noise, and her finger and thumb re-emerged, no longer white but red. She held up the bullet and regarded it with something that wasn't interest, not exactly.

'It's silver,' I explained.

She stared at me for more than a minute. 'You stupid child,' she said at last. 'Silver bullets are for werewolves.'

'Yes I know that, but he said . . . he said . . .'

There was a hiss of escaping air, or it might have been a sigh. '*Who* said?'

I suddenly felt very small. I said, 'Grauman.'

Something flitted across her face and was gone. 'Ah,' she said. 'I see.' Then she closed her eyes.

The minutes ticked away. She sat there unmoving, her shape blending into the shadows. I watched, even though there was nothing to see, and eventually I asked if she was going to kill me.

'There's no point,' she said.

She said nothing more, and neither did she move, not even when the limo arrived to take me to the airport.

We swung into Ladbroke Grove. I could see something blocking the street, further down, by the tube station. A bonfire, with a small crowd milling around it. Then I realized the flames were coming from a burning car. People were poking at it with sticks.

I got the impression there was someone still inside.

'Jesus,' I said.

'Not to worry,' said the driver. 'We'll go down here.' He was a thin, pale youth whose grey uniform made him look more like an overgrown schoolboy than a chauffeur. He turned right into Blenheim Crescent, and immediately had to brake. There were people all over the street in front of us, running and shouting. He slowed down, but didn't stop, edging ahead with his hand jammed down on the horn. Nearly everyone got out of the way. Those that didn't appeared not to care, one way or the other.

The front of the delicatessen had been kicked in. I saw a bevy of well-dressed women helping themselves to croissants and *pains au chocolat*. 'Well, they seem to be having fun,' my driver observed cheerfully. There were other people having fun too: someone was standing in the doorway of the wine merchant's, handing out what looked like bottles of claret to passers-by. There was a fine wisp of smoke curling out from the wrecked window of the electronics store, and an orderly parade of men and women emerging with camcorders, fax machines, and cordless curling tongs. A little further on, an old lady hobbled out of the hardware shop, bent almost double beneath a huge sack of compost.

Ruth's gallery was intact. Perhaps this had something to do with the detachment of cool-looking dudes in berets and army surplus who were lolling about on the pavement outside, each clutching a can of lager in one hand and an automatic weapon in the other. Several of them were puffing away on spliffs the size of torpedoes. Then I spotted Ruth. She was standing in the doorway, talking intently to Dino, who didn't appear to be paying her any attention because he was shouting into a walkie-talkie.

'Stop here, just for a minute,' I said.

The driver pulled up at the kerb, but kept the engine running. 'Don't be too long,' he warned. 'Traffic's getting worse by the second.' I got out and immediately found myself looking down the barrels of half a dozen machine-guns.

'Yo, mo, fo,' said one of the men in berets.

'Yo ho ho,' I said.

Ruth saw me and bounded forward. She was still wearing her samurai headband, but she'd swapped the flak jacket and drawstring trousers for strategically ripped olive-green overalls. 'Dora! Hi, glad you could make it. It's OK, guys, she's one of us.'

'The fuck she is,' I heard someone say as Ruth threaded her arm through mine and drew me to one side. 'Where've you been? I've been phoning you all day. Did you find out anything?'

'Oh yes, I found out lots. I found out about *Rotnacht*.'

'You *did*? And?'

'*Rotnacht* is scheduled to begin'– I looked at my watch, which appeared to be working properly again – 'in approximately three hours and forty minutes.'

Ruth put her hands on her hips and let out a long, deep sigh. 'Well, that's *really* helpful, Dora. Couldn't you have told us sooner?'

'Well, what did you think was going on here, exactly?' I waved my arm towards the toy-shop, where a crumpled Ford Fiesta was sitting amid a window arrangement of shattered glass and inflatable dinosaurs. Small, pre-school children were picking their way through the wreckage with their arms full of Barbie dolls and pastel-coloured furry animals.

'*This?* Oh, I thought this was run-of-the-mill civil disobedience,' said Ruth.

'Well, it's going to get worse,' I said. 'They're going to start killing people at midnight.'

'Really?' She seemed thrilled. 'I'd better summon the troops for a briefing.'

'Yo, what's up?' asked Dino, coming up behind us.

'*Rotnacht*,' said Ruth. 'It's tonight.'

All the colour drained out of Dino's face. '*Tonight?*'

Ruth nodded excitedly. 'Going to stick around for the party, Dora?'

'Nah,' I said, moving back towards the car. 'I'm out of here.'

'Where's *she* going?' Dino asked suspiciously.

I gave him a big, sweet grin as I slid into the back of the car. 'La Place de la Concorde,' I said, and slammed the door shut.

The radio crackled ceaselessly as we drove. 'Edgar Allan

Poe to H. P. Lovecraft,' said the driver. 'Come in, H. P. Lovecraft.'

'H. P. Lovecraft to Edgar Allan Poe,' said the voice from the radio. 'H. P. Lovecraft to Edgar Allan Poe. What's your position?'

'Approaching Harrow Road,' said the driver. 'Update on the situation, please.'

'Marylebone Road is no go. Repeat. Marylebone Road is *no go.*'

'What do you suggest?'

'Stay out of the West End. Repeat. The West End is a *war zone.* Your best bet is the North Circular. Repeat. The North Circular is your best bet.' The speaker sounded curiously jovial.

'Camden? Finsbury Park?' asked the driver.

'Dodgy. Very dodgy. Repeat. The North Circular is your best bet. Over and out.'

The driver grinned over his shoulder at me. 'Don't worry, lady. We're taking the scenic route, but we'll get you there.'

'I'm not worried,' I said, and I wasn't. I had one silver bullet left, and it wasn't for me.

We headed north. There were people out on the streets here, but the action was elsewhere, and they weren't hanging around. There was a lot of traffic, but my driver didn't let it put him off his stride. He wasn't sticking to the rules; he drove up on pavements, barged through red lights, and demolished a couple of sign-posts and a flower-stall. There were other sticky patches, but our car came off better than most of the others we encountered *en route.*

It was easier once we'd hit the North Circular, because most of the traffic was headed in the opposite direction. The driver relaxed, exchanged a few more words with H. P. Lovecraft, and fiddled with the radio dial until he was tuned into a music frequency. Presently he was whistling along to a disco version of the Anvil Chorus.

We were forced to take a minor detour through Palmers Green, but otherwise it was all plain sailing. I lit the last of Duncan's cigarettes and gazed through the tinted windows at the flickering light show in the skies to the south. It was Tottenham providing the fireworks now, but in a couple of hours it would be bonfire night all round town. And by then, I'd be swigging champagne at the Crillon.

As we swung south-east towards Wanstead, I felt the tiniest twinge of regret. But it soon passed. In a couple of months, Grauman had said, everything would be back to normal. Back to normal, if not quite the same as before. There would no longer be a train service during the day, he'd said. From now on, the trains would be running only at night.

But at least they'd be running on time.